Wilder than the Rest

MacLarens of Fire Mountain

SHIRLEEN DAVIES

Book Six in the MacLarens of Fire Mountain Series

Other Books by Shirleen Davies

Historical Western Romance Series

MacLarens of Fire Mountain

Tougher than the Rest, Book One

Faster than the Rest, Book Two

Harder than the Rest, Book Three

Stronger than the Rest, Book Four

Deadlier than the Rest, Book Five

Redemption Mountain

Redemption's Edge, Book One
Coming fall of 2014

MacLarens of Boundary Mountain

Colin's Quest, Book One
Coming in 2015

Contemporary Romance Series

MacLarens of Fire Mountain

Second Summer, Book One

Hard Landing, Book Two

One More Day, Book Three – Coming summer of
2014

For more information about Shirleen Davies and her books visit:
www.shirleendavies.com

For permission requests, contact the publisher.
Avalanche Ranch Press, LLC
PO Box 12618
Prescott, AZ 86304

Wilder than the Rest is a work of fiction. Names, characters, places and incidents are either products of the author's imagination or used fictitiously. Any resemblance to actual events, locales, or persons, living or dead, is wholly coincidental.

Cover artwork by idrewdesign
Book design and conversions by Joseph Murray at 3rdplanetpublishing.com

ISBN-10: 0989677389

ISBN-13: 978-0-9896773-8-7

Description

"A captivating historical western romance set in the burgeoning and treacherous city of San Francisco. Go along for the ride in this gripping story that seizes your attention from the very first page."

"If you're a reader who wants to discover an entire family of characters you can fall in love with, this is the series for you." –
Authors to Watch

Pierce is a rough man, but happy in his new life as a Special Agent. Tasked with defending the rights of the federal government, Pierce is a cunning gunslinger always ready to tackle the next job. That is, until he finds out that his new job involves Mollie Jamison.

Mollie can be a lot to handle. Headstrong and independent, Mollie has chosen a life of danger and intrigue guaranteed to prove her liquor-loving father wrong. She will make something of herself, and no one, not even arrogant Pierce MacLaren, will stand in her way.

A secret mission brings them together, but will their attraction to each other prove deadly in their hunt for justice? The payoff for success is high, much higher than any assignment either has taken before. But will the damage to their hearts and souls be too much to bear? Can Pierce and Mollie find a way to overcome their misgivings and work together as one?

Read Wilder than the Rest, another heartening story of duty, honor, passion, and love in book six of the MacLarens of Fire Mountain.

"If you're a reader who wants to discover an entire family of characters you can fall in love with, this is the series for you." – Authors to Watch

Dedication

This book is dedicated to my readers who have taken the time to send messages of praise and encouragement. My sincerest thanks to all those who have watched this journey unfold. Your enthusiasm and support has been a true blessing.

Acknowledgements

I want to thank my editors and proofreaders, Sue, Danielle, Shontrell, and Richard who offered their expertise and continued support.

Many thanks also go out to my wonderful resources, including Diane Lebow, an expert at guiding my social media endeavors, Joseph Murray who is fabulous at formatting my books for both print and electronic versions, and idrewdesign, the talent behind my wonderful book covers. Your talent is greatly appreciated.

Wilder than the Rest

WILDER than the REST

Prologue

Fire Mountain, Arizona, 1887

"Keep your head down," Pierce MacLaren growled at his partner as he placed a hand on her head, shoving her behind a stack of barrels.

"Damn it, Pierce. I don't need you to protect me." Mollie Jamison had followed him through the dark, dank alley, trying to catch up with Otis Tatum, the man they knew was responsible for the latest dump of counterfeit bank notes.

Mollie had confiscated the plates after they'd caught Otis cleaning up after his last printing session. They were tucked into a cubbyhole in the old brick building next to the barrels where she and Pierce now hid.

Otis had spotted them and bolted through the back door. For a large man, he was surprisingly quick.

"Such language," Pierce shot back with a slight grin.

Mollie ignored the jab. "What's he doing?"

"Hold on." He peered over the top of the barrels. Their forger had stopped outside the back door to the Desert Dove, the town's most popular saloon. "Looks like he may try to go through the Dove."

"You stay here. I'll go to the street." Mollie started to rise, stopping when Pierce grabbed her arm.

"Not likely. I'm faster. Besides, he'll plow through you when he comes out the front." Pierce took off, leaving her behind to fume.

"You're faster only because I have to wear this bloody skirt," Mollie hissed as she ran after him, her skirt hem in one hand, a Colt forty-five gripped in the other. "Damn him," she muttered when her skirt snagged on the rim of a barrel. She pulled hard, freeing herself by ripping the fabric, then dashed after Pierce and the counterfeiter.

Mollie came to a stop where the alley intersected the main street. Pierce stood motionless, looking into the business end of a pistol aimed at his chest. Otis Tatum wheezed, but held the gun steady. At five foot seven, he seemed as tall as he was broad, with a head that appeared to outweigh the rest of his body by several pounds. He adjusted his hat, trying to make it stay on his oversized skull while he kept his eyes trained on Pierce.

"Get out of my way, MacLaren, or I swear I'll put a bullet right through you."

"Not a chance, Tatum. There's no way you're leaving here alive," Pierce bluffed. He was a fast shot. He could try to raise his gun before Tatum pulled the trigger, but the odds were against him. From the noise level inside the Desert Dove, he realized that unless someone walked out, no one would discover what was happening just a few feet away. He rethought his plan. "How about we compromise?'

"Compromise?" Otis was a genius when it came to producing counterfeit money, but from what Pierce had determined, that was the only area where he mentally excelled.

"You lay down your gun, and I'll let you ride out of town."

Otis scrunched his face in thought as he tried to come up with a reason MacLaren would be willing to let him go. "Is this a trick?"

"Not at all. As long as you lay down your gun, I'll let you ride out of Fire Mountain."

"Let me think," Otis hedged, lowering his gun and removing his hat to scratch his head.

"What the hell are you doing, Pierce?" Mollie muttered to herself, keeping her Colt trained on Otis.

"No trick?"

"Absolutely." Pierce smiled, hoping he'd take the bait.

"Well, if this isn't a trick, okay. Now, you'll let me ride out?" Otis set his gun on a nearby chair, hurried down the steps to the street, and took off toward his horse tied up several yards away.

"That I will. Out of town."

Otis shrugged, still confused even though he would take the opportunity to escape. He galloped out of town, causing those in the street to scatter as he rode past.

Pierce's smile faded to determination as he watched Tatum head north, out of town. At the fork, he'd have two choices—continue north or ride west. Later, he could choose to go east or south. By then, however, he'd be in custody.

"What have you done?" Mollie's stunned, accusing voice brought his head around.

"Ah, Mollie, just the person I want to see. Tatum is riding out. Once he reaches the town limits, our deal is off."

"But you said he'd be free...?"

"*To leave town*. After that, Otis is fair game." Pierce strode to his horse, Bandit, and turned to Mollie. "You coming or what?"

She looked down at the barmaid outfit she wore—a floor-length red satin dress, now torn, with a scooped neckline that fell off her shoulders. And no time to change. She ran to Bandit, grabbed Pierce's hand, and let him haul her up behind him.

"Is your horse at the stable?"

"Yes."

"We'll get it then follow Otis. At the fork, I'll go north, you head west. One of us will catch him. He hasn't had time to go far and doesn't believe we'll follow. Whoever finds him will fire twice in the air."

"And if he pulls a gun?"

"This is his." Pierce showed her the pistol he'd grabbed from where Otis had set it. "Unless he has another, he'll give up without a fight."

Mollie slid off Pierce's horse and grabbed hers. They rode side by side for a few miles then split up. Within five minutes, Pierce saw Otis ahead of him. He urged Bandit on until he was within a few yards of Tatum, then fired two shots in the air.

"Hold up there, Otis," he shouted and trained his gun on the man.

Tatum reined in his horse, slid down, and started stomping toward Pierce. "You said I could go." He never stopped his pace.

"Out of town."

"You son-of-a-bitch."

Pierce fired a warning shot at the man's feet. "Stop right there," he warned, but it was too late.

Otis lunged toward Pierce, pulling him to the ground. Sitting on Pierce's legs, Otis pounded his chest and head with beefy fists. Pierce raised his arms to ward off the blows with little success.

The beating stopped abruptly.

"Stand up and put your hands above your head," a hard female voice ordered.

Tatum felt the cold metal of a gun on his back. In the man's moment of indecision, Pierce rolled sideways. Otis slid off as Mollie kept her gun trained on him.

"I won't tell you again, Mr. Tatum. Stand and raise your hands." Mollie swiped errant strands of hair from her face with her free hand. She took a quick glance at Pierce. "So he'll give up without a fight, huh?" She chuckled. "You're a mess."

"Yeah, well, I may have underestimated him," Pierce answered as he tried to stop the flow of blood from his nose. He could already feel the start of a black eye and bruising on his chest. "Jesus, you sure can hit, Otis."

"You lied to me." The disillusionment wasn't lost on either Mollie or Pierce.

"Not at all. You got your chance to leave town. That's all I agreed to." Pierce grabbed the water flask from his horse and took a long swallow then held it out to Otis, who brushed him off with a wave of his hand.

"Besides, what authority does a saloon girl—"

"Barmaid," Mollie corrected with a sweet smile.

Otis looked at her. "Fine. What authority do a barmaid and rancher have to make an arrest?" He sneered, his tone full of sarcasm.

Mollie and Pierce pulled out their badges and held them in his direction. Otis's eyes bulged as he read the inscriptions—United States Secret Service.

Chapter One

Noah Dodd, the head of the western United States Treasury Department's Secret Service Agency, sat in the upscale restaurant in downtown San Francisco sipping scotch while waiting for his guest to arrive, a well-respected and quite wealthy businessman with interests in industries ranging from steel mills to cattle to lumberyards. He had contacts across the country. They were the reason for tonight's meeting.

Noah looked up to see Louis Dunnigan walking toward him. "Hello, Mr. Dunnigan." He extended his hand. "Thank you for taking the time to meet with me."

"Please, Noah, I would appreciate it if you'd call me Louis, and I'm more than happy to get together." He took the offered hand before signaling the server for a drink, then took a seat across from Noah. "How'd you know I was in San Francisco?"

"You know the agency hired Pierce MacLaren, right?" Noah asked.

"Yes, I've heard Pierce had started working with you."

7

"He mentioned you were out here for a few weeks to purchase some property. I thought it might be a good time for us to talk."

Noah paused while the server placed a drink in front of Louis, then continued when the man retreated.

"I recruited him to work with us on a counterfeiting ring in Fire Mountain. Set him up with a partner. Not long after, he was able to determine the creative talent behind the plates being used to print the forged notes. The man is now in custody."

"Fast work. So what's the issue?"

"No issues other than he's headstrong, arrogant, controlling, and a general pain." Noah chuckled. "That's a direct quote, by the way."

"From whom?"

"His partner."

"Another man found those traits a problem?"

"His *female* partner," Noah clarified.

Louis chuckled. "Well, I can see why that might be a slight issue."

"To be honest, I can't afford to lose either one. The woman, Mollie Jamison, is good. Quick learner and not afraid to get in the middle of things. Plus, the criminals we pursue rarely think of a woman as an agent. It's easy for her to work undercover." Noah studied his drink and took a swallow. "Pierce has the skills, background, and experience that Mollie lacks."

"It appears that Miss Jamison can learn a lot from Pierce."

"You're right, she can. If only she would. The same traits she used to describe Pierce, he could fling at her. I guess it's all a matter of perspective. It will work out, with some rough spots along the way." Noah thought for a moment. "The issue I have is that they need a place to work from while they're here on their next assignment. I understand you're acquiring a building. The existing Treasury office here is small, and I can't afford to have confidential investigative work overheard by others."

Louis was beginning to see where this was going. "The deals aren't finalized, but yes, I will have offices that would work."

"The agency can't pay going rate, you understand."

"I'm sure we can work something out. When will you need it?"

"Within the month."

Louis thought a moment. "That will work. I must go back to Denver for a couple of weeks. I'll return to San Francisco by the time your agents arrive."

"Good. I'll let Pierce and Mollie know."

Noah got to the main reason for this meeting. He looked up at Louis. "They'll have a cover, which you'll need to be aware of."

"What is it?"

"The plan is for them to be a married couple, new to the city. Pierce will be working for Dunnigan Enterprises."

Louis suppressed a grin. "No issue at all setting him up with something that will provide a good cover. My other employees won't suspect a thing." He sat forward. "How did they take the news about the fake marriage?"

"I haven't told them yet."

Louis downed the last of his drink and stood. "You are a brave man, Noah. Be sure to have an escape route available when you tell them. You just might need it."

******

Fire Mountain, Arizona

Connor worked alongside his brother, Pierce, as they fixed fence lines and watched for strays. The physical work was hard, yet rewarding. Different from the work either had done in their past lives.

"Sounds like you've made up your mind to stay in Fire Mountain." Pierce's idle comment held more meaning than he wanted his brother to know.

"Appears so," Connor replied as he pulled a wire taut before securing it.

"The purchase of the other two saloons final yet?"

"Both will be by the end of this week, at least according to Jerrod."

Jerrod Minton had been the MacLaren attorney for years, handling all the ranch business as well as any other legal matters needed.

"That mean you won't be working the ranch?" Pierce asked.

"Nope. I'll manage the three saloons, but still do whatever else I can on the ranch. I don't understand much about the horse breeding program, so I'll work with the other men in the cattle operations. Learn from them."

The brothers fell silent, concentrating on the work in front of them.

"All right, let's move on." Connor stretched his arms above his head before mounting his horse, Crusader, to continue following the fence line. They rode at a slow, easy pace, watching for anything out of the ordinary as well as damaged wires.

"Hold up." Pierced reined Bandit to a stop and dismounted. "I think he picked up a rock."

Connor slid off his horse, grabbed his canteen, and took a deep swallow before handing it to Pierce. "You've made up your mind on continuing with Noah?" He didn't mention Mollie, a sore subject with Pierce.

"Might, if he finds me a new partner. Mollie's too damn stubborn, won't listen to anyone," Pierce said as he worked the stone out of Bandit's hoof.

"The way I hear it, she saved you from one terrific beating by Tatum."

Pierce glared at him. "I could've handled him. Just needed to catch my breath."

"That's your story?" Connor suppressed a smile, already knowing that Mollie had kept his brother from getting the tar beaten out of him. He and his cousins were grateful to her for interceding.

Pierce swung up on his horse. "Look, the woman's headstrong and overconfident. I get the headstrong part, but her overconfidence will get someone killed."

Connor followed a few paces behind. "Seems like confidence is needed for the types of jobs Noah gives you. You're not dealing with easy work or reputable people."

Pierce looked at his brother and shook his head.

"Look, I'm not defending her." Connor reached behind him to pull some jerky from his saddlebag, giving Crusader a soft kick to come alongside Pierce. "Just saying you might give it another try, see what happens."

"You trying to get rid of me?"

"Hell no. I just know the size of the bank draft you just got. Decent pay for a couple weeks of work."

Pierce knew Connor was right. Nothing he'd ever done had paid as well, except his previous work for Louis Dunnigan. The money would give him options if he stayed with the agency long enough. He liked choices.

Then he thought of how Mollie frustrated him more than any woman he'd ever known, and in a shorter period of time. He removed his hat to run a hand through his short, dark brown hair.

"Good pay, Connor, but no. It just won't work. Never again." He set the hat back on his head and turned Bandit down the hill toward home.

******

"You cannot be serious, Noah. I will not work with that man again. Ever." Mollie fumed, running a hand through her already windblown hair. "It will never work out." She paced the small office her boss had set up in the territorial capital of Fire Mountain.

"Why don't you wait until you've heard the proposition? I've passed it by my superiors and they like the plan. There are some stipulations, however—those requirements are a benefit to you and your partner."

"What stipulations?"

"Let's wait until Pierce gets here, so I can explain them to both of you at the same time."

Mollie turned at the sound of a knock on the door.

"Come in," Noah responded.

Pierce opened the door to see Mollie standing a few feet away. His first impulse was to close it and walk away. Noah saw his hesitation.

"Take a seat, Pierce." He turned toward Mollie. "You too."

Each lowered themselves into the two chairs facing Noah and edged away from each other. Not much, but just enough that their boss noticed.

He leveled his eyes on them. "The agency has ordered a new assignment, and they've approved both of you to be on the team."

"Team?" Mollie asked.

"I'll get to that in a minute. First, the preliminaries. This assignment is not being handled through normal agency channels."

"Why not?" Mollie interjected. The response was a stern look from Noah. "Sorry. I'll wait to ask my questions when you're done."

Pierce looked at the floor to hide his amusement. She just didn't know when to keep her mouth shut.

"Good idea, Miss Jamison. Now, as I was saying, this will be run differently and include some others we've recruited for this specific job only. This team is being established to handle federal crimes the Justice Department doesn't have the manpower to enforce. The two of you, plus the others on the team, will be considered independents as far as department guidelines. As such, I'm not bound by the normal requirements. That means the pay is higher. Considerably so."

Noah paused, wrote down a figure on a piece of paper, and slid it across his desk.

Mollie and Pierce stared at the number, stunned by the sum.

"Are you certain this figure is accurate? You didn't put an extra zero in there by mistake?" Mollie breathed out.

"No mistake. The number has already been approved, per person. Half now, half when the job is done." He pulled the paper back and placed it in the top drawer of his desk. "Before I am authorized to go any further, I need both of your commitments to take this assignment."

"Without details?" Mollie didn't understand how she could agree to something like this without any knowledge of the job.

"Take it or leave it. Makes no difference to me. Although, I believe the two of you are critical to the success of this particular assignment." He leaned back in his chair and regarded the two agents before him. "This may be a once in a lifetime opportunity."

The number Noah provided rolled around in Pierce's mind, an incredible amount that would take years to make as a standard agent. This job could set him up for quite some time, allow choices he'd never had before. The one issue holding him back from shaking hands on the deal with Noah was the woman who sat beside him. He'd have to work with her one more time.

Mollie appeared to be as conflicted as Pierce. At twenty-two, she had nothing stopping her from taking this assignment, earning the money Noah offered, and moving back east to flash her success in front of the man who'd told her she'd never amount to anything. She could still see her father's face hovering over her, and hear his liquor-laced voice telling her that she was worthless. This was a perfect opportunity to push it back at him, show him how wrong he'd been. Except for one thing— the assignment included Pierce MacLaren.

"There's nothing you can tell us about the job unless we agree up front?" she asked once more.

"That's the proposition. If you don't want it, for whatever the reason, no problem, I won't think less of either one of you. You'll both be eligible for regular assignments through the agency." He pushed up from his chair. "I need some coffee. Have a decision when I return."

15

The sound of the door closing echoed in the small office. Pierce stood and walked to the window, looking out on the crowded street below. The territorial legislature was in session, bringing more people to town than normal. His oldest cousin, Niall, was a council member of the legislature and, according to his wife, Kate, known to come home in a foul mood most nights that the legislature convened.

"I could use the money." Mollie sat clenching her hands in her lap, watching Pierce and wondering if his concerns were the same as hers.

"It's an impressive amount."

"It would take years to earn that amount by taking normal agency assignments." She stood, stepped around her chair, and rested her hands on the back of it. "I don't like not knowing the details."

"Neither do I."

"Or who else will be on the team." Mostly, she was concerned about one specific member of the team—the one standing a few feet away. Was the money worth the aggravation of working with this hardheaded man one more time?

Pierce didn't respond, too focused on deciding which way to go—take the assignment and the money or walk away from Noah and the female agent who caused him nothing but grief. A short assignment might work. A long one might drive him over the edge.

Both turned at the sound of the door opening and looked at the man walking through it holding a half-finished cup of coffee. Noah didn't

16

acknowledge either of them, just returned to his spot on the other side of his desk and settled into the large leather chair. He set down the cup, placed his arms on the desk, clasped his hands, and leaned forward.

"Your decision?"

"I'm in," they replied in unison. Each snapped their gaze to the other, stunned they'd made the same choice, and neither looking happy about it.

Noah didn't miss a step. "Good." He pulled two documents from his desk drawer and handed one to each. "Sign these so we may continue."

Pierce glanced at the document. It was simple, an acknowledgment of the fee for the job and that assignment details would be provided. He accepted the pen Noah offered and signed his name, hoping he wasn't making a colossal mistake.

Mollie watched Pierce sign, then took the pen from his hand and did the same. Each handed their copy to their boss.

"Wonderful." He took a satchel from underneath his desk and put the agreements inside, then looked toward them and took a deep breath. "There are three items you need to know about today. The rest we'll review in a few days, once I receive final details from my colleagues."

Pierce and Mollie nodded, trying to remain patient.

"First, there is another team of agents investigating all of the same leads and sources you'll be provided. We don't have enough information to know if this is East or West Coast based. Regardless, the two groups will share information until such time as we identify more specifics. Second, you'll have three team members. One you don't know, two you do."

Noah took a sip of his coffee and continued. "Eva Gagnon has been with the agency for quite a while. She has excellent clandestine skills and a file full of arrests. Lee Hatcher normally works for Alex McCann. He only comes back to the agency for the most difficult assignments, and always with McCann's approval. He will continue with McCann Investigations once this job is done." Noah looked up to see that Pierce's eyes had widened at the name of a man he knew. "Lee was one of our most successful agents. He and Eva have worked together before, so their joint experience will be invaluable. Lee will stay in New York unless it's found his presence is required. He'll be my main contact, and you'll take your orders from him. Last is Chaz Yarbrough."

"Chaz?" Mollie asked. "But he's a merchant. How does he fit in?"

"Chaz was an agent for several years and has agreed to come back for this job. His assignments were in Europe and focused on criminal intelligence in conjunction with Scotland Yard. When the last assignment ended, they offered him a position, which he refused. He's fluent in several languages, although I doubt he'll need them for this job." Noah leaned back in his chair, resting his elbows on the armrests, and brought his hands together to steeple his fingers. "Now, I'll explain how this is going to work."

It didn't take long for him to explain the basics of the assignment. He told them covers for Eva, Lee, and Chaz would be arranged as needed, but they would be a part of the team. Lee was the lead for their assignment, with Eva as the main contact between him and everyone else. For the most part, Noah would stay at a distance and handle requests from Lee.

"Most, if not all, of the assignment will take place in San Francisco," Noah added.

"And our cover?" Pierce asked.

Noah's face remained impassive. "You'll be posing as a married couple."

Chapter Two

Neither his brother, Connor, nor his cousins—Niall, Jamie, Will, and Drew—could contain their laughter. All six were working on an extension to the horse birthing area next to the barn at the main ranch house. It was the first time in weeks they'd all been together, without the women.

"Are you still planning to work for Noah?" Drew straightened to stretch his arms and legs.

The turn of events the day before still angered Pierce. He believed Noah had set the two of them up. He'd almost walked out until he realized he was truly hornswoggled. Mollie had looked as if she would jump over the desk and attack the man.

"What the hell was I supposed to do at that point?" he asked, clearly exasperated. "I'd already signed the agreement, learned about the others and how they'd be involved. He knew how Mollie and I would respond, that's why he insisted we agree beforehand based on the money." He pulled off his work gloves and threw them on the ground. "What a mess."

The others watched him put some distance between them. The five glanced at each other, sobering at the thought that Pierce would be holed up for who knew how long, with a woman he disliked intensely, but was drawn to like a moth to a fire. It was a true mess. Either way, he'd get burned.

Connor walked up and placed a hand on Pierce's shoulder. "You did what any of us would have done—accepted it. Now, you'll do your best to honor the commitment you made. There was nothing else you could have done."

The four cousins nodded their agreement and broke off, each returning to the work before them.

"Hey, supper's ready." Grace walked up and slid her arms around her husband, Connor.

They'd been married a few weeks, and it was rare to see one without the other nearby. His cousins understood the newness would fade a little in time. For now, however, they all enjoyed watching and ribbing him about being on a short rope.

******

Alicia MacLaren looked around the table at her family. It was a good thing that her deceased husband, the boys' uncle, Stuart MacLaren, had planned the house for a large family. Even though they both wanted children, it had never happened. Now, with six grown nephews, four wives, a niece and her husband, plus several grandchildren around the supper table, the house felt full—and wonderful.

"When do you start the new assignment, Pierce?" she asked. The men had mentioned it while eating supper, and she wondered if it would take her nephew away from Fire Mountain and the family.

"Just waiting for word from Noah Dodd, Aunt Alicia. Shouldn't be long." Pierce continued to focus on the roast beef in front of him, his mind filled with second thoughts. He wished he'd walked away, ignored the large sum of money, and waved goodbye to Dodd, as well as the female agent who was nothing but trouble. His gut had told him something wasn't right and he'd ignored it.

"So it's the two of you, no one else involved?" Connor pushed back his empty plate and laid an arm across the back of Grace's chair.

"For the most part, yes. Dodd says there are some others, but he didn't share with us their exact roles." Pierce wasn't at liberty to share the names of the others involved, at least not yet. He took a deep breath and let the air escape in a slow stream. "Damn, but I hate waiting." He looked around the table. "Sorry, ladies."

"As far as I recall, you've been impatient most of your life," Mr. Jericho commented. An older man, he'd known Connor and Pierce since not long after they'd come to America with their sister, Meggie. He had been involved in their lives in some fashion ever since. Now, he made his home at the ranch.

"Guess you're right about that," Pierce replied on a sigh.

Alicia looked at her youngest nephew and smiled. "Pierce, all you need to understand is that you always have a place here. No matter what transpires, this will always be your home."

"How did Pierce and Mollie take the news?" Chaz Yarbrough sat in Noah Dodd's office smoking a thin cheroot as he leaned back into the large leather chair.

"Not well, I'm afraid." Noah hadn't been surprised when Mollie had jumped from her chair, demanding to tear up the agreement. He'd calmed her down after some quick talking and a reminder than he'd already shared a portion of the details about their new job. "However, they did accept the plan, such as it is at this point. Of course, they will need to work on the way they communicate in public, lest people catch on that they're not married."

Chaz chuckled. "I know what you're saying. They either want to throttle each other or..." He let the rest trail off, sure that Noah knew what he alluded to.

"That is the one potential flaw in this plan. They can be brilliant working together or go up in flames. I'm betting each will work through any personal issues with the other to make this assignment a success."

"You wouldn't have set them on it if you weren't sure of their ability to follow this to the end."

"Now, what do you have for me?" Noah was ready to get down to the reason for their meeting. He liked Chaz, the way he operated, his cool professionalism, and willingness to take risks other agents avoided. They'd both served in Europe, which, in Noah's opinion, was a benefit and provided them with contacts that might very well be needed for this assignment.

"There isn't much right now." Chaz slid a file across the desk. Scattered bits of information that he and Lee had pulled together for both teams the agency had established for this assignment. "This is all we have."

Noah pulled the file toward him and began to review the contents, shaking his head at the utter lack of detail. He wondered if they'd gotten involved too soon in the investigation. "The East Coast group has been provided the same material?"

Chaz nodded.

"My understanding is they will be working from New York City. My counterpart, in the Eastern region at the Treasury, has arranged a place for them to work." Noah continued to scan the small amount of information.

"Do you have anything identified for Pierce?" Chaz asked.

Noah looked up from the file. "Yes. We were lucky on two counts. First, Louis Dunnigan is providing offices for our use. Second, it turns out that Victoria MacLaren, Jamie's wife, owns a mansion in the society district of Nob Hill. The team will hold most of its meetings at her home."

Chaz's eyebrows lifted at the news. "Torie MacLaren?"

"The same. A long story, but suffice it to say, the woman has substantial assets in California."

"I'll be damned. I never would have figured her to come from money like that."

"You wouldn't expect to. Nothing about the family indicates their standing or money, but, trust me, the family has both. Victoria MacLaren happens to have an over-abundance of it."

"She's agreed to the use of her property?"

"Yes. I met with her and Jamie yesterday. All the MacLarens know of its existence, but she and Jamie are the only two who know its location." Noah handed Chaz the address.

"When do they leave?" Chaz asked.

"Within the next few days, once Lee Hatcher gets back to me. He's got Eva on a train to San Francisco already. He'll head out only if he's needed."

"You do live dangerously, don't you?" Chaz smirked.

"What are you talking about?"

"Lee and Eva."

"What does that mean?" Noah thought he knew most of the secrets of his various agents. Perhaps he'd missed something.

"Nothing much, except they used to be married."

******

Mollie packed the last of her clothes and shut the lid of the trunk. She'd given the outfits she'd used while undercover at the Desert Dove to one of the working girls, a young woman who'd started just after Mollie began her last assignment. The same time she'd first met Pierce MacLaren.

She leaned against the frame of a window overlooking the main street and fingered the thin black ribbon around her neck. Dangling from it was the cameo her mother had given her many years ago, just before she'd left for her job at a small laundry several blocks away. She'd never returned, leaving ten-year-old Mollie and her father to carry on alone.

Twelve years later, Mollie was still plagued with the notion that her mother had not walked out on them, but had become a victim. She was certain her mother was dead.

Her father had insisted otherwise, said that she'd gotten tired of living with so little, and walked out. The police had sided with him, explaining that a body had never been found, nor had anyone heard screams or pleas for help anywhere between their house and the laundry.

She glanced out the window and pulled her thoughts from the past to the real dilemma that had her so on edge—her partner.

Mollie had been raised by a single father, she'd worked alongside men as a clerk in a lumberyard, served drinks to them while at the Desert Dove in Fire Mountain, and yet none of them had made as significant an impact on her as Pierce MacLaren. He'd walked into the Dove alone one afternoon, taken a seat at a back table, and introduced himself. She knew who he was. Everyone knew the six MacLaren men, or at least knew of them.

She'd served him a whiskey then lingered for a moment wanting ... something. She hadn't known what. All Mollie remembered was the way she'd felt when he'd walked into the saloon. Tall and lean, rugged looking with broad shoulders, short dark brown hair, and clear blue eyes that had locked with hers the moment he'd walked in. Her stomach had tripped over itself and her breath had caught in her chest. Never in her life had she felt such an immediate attraction to a man.

Now, they were partners. Mollie winced, irritation at the current situation coursing through her. She still felt the same pull toward the man, yet that pull was mixed with equal parts frustration and exasperation. He was an arrogant, self-righteous, controlling troublemaker who wreaked havoc on her patience whenever they were together. She didn't understand how one man could affect her so much.

Mollie turned toward the bed and looked at the small trunk that held everything she owned. She straightened her spine and resolved to get through this one last assignment with him. After that, she'd collect her money and take the first train to Boston, leaving the bigheaded MacLaren and her job as a Treasury agent behind.

******

New York City

Lee Hatcher finished his coffee and set the empty cup on the desk. He'd been studying the report in front of him for over an hour, jotting down notes and trying to figure out what it was about the information that sent cautionary sparks through his body. He was a perceptive man, had stayed alive more than once by recognizing the red flags and heeding their warnings. The newest report signaled that what Noah Dodd and many others thought to be isolated cases were, in actuality, tied together. The problem was no one had any information on how all the disparate occurrences were related.

A knock on his door had him looking up to see his other boss, Alex McCann, walk in with another gentleman behind him.

"Good morning, Alex. I thought you were in Philadelphia this week?" Lee stood and walked around to face the two men.

"Something came up that we need to discuss. Alex, this is William Rents. He has some information that might prove interesting." Alex McCann owned a well-respected investigation firm whose clients included some of the most wealthy and influential men in the eastern United States. Lee, as his chief investigator, was aware of all the cases handled by McCann Investigations.

"Mr. Rents," Lee said and held out a hand. "Have a seat."

The three men settled into their chairs before Alex indicated for Rents to begin.

"It's hard to know where to start," Rents began. "A good friend of mine is, or *was*, a banker here in New York. We'd meet for supper a couple of times a month, talk about work, families, and such. The last few times we met, he seemed agitated, would order his meal then hardly take a bite. He was a big man and enjoyed his food, if you know what I mean."

Lee nodded in understanding. "What happened to your friend?"

"That's just it—he disappeared for several days before knocking on my door early one morning. He's got a black eye like he's been beaten, clothes torn up and such. Told me he'd been bothered by some odd activities at work and needed to speak with someone who could help. Problem was he didn't know who he could trust, except me. I'll tell you, he was scared. I told him about Alex and that I'd set up a meeting. Trouble was Alex was in Philadelphia. My friend got nervous about waiting and took off. Next thing I know, his body's found near the docks. Guess he'd been dead a couple of days."

"I see." Lee glanced at Alex before leveling his gaze back on Rents. "Have you spoken of this to anyone besides Alex and me?"

"Not a soul. I got a message off to Alex as soon as I learned of Edward's death."

"Last name?"

"Franks. Edward Franks."

"Have the police figured anything out, found the killer?"

"They won't talk much to me, but I heard from an acquaintance at the station that they've got nothing. Not one clue."

"Did Franks give you any idea what he wanted to talk to Alex about?"

Rents leaned forward, resting his arms on his knees. "Only that he'd overheard a conversation about how to best get rid of someone. He seemed to think it involved some very influential person." He paused a moment. "Wish I had more, but I don't."

"You did right coming to Alex. Do we know how to reach you, Mr. Rents?"

"Alex has my information."

Alex stood. "William, I'll walk out with you. One of us will let you know if we learn anything." He looked back at Lee. "Don't leave until we've had a chance to talk."

Five minutes later, Alex had returned, a grim expression on his face as he took a seat. "My gut tells me there's a connection between what Rents reported and what you're working on for Dodds."

"How's that?"

Alex reached into his pocket, pulled out a piece of paper, and handed it to Lee. It was a report about a man who was looking for contacts to do some particularly nasty work for one of his clients. The source who'd overheard the conversation seemed to think it involved someone well known. The report had come from one of Alex's investigators who'd been working another case.

Lee let out a breath. "I don't believe much in coincidences."

"Neither do I," Alex responded as he walked out the door.

Chapter Three

San Francisco

Pierce stepped off the train before helping Mollie down. They'd talked little during the entire trip, each lost in their own thoughts. Mollie had surprised him by pulling out one of the dime novels that were popular and reading for most of the ride, effectively stopping any conversation between them.

He flagged a carriage to take them to Torie's large house. Even though Jamie had described the property, Pierce was still unprepared for the imposing structure and lavish interior. Torie had lived here when she'd been married to her first husband, Hamilton Wicklin, a miserable human being who was now out of her life forever.

A nice-looking woman of about thirty answered his knock and smiled. "You must be Mr. and Mrs. MacLaren. I'm Penelope. Miss Victoria sent word that you'd be using the house." She opened the door wide. "Please come in. I'll get your bags and show you to your room."

Room. The word hung in the air between Pierce and Mollie. Both knew one room would never work.

"Hello, Penelope. I'm Pierce and this is my, uh, wife, Mollie." He'd almost choked on the word

31

wife, and hoped the housekeeper hadn't noticed. He carried his own bag, letting Penelope assist Mollie with her small trunk. "If it's not too much trouble, we'd like to have separate rooms."

Penelope split a look between the two, not commenting. It wasn't unusual for married couples to have separate rooms, yet when she'd mentioned individual bedrooms to Miss Victoria and her husband, Jamie, he'd about bit her head off.

"No trouble at all, Mr. MacLaren. Follow me and I'll help you get settled before supper."

She set Mollie's trunk down in a beautiful bedroom with rose, soft green, and gold flowered draperies and matching bedspread. Mollie's breath caught at the lovely furnishings. She stepped to the window and pulled back the sheers to look out on a magnificent garden with walkways and a large gazebo covered in vines.

"I'll be right back, ma'am, to help you get settled." Penelope left the door to the hallway open as she showed Pierce his room.

"Here you go, sir," she said to Pierce. She walked to the large window and drew open the heavy fabric curtains. It was larger than Mollie's room, with dark wood furnishings and draperies of deep green, blue, and burgundy. The bedspread was of similar colors with a different pattern. "Shall I help you unpack, sir?"

"No, thank you, Penelope. I'll take care of it."

The servant nodded and closed the door behind her.

Pierce looked around, trying to imagine his taciturn cousin in this room. He grinned, thinking of what Jamie's reaction would have been the first time he'd seen it. He thought of the smaller home Jamie and Torie shared in Fire Mountain, wondering how a woman coming from this had been able to accept life on the ranch, which offered so little in the way of comforts compared to the opulent mansion overlooking the sprawling San Francisco bay.

He gave Mollie some time to unpack then walked down the hall to knock on her door. She pulled it open, not offering to let him enter.

One hand on the doorknob, the other on a hip, she looked him up and down. "You need something, MacLaren?"

His eyes narrowed. "We need to talk, work out some details before tomorrow. Meet me downstairs." He turned to leave and chuckled at her mumbled reply.

"Yes, sir, MacLaren. Whatever you say."

He ignored the sound of her slammed door and made his way downstairs thinking that this was going to be a very long few weeks.

Mollie leaned against her bedroom door, taking a deep breath to still her racing heart, and closed her eyes. She needed to figure out a way to control her reactions to the handsome MacLaren. She hated the feelings that rippled through her when he was around. The train ride had been excruciating. She just couldn't seem to relax when he was anywhere around.

"Damn him," she murmured, and vowed to find a way to keep her attraction to the man concealed, whatever the cost.

******

Eva Gagnon glided down the wide staircase of the opulent San Franciscan Hotel and walked toward the large dining area. She'd been staying in Canada, taking time off after her last assignment, when Noah contacted her.

She stopped to check her image in the gilded mirror to the left of the dining room entrance. Tall, at five nine, and slender with jet-black hair hidden under her fashionable hat, Eva knew she created a presence. It was her job to turn heads, distract, and occupy those under suspicion while her associates dug into their affairs. This assignment would be much the same.

"May I help you, madam?" the maître d' inquired, his eyes fixed on the statuesque woman.

"Yes. I am meeting Mr. Theodore Crow."

"Of course. Mr. Crow is waiting for you."

She followed him toward a kind-looking man in a fashionable suit who sat at a table near the front window. He stood when she approached.

"Ah, Miss Gagnon. It is a pleasure to see you again." He lifted her hand to place a kiss on her delicate fingers.

"Thank you, Mr. Crow. The pleasure is mine." Eva sat down and smiled at the older gentleman. She'd arrived in San Francisco the week before and wasted no time beginning her charade as a wealthy widow looking to make contacts in the rapidly expanding West Coast city.

Eva met Crow and his wife the previous night at a party hosted by the mayor of San Francisco, Edwin Pound, and his wife, Lydia. Noah Dodd had provided her with a list of businessmen most apt to assist a wealthy widow assimilate into the city's higher social circle, the kind of men who would have a feel for what was happening around them. All the men on the list possessed the required connections, and Eva was determined to identify those who could provide the answers the agents needed.

Theodore Crow sipped his wine and exchanged pleasantries with Eva. He wasn't an unattractive man. His medium height and average appearance, with curly red hair mixed with gray, made him seem approachable and sincere. Those qualities, paired with the massive wealth his family had accumulated from generations in the shipping business, made him high on Eva's list. He'd married a woman a few years his senior who'd inherited an unthinkable sum when her parents died in a train accident. It was a marriage of social and financial equals, which suited them both. Mrs. Crow lived her life of charity events, social issues, and luncheons, and Theodore pursued his own business interests. He was known for helping those new to San Francisco get to know the city.

"The mayor and his wife will be hosting their annual ball this month. His wife is quite the hostess, as you know from last night's supper party. Do you plan to attend?" Crow finished his wine and watched as their efficient server hastened to fill his glass.

"Yes, I do. The mayor's wife, Lydia, invited me and a guest." Eva smiled, planning to get a message off to Lee Hatcher the following day, requesting another agent join her to act as an escort. It would be easier to flow through the social circles on the arm of a wealthy bachelor. "I have some close friends who have recently moved to the city, and Lydia graciously invited them to attend. He works for a wealthy businessman from Denver and will be expanding the gentleman's operations on the West Coast. His wife is a beautiful woman and quite charming. However, they're in need of a proper introduction."

"I'd be happy to introduce the three of you to those I know."

"What a marvelous idea, Theodore. I'm sure we'll all have a wonderful time." Eva relaxed, having already accomplished her objective for the evening.

******

"Mr. MacLaren?"

Pierce looked up from his breakfast to see the housekeeper standing at the entrance to the dining room. "What is it, Penelope?"

"There's a Miss Gagnon here to see you." The servant stood erect, keeping her hands clasped in front of her as she waited for his response.

"Please show her to the library."

They'd been in San Francisco two days without contact from the other female agent. Pierce was glad the waiting was over. He gave Penelope a few minutes to get their guest settled before joining her in the library. He was ready to move this assignment forward.

"Hello, Miss Gagnon. It's a pleasure." Pierce walked into the wood-paneled room and took a seat near his guest.

"Thank you for receiving me without notice, Mr. MacLaren. I appreciate your courtesy," Eva said for the benefit of the housekeeper who still stood at the door.

"Please bring us some coffee, Penelope." Pierce watched as she left the room then turned to face the woman in front of him.

He wasted no time. "Tell me what's going on."

Eva arched a brow as her mouth turned up at the corners. "Anxious, Mr. MacLaren?"

"Pierce, and, yes, I'm ready to move this along." His response was clipped, not rude, yet his impatience was clear.

Eva opened her reticule and withdrew a piece of paper. She handed it to Pierce and watched as he read through it.

"Mr. Theodore Crow?"

"I met him a few nights ago. He's wealthy, well connected, and has lived in San Francisco for many years. You, Mollie, and I have received an invitation from the mayor's wife to attend their annual ball and Mr. Crow has offered to make introductions for us." Eva shifted to look at a beautiful young woman who entered the library, closed the door, and walked toward her. "You must be Mollie Jamison." She stood when Mollie came to a halt in front of her chair.

Mollie said nothing at first, staring at the woman before her. She was taller than Mollie by at least two inches, slender, with black hair and striking features that gave her an exotic look. Eva was perhaps the most stunning woman she'd ever seen, and the way Pierce looked at the woman told her he agreed. For some reason, the thought of the gorgeous woman working alongside her partner irritated her.

"Mollie, this..."

"I know who this is, Pierce" Mollie cut him off, not taking her eyes from the woman before her. "Eva Gagnon, correct?"

Eva's brow arched. "That is correct." She settled back in her chair and looked at Pierce. "The ball will be the perfect place to move about freely and meet the types of people we need to gather information."

"What ball?" Mollie asked, miffed that Pierce hadn't sent for her when Eva arrived.

"The mayor and his wife host an annual ball," Pierce said. "It will be held later this month, and I was able to secure an invitation for us to attend."

Mollie understood the significance of an invitation to such a sought-after social affair. They could acquire more information in one night than they could learn through weeks of meeting people and searching for answers on their own.

"What do we do in the meantime?" Pierce asked while keeping his eyes on Mollie, uncomfortable with her behavior toward Eva. He'd watched her scrutinize the other agent as if she were the enemy and not part of the team Noah had formed.

"Pierce, you'll go to the office each day while Mollie begins to make friends with some of the more influential women in San Francisco."

"And how do I go about doing that?" Mollie had taken a seat between Eva and her partner, effectively blocking Pierce's view of the other agent.

"You're quite fortunate in that Torie MacLaren is well liked and accepted in the highest circles. She offered to send letters to some of her friends, asking that they accept you as part of her family. I would expect you to hear from most of the women quite soon." Eva looked at the small enameled brooch pinned to her dress, popped it open, and checked the timepiece housed inside. "I should be going, but we'll all meet again soon."

"I'll see you out." Pierce stood and glanced at Mollie. "I'd like a few words with you." He didn't wait for a reply before escorting Eva out. Within moments, he'd returned to the library and shut the door behind him.

"Do you want to tell me what that was about?" He walked over to the small bar and poured himself a drink, not offering anything to Mollie.

She watched him open the bottle and take down one glass. She didn't want to answer. Not because she intended to appear obstinate, but because she didn't know what had caused her to behave that way toward Eva. Granted, she'd never worked with another female agent and hadn't expected one as striking as Miss Gagnon, yet that didn't excuse her odd conduct. She hadn't been outright rude, yet she'd offered no welcome to the woman who was only doing her job as part of their assignment.

"Well?" Pierce had walked over and now stood a few inches in front of her.

"Well, what?" Regardless of how Mollie felt, it wasn't Pierce's place to question her actions.

"Are you going to pretend your behavior toward Eva wasn't rude?"

"It was no such thing." Mollie's retort lacked conviction. She folded her arms across her chest and stalked to the window, drawing back the heavy draperies. She'd taken a walk through the spacious grounds that morning, admiring the flower gardens and various shrubs, and wondered what it would be like to live in a place like this all of the time.

Pierce watched his partner as she tried to distance herself from both him and the subject. She may be frustrating and strain his patience, but Mollie wasn't stupid. He knew she wouldn't risk alienating another agent without a reason.

"Are you suspicious of her?" Pierce fished for an answer.

"Of course not. If Noah brought her in, then I'm sure she's more than capable."

"Plus, she's had more experience than you and I combined."

"Yes."

"And she's already accomplished more in two days than we have."

"I agree."

"And, of course, there is the fact that she's a stunningly beautiful woman." He watched her face for a reaction.

She turned from the window to glare at him. "You find her pretty?"

"Don't you?"

Mollie didn't respond. This wasn't a conversation she intended to have with Pierce. "It doesn't matter what I think as long as her skills bring us what we need to finish this assignment."

"So you do think she's beautiful?" Pierce persisted.

She narrowed her eyes, but didn't respond. "I'm going upstairs. I'll see you at supper." She avoided eye contact as she brushed past him and left the room.

Pierce watched her leave, barely able to restrain a smile until she'd closed the door. Her behavior had baffled him until he realized that his partner might be jealous of the beautiful female agent who was part of their team. From his point of view, there was just one reason one female would be jealous of another, and he was unwilling to go there.

He'd been able to control his body's response to Mollie over the last few months, even though it had become increasingly difficult. He found Mollie to be the most achingly beautiful and annoyingly desirable woman he'd ever met. Before their partnership, he had spent many hours fantasizing about her. Now, he had to ignore his normal reactions, and treat her like anyone else he worked around—except they were partners and forced to be together almost every day.

If he could bed her, let his strong attraction run its course, he'd be able to get her out of his system, and his automatic response to her would end. He was certain of it.

Chapter Four

New York City

Lee studied the latest message from Eva. Even though it had been four years, he still felt a twist in his gut whenever he heard her name or saw her, which, thankfully, wasn't often, and generally from far away. He hoped to keep her at a distance for this assignment, at least several thousand miles away. The telegram he held in his hand caused that hope to fade with each word.

Eva recommended that they'd be able to accomplish more with another agent, someone from wealth who had a high enough pedigree from the East Coast that no one would question him. She'd leave the final decision to Lee.

It was cloaked as a recommendation, even though both Eva and Lee knew otherwise. She had a knack for making her demands known, even if they appeared subtle to those unfamiliar with her tactics.

What bothered him above all else was the fact that there was no one he could think of who fit the description of the perfect agent—no one except him. If she'd been hinting for him to travel to the San Francisco, she would have said it straight out. She hadn't. He knew he was the last person she wanted in her presence, not after what happened four years before.

Lee grabbed the message and marched across the hall to Alex McCann's office, knocked once, then entered. Alex looked up from his desk.

"What do you need, Lee?" Alex knew Hatcher well enough to know the man had little time or patience for small talk.

"Advice."

Alex tossed down the pen in his hand and sat back. "All right."

"Eva Gagnon has requested another agent. Someone well trained with the right social standing to act as her suitor and escort in San Francisco. I need your help to identify someone."

Alex McCann handled many off-the-books investigations for Noah Dodd and several other well-placed government employees in various agencies. His company was working behind the scenes on the current assignment led by Noah and Lee. A request for a certain type of agent with specific skills wasn't unheard of, and was most often passed by Alex for his input and approval.

"Ty Bonnefield would fit the requirements nicely, however, he's in the middle of a four month assignment for another agency. John Hamilton would be an excellent choice if he hadn't broken his leg on his the job. He'll be laid up for months."

Alex pulled open a desk drawer and pulled out some files. He thumbed through the stack, setting a couple aside and placing the rest back into the drawer. He opened the first, closed it, then picked up the second file to read the contents.

"Owen Kendall. He'd be perfect. About your size, excellent skills, from a wealthy family with banking interests in New York and Boston. He's a lawyer by trade, graduated from Columbia, and keeps a home in the city. If I'm not mistaken, I believe he may also have a house in San Francisco that was left to him by one of his relatives." He looked up to see that Lee's face had turned to stone.

"No, not Kendall. There must be someone else."

"There is only one other person I know who could make this work." Alex folded his hands on the desk and leaned forward.

"Who is that?"

"You."

Lee stood, shoved his hands in his pockets, and paced to the large set of windows that looked out onto one of the busiest streets in New York. He had a love-hate relationship with this city and some of the people in it. He loved it for the same reasons he hated it. Privilege and power were wielded without regard for those who stood in the way. Educated, wealthy scions with questionable character and back room business dealings were revered, while those who made their money through honest hard work and respect for the law were spurned. He'd been born into privilege and affluence, was an almost embarrassingly wealthy man from a well-respected family, yet he still felt the chains that came with the opportunities which had been handed to him. That he hadn't been disinherited by his father still amazed him.

He turned back to Alex. "I can't."

"It's been over four years. You're both professionals. I'm betting the two of you could pull this off better than any other two agents."

"Perhaps, but we could just as easily fail."

"She's over it."

"So she's told you and everyone else." He ran a hand through his thick auburn hair and took a deep breath, never moving from his spot by the window. "Eva believes I destroyed our marriage. She may never trust me again. This assignment is too important. It's not worth the risk."

"Then Owen Kendall it is." Alex closed the file. "I'll contact him today and set up a meeting for tonight."

"No, not Kendall," Lee hissed then walked back to his chair in four long strides.

"For God's sake, Lee, there isn't anyone else."

The room fell silent as Lee struggled with a decision that could mean success or failure for their current assignment—an assignment that, as yet, wasn't fully understood by anyone. Alex was right. There were few men who could meet the needs of this job, and only two of them were available—he and Owen—and there wasn't a chance in hell he'd let Kendall get anywhere near Eva.

He stood and straightened to his full six foot four inch height. "I'll make travel arrangements for San Francisco."

Alex nodded, knowing that this was not the best solution. But it was the only one they had under the circumstances.

******

San Francisco

"Mr. Dunnigan. It's good to see you." Pierce stood in the lobby of the large building and extended his hand to the man who'd once hired him to work on a decoding case. Pierce's current assignment included a cover as an employee of Dunnigan Enterprises in the San Francisco offices.

"Hello, Pierce. It appears that life is treating you well." Louis Dunnigan accepted the offered hand then indicated that Pierce should follow him upstairs to the third floor. "Here you are." He opened the door to one of the offices facing the main street and waved Pierce inside. "As you can see, your office is furnished with everything needed by an executive of my company. Although Dunnigan Enterprises purchased the building, it is used by several of my companies, including Taylor-Dunnigan Cattle & Timber. Since you know most of the people involved in Taylor-Dunnigan, that is what we'll go with for your cover. You'll be helping us expand our timber, lumberyard, and cattle operations in northern California."

Louis walked into the hall. "Miss O'Connell, I'd like to introduce you to Pierce MacLaren, the new director."

Pierce followed Dunnigan into the hall, expecting to see an older woman. What he found surprised him. Martha appeared to be in her early twenties, with dark reddish-brown hair pulled into a loose bun. Her soft, green-gray eyes were set wide, giving her a perpetual look of innocence. She stood about five foot five, and her petite frame was covered in a long-sleeved, high-necked green dress that hugged her slim waist.

"Pierce, this is Martha O'Connell. She'll assist you with whatever you need. Martha, meet Pierce MacLaren."

"It's a pleasure to meet you, Miss O'Connell." Pierce studied her serene expression and wondered how much she knew about him and his work at Taylor-Dunnigan.

Martha smiled as she looked up at the much taller new director who would be her boss. He was handsome in the extreme. "Nice meeting you also, Mr. MacLaren. My desk is just down the hall. Please let me know if there is anything I may do for you."

"Miss O'Connell, please see that Mr. MacLaren receives a complete tour of the building and meets the other managers and staff." Louis turned to Pierce. "I must leave for an appointment, but Miss O'Connell will take good care of you."

"Let me know when you'd like your tour, Mr. MacLaren," Martha said and began to turn away.

"Now is fine, Miss O'Connell."

She inclined her head and motioned for him to follow. "All right. We'll start with this floor."

They walked through the three-story building, Martha introducing him to perhaps twenty employees. There was considerable empty space, which Martha said would be leased to a law firm for at least two years.

"Mr. Dunnigan told me you and your wife just moved here from the East Coast. Do you have children, Mr. MacLaren?"

Wife? Pierce almost said before he caught himself. "Uh, no. Mrs. MacLaren and I were only recently married."

"Congratulations. Please let her know that I would be delighted to help her with anything she needs regarding the city. I've lived here my entire life and know all the good areas, as well as those she should avoid. It's a wonderful place, but women must still be careful which neighborhoods they frequent."

"Thank you, Miss O'Connell. I'm sure she'll be appreciative of your offer."

They finished the tour before returning to his office.

"Did Mr. Dunnigan provide you with a key?" she asked Pierce.

"Key?"

"To your office."

"No, he didn't."

"I'll make sure you have one by the time you leave today." She made a note on the pad of paper she always carried. "Will there be anything else, Mr. MacLaren?"

"Nothing else now, Miss O'Connell. Thank you for the tour and introductions."

Martha nodded before turning to walk back to her desk. Pierce watched her walk away, appreciating the sway of her hips and damning Noah once more for creating a situation that was as frustrating as it was lucrative.

******

"Is Mrs. MacLaren home, Penelope?" Pierce walked into the large entrance hall, placed his hat on the hallstand, and reached for his gun belt before realizing he'd left it in his bedroom. Noah had ordered a special holster to conceal the forty-five Peacemaker that Pierce preferred to carry, plus a special holster for Mollie's use, but they had yet to arrive.

"Yes, Mrs. MacLaren is in the drawing room having tea."

Pierce loosened his shirt collar while walking toward the drawing room. He needed to arrange for Mollie to come to his office, meet the employees, and speak with Miss O'Connell. Mollie had good instincts and he valued her opinion about people—everyone except himself, of course. He believed she was dead wrong in her judgment of him.

"Good evening, Mrs. MacLaren." He bent to place a quick kiss on her cheek, knowing that Penelope had followed him with a glass and decanter of whiskey. The kiss had an unanticipated effect on Pierce as he found himself fighting the urge to place a proper kiss on her lips. It unsettled him to know that even a slight touch, his lips to her skin, could trigger such an intense desire and impulse to take more.

Mollie froze at the feel of Pierce's lips on her face. The contact was brief, yet the impact was profound. She fought to keep her gaze forward and not raise her eyes to his, seeking what her body had craved since the first day she'd met him. Her hands stayed clasped tight in her lap until he pulled back and turned to take a seat across from her.

"How did it go?" To her dismay, her voice wavered. She reached for her cup of tea and took a long swallow of the warm liquid to hide the momentary lapse.

"It will more than suit the purpose. Mr. Dunnigan introduced me to Miss O'Connell, the woman who will help with any of my needs." He glanced at Mollie to see her eyebrows lift at his comment. Pierce knew he was baiting her, wanting to see her react to the implication in his remarks, and perhaps comment—show the slight vein of the jealousy that surfaced when she'd met Eva—but she didn't respond.

He cleared his throat. "I'd like you to visit tomorrow, meet Miss O'Connell and a few others. I believe it's a good idea to get in the habit of showing up at odd times, letting everyone know that you'll come and go as you please."

Mollie thought his request made sense. The more she visited Pierce, the more her appearances would be seen as normal, and those who worked around him would relax and perhaps speak with her. She'd heard from Noah that Dunnigan had hired locals who either grew up in San Francisco or knew the area well. Exactly the type of people who might know the city from another point of view—a vantage point different from those considered newcomers. She turned at the sound of Penelope entering the room to announce supper would be ready in ten minutes.

"Thank you, Penelope." Mollie turned back to Pierce. "It would be my pleasure to come by your office tomorrow. Shall we say noon?"

Pierce waited until Penelope closed the door. "That's fine." He leaned forward in his seat. "There are several banks a short distance from the office. It would be a good time to visit each one and meet the managers. They're in a position to know about activities that seem out of place and provide us with additional introductions."

Mollie agreed. She knew they had to make acquaintances with those powerful in business, as Eva was already doing.

Penelope came back in to let them know their meal was ready.

Pierce stood, took a couple of steps toward Mollie, and extended a hand. "May I accompany you to supper?"

Mollie took his hand and quickly wrapped her fingers under his as they turned to leave the drawing room. The same sensations she'd felt when he'd touched her cheek with his lips rippled through her body when his hand touched hers. This time, the awareness excited and troubled her. By the time they reached the beautifully set table, she'd made a resolution to steel herself against her body's reaction to Pierce MacLaren. They had a job to do, and neither could afford to jeopardize it over some passing attraction.

Chapter Five

Fire Mountain

"What's the news from Pierce?" Aunt Alicia passed the large platter of roast beef to Jamie then picked up the bowl of potatoes.

Connor spent most days in town managing the three saloons owned by Niall MacLaren and taking care of family business which included a stop at the post office. Today, he'd been surprised to find a letter from his younger brother.

"They're all settled in Torie's house and he connected with Louis Dunnigan." Connor nodded to Jamie's wife, who, with a small wave of her hand, brushed off the use of her mansion as nothing unusual.

Truth was Torie had never reconciled herself to the wealth she'd inherited from her first husband's aunt. Although she was no fool and would keep the estate in the booming West Coast city, she rarely thought of it and had only traveled back four times in the years she'd been married to Jamie.

"That's it? Nothing about how it's going with Mollie?" Will filled his plate and tucked into the evening meal.

"Only that he's more than ready for the assignment to end, which could take weeks or months. Poor guy, cooped up in a mansion that overlooks the bay with a beautiful woman. Sometimes, I don't think Pierce knows when he's got it good." Connor smiled at his wife Grace then fell silent.

"Dunnigan sent me a letter a few days ago. I may need to travel out to the new offices in San Francisco to meet the employees and go over some of the legal issues regarding the lease of space to a law firm." Drew MacLaren handled all the legal work for Taylor-Dunnigan as well as a good portion of the work for Dunnigan Enterprises. "Don't know why he'd need me out there, it's a simple contract."

"Isn't there another attorney that you hired to work on those types of transactions?" Jamie asked.

"Henry Thompson. Dunnigan says he's back east working on the acquisition of another building in New York. That leaves me. I still hope to work it out so it won't be necessary for me to go to San Francisco. There's just too much work around here to do, and with Tess being pregnant..." He stopped at stunned expressions.

"Pregnant?" Aunt Alicia's eyes widened at the news.

"Doc McCauley confirmed it a few days ago," Tess smiled and leaned into Drew, who'd draped his arm across her shoulders. "I haven't even had a chance to send a letter off to my parents."

"We'll do that tomorrow when I send a response to Dunnigan." Drew stood and pulled out her chair. "By the way, Connor, I heard from Dunnigan that a man named Lee Hatcher may be traveling out to San Francisco to work with Pierce. You know him?"

The news surprised Connor. Lee worked for Alex McCann, a long-time friend to Connor and Pierce. From what Pierce had confided in him before leaving for San Francisco, Lee planned to work from the New York office on this assignment. Something important must have come up for him to travel across the country.

"I know Lee, he's a good man. How'd Dunnigan hear about it?"

"He uses Alex's firm on occasion. You know Noah arranged for Pierce's office to be located in the building Dunnigan purchased in San Francisco, right?" At Connor's nod, Drew continued. "All I'm saying is these men inhabit a tight circle. It's interesting how much each knows about the other." He looked at his wife. "How about a walk?"

Connor watched Drew escort Tess out the front door and into the cool night air, and wondered how Pierce truly was doing with his new assignment.

******

San Francisco

"Good afternoon. I'm Pierce MacLaren, and this is my wife, Mollie. We're here to see Mr. Benstead." Pierce and Mollie had already made the rounds to two other banks, discussing services and meeting the managers. This was the last one for today.

The middle-aged woman looked up from her desk at the handsome couple. She knew they didn't have an appointment, and her boss had been quite specific about not seeing anyone who stopped by without being on his calendar. "Let me see if he's available." She started toward her boss's office.

"Please tell him that Louis Dunnigan asked us to meet with him," Pierce added.

Within minutes, the woman walked back to her desk with Mr. Benstead following a few paces behind. He held out his hand to Pierce.

"I'm Carlton Benstead."

"Pierce MacLaren. This is my wife, Mollie MacLaren." Pierce marveled at how accustomed he'd gotten to calling her his wife.

"It's a pleasure. Please, come into my office."

Benstead took a seat behind what Mollie thought to be the largest desk she'd ever seen, or perhaps the diminutive man was simply dwarfed by it. She guessed the banker stood at no more than five foot five, and was as thin as a knife blade. He sank into a tall leather chair and she found herself wondering if his feet touched the floor.

"You know Louis Dunnigan?" Benstead stroked the thin mustache above his upper lip, watching as Mollie took in her surroundings. Pierce's eyes, however, were trained on him.

"Yes, I work for Mr. Dunnigan. Mostly with Taylor-Dunnigan, their cattle and timber business."

"I see." Benstead rested both arms on his desk and leaned forward. "I'd hoped to work with him on the purchase of the office building. Unfortunately, someone else beat me to it. He did, however, leave the door open for future business."

"Mr. Dunnigan has had long-term relationships with a bank in New York and one in Denver. He is a very loyal man. I'm quite surprised he even discussed the transaction with you." Pierce relaxed and watched the banker squirm in his chair then begin to finger his thin mustache once again.

Benstead cleared his throat. "So, what is it I may do for you and Mrs. MacLaren?"

"My wife and I are deciding where we would like to place our funds. We're new in town, and unlike Mr. Dunnigan, plan to be long-term residents of this fine city. You were referred to us by my assistant, Miss O'Connell."

"Ah, yes, Martha O'Connell. I've met her several times. She keeps a small amount of savings with us. Not much, you understand, lower than most of our customers. She'll be married soon, you know. Her fiancé works for one of my finest customers, Gerald Black."

"I hadn't heard that," Pierce replied. He felt that, with time and encouragement, the banker might be just the contact to supply insights on other customers. They wanted to learn as much as possible from him and establish a social connection with both him and his wife. "It is quite kind of you to handle small accounts for women with little income, such as Miss O'Connell."

57

Benstead tilted his head and shrugged. "We do what we can for all of our customers, Mr. MacLaren."

Pierce and Benstead discussed general details about moving funds to San Francisco, and then made plans to meet for lunch the following day. Mollie heard every word, yet acted bored and disinterested, as was the custom of most women in Benstead's circle. The banker turned his attention to her once he and Pierce finished their business.

"I would very much like for you and my wife to meet, Mrs. MacLaren. She is quite involved in many projects. Perhaps something will catch your fancy."

Perfect. This was exactly what Mollie had hoped to accomplish. "I'd be delighted to meet your wife, Mr. Benstead. Please, have her call on me when she has some time." Mollie had already scheduled luncheons with two other women Torie MacLaren knew from her time in the city. Her social calendar was filling up much faster than expected.

******

"We've been invited to supper at the Benstead home on Saturday." Pierce had returned home early after his lunch meeting with Carlton Benstead. He and Mollie sat in the library trying to figure out where various connections lay between people they'd already met. "There will be two other couples, prominent businessmen and their wives."

"Mrs. Benstead visited today. She and I are to have lunch next week with two of her friends. Perhaps they're the same women who will be joining us at supper." Mollie disliked the social functions she and Pierce were being forced to endure, yet she knew they were part of the job. She preferred to work alone, at a safe distance from society as well as Pierce MacLaren. The sooner they finished their job, the faster she'd be able to collect her money and leave.

A soft knock on the door interrupted them.

"Yes?" Pierce called out.

Penelope opened the door. "Miss Gagnon is here to see you."

"Please show her in," Mollie said and stood to greet the woman she had slighted on her last visit.

Eva Gagnon was one of those women incapable of entering a room in a subtle fashion. She didn't have to say a word, yet she commanded space—attention really—from those who stopped in mid-conversation to follow her path.

"Eva, it is good to see you again." Mollie took Eva's parasol and set it aside as Penelope disappeared behind the closed door. Mollie looked up to ensure they were alone. "What news do you have for us?" She hadn't failed to notice the way Pierce's gaze followed Eva into the room, a look of appreciation on his face. She felt herself stiffen at his obvious interest in the other agent.

Eva walked to the large window which overlooked the extensive gardens outside. Although she believed no one had followed her, she couldn't shake the prickling sensation that had accompanied her the past few days.

She reached into her reticule for the newest message then took a seat in a large, upholstered chair, arranging her skirt as she settled back. "I sent a message to Lee Hatcher, requesting that a trained agent be selected to join us. Someone of impeccable background from within the East Coast social set who would be accepted without thought into the social circles of San Francisco. Between the four of us, we are bound to find the information we seek more quickly and connect all the various messages stemming from odd transactions."

"What about Chaz Yarbrough?" Mollie held her glass, but had yet take a drink.

"Chaz is an exceptional agent, and one who will be used extensively for this assignment. Although he has excellent contacts in the southern states, he is not well known in New York or Boston. The agent I'm requesting must be from that area, wealthy, with an impeccable pedigree."

Mollie nodded in understanding and took a seat next to Eva.

"Has Lee found someone?" Pierce watched the two women, both competent and committed to this assignment, yet so different in appearance and approach. Where Eva was all cool finesse, patiently working every detail of their assignment, Mollie was like a finger itching to pull the trigger. Eva's exotic features and poise set her off as a woman few would forget, while Mollie captured you with her down-to-earth approach and street sense. He was captivated by one, yet drawn to the other.

Eva opened the message. "I received his response this morning. He and Alex McCann identified an agent who has already been dispatched to San Francisco. He'll arrive in time for the Mayor's Ball."

"Any idea who it is?" Pierce now stood facing the women, leaning against the edge of the desk with his arms folded, his shirt pulled taut across his muscled chest.

"My guess is an agent I've worked with in the past, Owen Kendall." She rolled the glass of sherry between her palms, remembering the last time the two of them had worked together. She'd been married to Lee and incredibly in love. Owen had been the one to introduce them. Lee, a wealthy and very eligible bachelor, had proposed within weeks. They'd married and Eva had thought they were happy. The truth had been devastating, but at least they'd divorced sooner rather than later.

"What should we expect?" Pierce had watched the expression on Eva's face change from wistful to emotionless within the span of a few seconds. He wondered what she was thinking.

"Owen is a professional, from a well-established family in Boston and is associated with some of the biggest names in East Coast society. He can be somewhat hot headed, but then all of us can be at times. He'll do a good job." At least, that's what Eva hoped. She'd heard he'd changed over the last few years, growing more and more distant from the other agents and taking jobs where he was the only person involved. She hoped she'd made the right decision in requesting an additional agent.

She set down her empty glass and stood. "I'll be in touch."

Chapter Six

"Mollie? Are you ready?" Pierce stood outside her bedroom door, already dressed and waiting to leave for their supper engagement with the Bensteads. He wore a long tailcoat with a white shirt and white tie. He thought he looked good, if somewhat uncomfortable. Then Mollie pulled her door open and smiled, the first genuine smile she'd given him in weeks.

Pierce's eyes widened and he sucked in a slow breath at the sight of her. He knew she was a pretty woman—her beauty had been all too apparent the first day he'd met her months ago. She'd been working as a barmaid at the Desert Dove, a saloon in Fire Mountain owned by his cousin, Niall MacLaren. At the time, Pierce hadn't known she was undercover, trying to find the source of counterfeit bills being circulated in the territorial capital and taking orders from Noah.

He ignored the blood thrumming through his temples and the tightening of his body. Pierce couldn't allow himself to think of her as anything other than a colleague, even though it took all of his self-control to stop from reaching for her and drawing her to him.

"We should be leaving. Are you ready?" His words were clipped, hard. He could see her face fall, her smile vanish, and wished he could pull the words back.

She didn't say a word, simply grabbed her wrap and walked into the hall, passing him on her way to the stairs.

The ride to the Benstead's was short, taking them to a large home a few blocks away. Both were silent, already knowing what needed to be accomplished and how they'd approach the guests.

"Ah, Mr. and Mrs. MacLaren," Carlton Benstead greeted as his butler escorted them into the moderate-sized parlor. Three other couples were already present. Mollie recognized Mrs. Benstead, who sat alone on a small settee.

"Mrs. MacLaren, I believe you've already met my wife, Henrietta." At Mollie's nod, he went on to introduce them to Thomas and Virginia Traxton, and Gerald and Viola Black, both prominent couples. A third couple, Harold and Lottie Goss, had been added to the guest list. Pierce had met Harold Goss when he'd had lunch with Carlton a few days before.

Supper was served in a well-appointed dining room. Rather than sitting side-by-side, Henrietta Benstead distanced each couple, placing Mollie between Thomas Traxton and Carlton, who sat at one end of the table. Pierce was on the opposite side, between Virginia Traxton and Henrietta, who sat at the other end.

"Pierce, tell us of your experience working with Louis Dunnigan. Have you known the man long?" Harold Goss asked while enjoying both the food and wine offered by the Bensteads. He was a large man, both in height and girth, and offered an easy smile. Pierce came to learn he also possessed a quick mind.

"I've worked for Dunnigan long enough to respect the man and the way he conducts business. Not many are his equal." Pierce sipped the French wine then replaced his glass on the table.

"Are you originally from the east?" Virginia Traxton asked. Pierce hadn't failed to notice the way her eyes roamed over him, or her predilection for touching his arm when she spoke. He shook off his initial unease at her obvious interest.

"Yes, Boston and New York." He kept his answer short, hoping to dissuade further questions from the woman next to him.

"Oh, then perhaps you know the Kendall's? One of their sons, Owen, attended university with my brother."

Although Mollie sat at the opposite end of the table, their eyes shot to each other, recognizing the name as that of the other agent Eva had indicated might join their assignment. Both knew it could be pure coincidence that his name came up, but neither was willing to write it off as pure chance.

"Yes, I've heard of Owen Kendall. I've never had the pleasure of meeting him," Pierce answered.

"Oh, you'll remember him if you ever do make his acquaintance. He's quite impressive." Virginia smiled at Pierce.

"What she means, Pierce, is that he is quite wealthy, mainly family money, and eligible," Thomas Traxton added in a mild tone.

Virginia's eyes fell to her lap, and Pierce noticed how she fidgeted with her napkin. He thought perhaps the woman might know quite a bit about Kendall's past.

"However, he's rumored to have become quite successful on his own," her husband finished.

Mollie listened, trying to assimilate the comments Virginia made against what Eva had told them of the man who might join their assignment. She hadn't mentioned anything other than his wealth and temper. It appeared there might be more to the man than she'd shared.

"We'll take our dessert and coffee in the parlor," Henrietta instructed the butler, ending a conversation that had just become interesting, in Pierce's point of view.

Virginia latched onto Pierce's arm as soon as he'd pulled out her chair. He glanced at Mollie, not missing her questioning stare and arched brow.

"May I?" Thomas Traxton offered his arm to Mollie and escorted her into the parlor. She kept her eyes fixed on Pierce, not missing the intimate way he leaned down to hear something Virginia had said. She was one of the women scheduled to attend the luncheon the following week, and Mollie already found herself disliking the woman.

Pierce escorted Virginia to a large divan and stepped back, expecting her husband to occupy the spot next to her. Instead, the woman tugged on his hand. "Come, sit by me, Pierce. There are so many questions I'd like to ask you."

He shifted his attention to Mollie, who sat across the room, Thomas beside her.

"My pleasure, Mrs. Traxton." He tried to emphasize her married status, already knowing his subtle hint would be lost on the voluptuous blonde. Unlike the other women in the room, Pierce pegged her as someone who went after what she wanted, whether it was a married man or a prized horse. He guessed she was unaccustomed to being refused any overture.

"Now, tell me how you find our city." Virginia looked up at him and smiled. She'd rested her hands in her lap at first, but as she spoke, Pierce felt one hand gently tap his leg as if emphasizing a point before she settled it on his thigh. Her fingers squeezed just enough to gain his attention. It surprised him that no one seemed to notice her unseemly behavior.

"I believe we'll like it here once we've had a chance to settle in."

"And what do you do for pleasure, Pierce?" She'd removed her hand from his thigh and held a cup of tea to her lips, glancing over the brim at him, her eyes sparking with a wicked glimmer.

He narrowed his eyes at her then curved his lips into a half-smile. "Why, Mrs. Traxton, are you flirting with me?"

She laughed and placed her cup on a nearby table. "Of course I am, Mr. MacLaren. Are you not interested?" Her voice had become soft, a husky whisper that only the two of them could hear.

Pierce didn't know how to respond to such a direct offer. He wasn't immune to her beauty, yet had no interest in the woman for anything other than information which would help solve the strange mix of messages Noah and Lee fed them. He dragged his eyes over her, wondering if her husband knew her true nature, or if he cared.

He leaned forward, close to her ear. "I wouldn't want this to be spread around, but, as unfortunate as it sounds, I'm in love with my wife." He pulled back and stood. "I know Mollie is looking forward to your luncheon this week, Mrs. Traxton. It has been a pleasure." He made a slight bow and turned toward Carlton Benstead, who stood several feet away talking with Gerald Black. Pierce glanced at Mollie, who was in deep conversation with Thomas Traxton and Lottie Goss. He wondered what she would think of his conversation with Virginia.

"Ah, Pierce, Gerald and I were just speaking of you." Carlton took a quick look toward Virginia then back at Pierce. "So, you've had your invitation from Mrs. Traxton, I presume."

Pierce's face remained impassive at Benstead's comment.

"Come now. The woman is notorious for her boldness. Has she ensnared you yet?"

He took the glass of whiskey Carlton's butler offered. "I'll only say that the lovely Mrs. Traxton made her intentions known."

Both Carlton and Gerald chuckled.

"The woman is nothing, if not tenacious. Best you keep a level head around her." Carlton offered a vague smile as he sipped his whiskey.

"Good advice." Pierce took a small sip from his glass.

"Yes. She and—" Gerald stopped as his wife, Viola, walked up to the group and laced her arm through his.

"Excuse me, gentlemen, but I do believe it is time we say our goodnights." She looked at her husband then the others.

Pierce turned to find Mollie smiling up at Thomas Traxton, who stood not six inches from her. It appeared the husband was just as bold as his wife. Pierce watched as Mollie laughed at something Traxton whispered in her ear before he reached down to take her hand in his. She quickly slid it free and dropped her arm to her side.

Pierce felt himself chill. In a single, fluid movement, he was by her side, taking her arm in a gentle but firm grip before focusing his attention on Traxton.

"My wife and I will be leaving now. It was a pleasure meeting you." He held out a hand to Thomas, his other hand not releasing its hold on Mollie.

Traxton shifted his gaze from Pierce to Mollie then back to Pierce. "The pleasure was mine, MacLaren. I'm sure we'll be seeing each other soon." He nodded to Mollie before leaving to join his wife.

Pierce loosened his hold on Mollie as they thanked the Bensteads then escorted her to their waiting carriage. He took a seat next to her, crowding her space.

Mollie could feel heat radiating from him, not understanding his actions and not liking the way he'd manhandled her. "What was that about?" she demanded as she tried to create some space between them.

Pierce worked to control his temper. He'd been asking himself the same thing for the last ten minutes and hadn't come up with an answer. All he knew was that the moment he'd seen Mollie's rapt attention on Traxton, the man whispering in her ear then taking her hand, he'd seen red.

"Pierce, did you hear me? What just happened back there?" Her voice was uneven, anger coursing through her blood. Anger that she knew wasn't just from the way he'd acted. Her fury had started as soon as she'd seen the way Virginia had laid her hand on Pierce's thigh, the subtle way the woman had massaged his leg, Pierce doing and saying nothing to stop her.

He ran a hand through his short brown hair, but didn't speak. He had to get himself under control, fast. This was a job, nothing more, with a woman he wasn't certain he liked, and certainly didn't want to be partnered with. *What the hell was wrong with him?* Even as the logic of his thoughts penetrated, his body tightened as their legs and shoulders touched in the close quarters of the carriage.

The short ride felt like hours. He helped her from the carriage and escorted her into the entrance hall and up the stairs, not stopping until they'd reached her bedroom. She'd just extended her hand to grasp the door handle when she felt his hands grip her shoulders and spin her toward him.

Mollie looked into eyes that appeared tormented and hostile. Her voice caught in her throat. She lowered her thick, golden lashes and tried to step back, but he held her firm.

Without warning, Pierce pulled her to him, his mouth coming down on hers in a hard kiss. She tried to ease her hands between them and push away, but stopped as he softened the embrace, his warm, firm lips claiming hers, causing heat to course through her body, all thoughts of pulling away were now gone. Her eyes, strangely heavy, fluttered shut. His grip loosened and she leaned into him, feeling the warmth radiating from his body to hers.

Mollie's hands eased up his arms to his shoulders as his mouth shifted over hers, his gentle ministrations fogging her mind while her body thrummed with need. She wrapped her arms around his neck and drew him closer.

He guided them toward her room, moving through the entrance and kicking the door closed. He wrapped his arms around her, letting his lips find the soft, sensitive area behind her ear before traveling down her slender, ivory neck then back up to her lips. She moaned into his mouth, her body surging against his.

Pierce didn't know what it was that made him stop, pull away, and step back, letting his arms drop to his sides. He took a deep breath, closed his eyes, and paced a few feet away, lifting his arms to spear his hands through his hair. His eyes opened to see Mollie, lips slightly swollen, confusion on her face, and breathing heavily.

"Mollie, I..." Pierce began then trailed off. He wasn't sure what it was he wanted to say.

She blinked a couple of times in an attempt to recover her composure and took a deep, steadying breath before opening the door.

"It would be best if you'd leave." She nodded once toward the hall.

Pierce's eyes narrowed on hers before he stepped past and into the hall, hearing the door close behind him. He shoved his hands in his pockets and looked toward his bedroom. The walk seemed like miles, yet it was just a few yards.

He made his way to his bed, dropping clothes as he went, and fell across it, resting an arm over his eyes and wondering how he'd let that happen.

Chapter Seven

Mollie took one last look in the mirror, and satisfied, picked up her reticule to leave for her luncheon.

She'd been struggling with her body's intense reaction to Pierce a few nights before. The encounter had been unexpected, but not unwanted, at least from her perspective. She had an inkling of what had triggered his sudden desire for her, even though Pierce had yet to utter a word about that night. Their few, brief meetings since had been all business, as if the passion they had experienced never happened.

Mollie had been attracted to Pierce from their first encounter, but had kept her distance, in part because of her job, but also due to his status as a MacLaren. Everyone in Fire Mountain knew and respected the wealthy ranching family. She'd grown up barely able to survive from week to week, her father's work never providing for anything besides the bare minimum. Pierce was used to a life only wealth and status could offer, two things she knew little about.

It had surprised her when he'd joined the agency. She'd vowed to keep her distance, her attraction at that point already too strong. Then Noah had partnered them on the counterfeiting assignment. As much as she'd resented it, felt he would hinder the progress she'd already made, Pierce had been the one to identify the leader and close down the operation. To her distress, working with him had done nothing to lessen her attraction to the tall, handsome man.

Mollie had been angry when he'd insisted they leave the Benstead's house. Even though it had grown late and others were saying their goodbyes, Pierce's sudden appearance by her side, the way he'd clasped her arm, forcing her to his will, had infuriated her. Now, looking back, his anger was no more than she'd felt when Virginia had thrown herself at him. The short ride home had done nothing to relieve the tension between them. She'd simmered while trying to control the urge to vent her frustrations. At the same time, she'd wanted to wrap her arms around him and pull him to her. Her instincts told her that Pierce had been fighting the same temptation.

While Mollie had tried to ignore and fight it, Pierce had given in to it and she'd been swept along as a willing participant. Until he'd stopped. Now, they were as far apart as ever.

Mollie pulled her thoughts to the present as the carriage stopped outside a fashionable restaurant. She could see Henrietta Benstead, Lottie Goss, and Viola Black through the large windows. Each of the women was older than Mollie by a few years. Only Lottie and Viola were originally from the area, Lottie from a small town on the other side of the bay and Viola from the city. Henrietta was from Philadelphia.

"Good afternoon, Mollie." Henrietta beamed as Mollie was shown to her seat.

She greeted the others, noting that Virginia Traxton had not joined them.

"Is Virginia ill?"

The three glanced at each other before Henrietta spoke.

"She sent a note with her apologies, indicating she was indisposed." Henrietta looked at the others again before continuing. The three knew the woman's life with her husband, Thomas, was strained. They suspected he kept a mistress, yet no one had dared bring it up with Virginia. "We so enjoyed having you and your husband over for supper. It's always nice to meet people new to San Francisco."

"Thank you again for having us. We enjoyed ourselves immensely."

"You seemed to spend quite a good deal of time speaking with Thomas. Did you find some common ground?" Lottie asked, remembering how Traxton's gaze had rarely lifted from Mrs. MacLaren.

"I don't know about common ground, however, he was gracious enough to explain a little bit about how all of you are connected. It seems each of your husbands work together in some way."

"Yes, that's true. My husband, Harold, is an engineer, involved with the railroad and planning additional bridge systems," Lottie explained. "Viola's husband, Gerald, handles distribution of building supplies—steel, iron, and other products. And, of course, Henrietta's husband is in banking."

"And Mr. Traxton?"

No one said a word until Viola broke the silence. "Thomas owns several businesses. He doesn't speak too much about them, although, I'm certain the men understand what he does. He and his wife haven't been in San Francisco more than a few years. According to my husband, his businesses are doing well."

"Sounds intriguing."

"Yes, Mollie, that's an excellent word for it." Henrietta opened her menu. "Well, ladies, shall we order?"

******

Pierce was on edge. He'd spent the last few days poring over various bits of information that funneled in from Lee and Noah. As necessary as it was, and as much as he usually enjoyed solving puzzles, he needed more to do, something to take him out of this office and into the streets.

Eva had been to the office twice, garnering the attention and, Pierce surmised, the suspicions of his assistant, Martha O'Connell. He had deflected the speculation by introducing Eva as a business associate of Louis Dunnigan.

"What do you make of it, Eva?"

"Lee's message says that several prominent New York and Boston businessmen are being investigated, quietly of course, regarding steady withdrawals of cash from a bank where most were original investors. There are several men involved in the withdrawals, all wealthy and successful. The team on the east is attempting to get someone placed inside the circle, close to at least one of the men, to see if they can discover what is happening. It may all be quite innocent, but that's not the sense Lee or Noah gets. Both believe something isn't right, but they just can't identify what. From experience, I would trust their instincts."

"And the same investors are involved in a bank here in San Francisco," Pierce muttered, more to himself than Eva. "They could simply be shoring up the new bank through profits from the one on the East Coast. That doesn't seem odd to me, but I have little knowledge of banking and money transfers."

"That's my thought as well, that Treasury may be jumping to conclusions. There is something else pushing the agency to learn more about the actions of these men. All have been quite vocal in their negative reactions to President Cleveland's stand on certain issues and his vetoes of legislation they believe to be in the best interests of the country. From what I know, their comments have been no more vociferous than those who support the president's actions. We could find that this whole assignment is a waste of our time." Eva began to fold the various messages and place them in a file that Pierce would place within a wall safe.

"What do you suggest? Wait for more information? Try to dig something up on the bank investors at this end?" Pierce wanted some firm directive.

"Chaz is on his way and is expected to arrive within two to three days. Let's wait until he arrives then meet again."

******

Pierce walked to the window and stared out at the street below. Frustrated at the lack of information on their assignment, he wondered if they were wasting their time in San Francisco, and pondered the one person he'd been trying to force from his mind—Mollie. Memories of their brief encounter a few nights before played over and over in his mind, tormenting him in a way he'd never experienced. He was through telling himself she wasn't what he wanted. He now knew better.

The touch of her mouth on his had a strange effect on him, quite unlike anything he'd felt with other women from his past. He'd felt a tightness deep in his chest, a heating of his blood that made him feel as if he were on fire. If sanity hadn't returned to save them, Pierce felt certain he would've seduced Mollie and taken her that night in her room, destroying their already tenuous partnership in the process.

They'd met a few brief times to discuss the progress of their assignment, awkward and strained encounters. He'd left each meeting frustrated with their lack of progress on the assignment and hollow inside from the tension between them. He had no idea what to do at this point except close the current job, find a way to diffuse his growing attraction to Mollie, collect his money, and head back to Fire Mountain as soon as possible. The one other option was to bed her, get this burning desire for her out of his system, and get on with his life. Neither choice felt right.

******

Chaz Yarbrough left the train station, climbed into the waiting carriage, and instructed the driver to take him to the San Franciscan Hotel, the same hotel where Eva was staying. He wanted to arrange a meeting with her, Mollie, and Pierce soon, today if possible. Chaz had a growing suspicion that there was significance to what the agents were investigating. He had nothing to prove his belief except the burning sensation in his gut that something major was looming.

It didn't take him long to get settled. He'd sent a message to Eva and was now impatiently awaiting her response. He didn't wait long, evidence that she and the others were just as eager to learn what was going on.

An invitation had arrived at the hotel from Mr. and Mrs. Pierce MacLaren, inviting him for supper at their home that evening. A carriage would be sent for him. Chaz unpacked his few belongings, strolled to the downstairs lobby, and waited for his conveyance. He'd just settled into a large wingback chair when the carriage arrived for the short trip to the area referred to as Nob Hill.

"Good evening, sir," Penelope greeted the tall, slender man.

"Chaz Yarbrough," he said and handed her his hat.

"Chaz." Pierce walked in, shook Chaz's hand, and led him into the nearby parlor where Mollie and Eva waited.

Chaz greeted the women, accepted a drink from Pierce, and took a seat next to Mollie.

"I'm wondering if we may have been sent to San Francisco too soon, without enough information." Eva's voiced what all, except perhaps Chaz, were thinking.

"It doesn't appear that we have much to go on or check out. At this point, it all seems like a waste of time." Pierce was exasperated with the assignment. Sitting and waiting wasn't high on his list of things to do, especially in such close proximity to Mollie.

"I have to agree with Pierce and Eva. Besides meeting some of the local bankers and attending social functions, there doesn't seem to be enough coming from Lee or Noah to keep this going." Mollie leaned forward in her seat, focusing her attention on Chaz.

"It does appear to be a bit of a waste," Chaz said as he finished his drink and set down the glass. "There's little detail, and what we have, is conjecture. Nothing proves anything illegal is happening yet. My guess? There is someone in Cleveland's government stirring things up to see what happens. He may have his suspicions, genuine concerns, and Noah's boss may side with whoever has triggered our involvement.

Unfortunately, when someone at the stop snaps their fingers, we must jump."

"But to what end, Chaz? Yes, there are records of large sums of money being withdrawn from one East Coast bank by members of the original investors group, but what does that prove? These same men are original investors in Carlton Benstead's bank. Perhaps the money is being used for that, or some other very legitimate investment. There must be something more that neither Lee nor Noah are sharing."

"Perhaps they're in the same fix we are," Chaz interjected. "They must respond to an order from their bosses the same as us." He stood, walked to the liquor cabinet, and poured another drink, offering more to the others, who declined. "And they may not be sharing everything they've learned. I will guarantee you, if anything of note occurs, we will be given instructions." He paused a moment to swallow some of the amber liquid in his glass. "There is one piece of information that may interest you. One of my sources has heard multiple rumors of an American, connected with the government or possibly an actual government employee, who is seeking contact with people my source says are less than honorable men. His sources are distinct, so he believes there is some truth to the rumors."

"What is he asking? Has anyone given a description?" Eva set her glass down and stood, becoming more intrigued as this new revelation unfolded.

"The rumors are that he is an American connected to the government, that's it. No one is saying what business he is discussing or services he needs, or what the man looks like. Are they afraid to talk? I don't know. Nothing more specific, yet it's a start and confirms that something is in the works. Is it connected to what Lee and Noah have us doing? I don't know that either." Chaz knew the assignment would not be cancelled, at least not until Noah was ordered to shut it down. "Right now, all we can do is continue to learn what we can from those in San Francisco financial and business circles. At some point, our endeavors may mean something."

Pierce turned at the soft rapping on the door. He opened it to find Penelope.

"Supper is ready, sir."

Chapter Eight

Lee Hatcher looked around his room at the elegant San Franciscan Hotel. He'd been given a suite, one of only three in what was considered the most prestigious hotel in the city. He knew Chaz and Eva had rooms in the same hotel and tried once more to quell both the dread and anticipation he felt at knowing he would be near Eva again after more than four years apart.

He'd seen her a few times since their divorce, or more accurately, since the evening she'd shown up at his hotel room at the urging of Owen Kendall, his partner and close friend—at least until that night. Now, he would not only see Eva, but also be partnered with her until the assignment was over.

He knew she'd be furious and might quit, or refuse to continue until a replacement could be found. It was a chance he'd have to take. Even though she'd judged him and filed for divorce without allowing him to explain, Lee still loved her. He didn't know if he could ever take her back, not even if she learned the truth and came begging. He'd learned Eva's true nature—beneath the exotic beauty, keen mind, and charming exterior was a woman incapable of fully giving her heart or her trust. He doubted he would ever be able to entrust her again with his.

Lee stopped his musings at the sound of a soft knock on the door. The hotel messenger handed him a note then disappeared. It was from Chaz, informing him of his room number and that he'd be out that night. He wanted to meet Lee for breakfast the following morning at seven o'clock in a small restaurant two blocks from the hotel. He'd scrawled the address at the bottom of the message. Lee smiled, knowing his fellow agent had picked a place Eva wouldn't patronize.

He laid the note on his dresser, glad to have a meeting already arranged. Once he met with Chaz, he'd decide what to do next.

******

Penelope had a prepared a wonderful meal. Pierce had overindulged in both food and spirits. It was fortunate he was a man who could hold his liquor.

"We'll take our dessert and coffee in the parlor, Penelope. Shall we?" Pierce stood and pulled out Mollie's chair, then offered his arm.

"You're good at this, playing a role, pretending." Her comment hit a nerve with Pierce.

"What's that supposed to mean?"

"You're a natural at it."

"At what?"

"Pretending to be someone you're not." Her tone wasn't accusatory, more a statement of fact.

"Do you want to tell me exactly what you're talking about?" He let her arm slide from his then took a step back to look at her.

"Slipping into a role comes easy to you, like putting on a different shirt, or hat. You're a natural at fitting into unfamiliar situations and making people believe that's where you belong."

"Not any better than you. Your performance at the Benstead's couldn't have been better. You had Traxton right where you wanted him." Pierce clenched his teeth, remembering how he'd felt when he'd seen Traxton's interest in Mollie.

"I was doing my job, trying to gain his trust. Nothing more. Certainly not as entertaining as watching you and Virginia Traxton circle each other." She took another step away from Pierce, turning toward the parlor. "Tell me, how far will you let the pretending go?"

"As far as it needs to go if I think she has information we need." His eyes were like knives, razor sharp and penetrating.

Their sparring had taken an uncomfortable turn and Mollie wished she'd never brought it up.

"Just forget it." Mollie walked into the parlor and took a deep breath. She'd done this her whole life, opened her mouth before she'd thought through her words. Most of the time, everything turned out all right. Once in a while, they didn't. Tonight, she was afraid, was one of those times.

Pierce didn't budge, hands on his hips, looking through the open parlor door, and wondering what was bothering her. Certainly not anything he'd said during supper, they'd hardly spoken. It couldn't be her part of the assignment. Even though they were all on edge, tired of trying to figure out what they should be doing with so little information, she'd been handling her part for several weeks without incident. He started into the room then stopped. *The Benstead's supper.* In an instant, he knew it had to do with that night, in her room, and the lousy way he'd handled everything. He should have talked with her the following day, told her it was a mistake and it wouldn't happen again. Instead, he'd been a coward and allowed the tension between them to build.

He entered the parlor to see Penelope walking out the other door, having finished serving dessert and filling their coffee cups.

"We won't be needing anything else from you tonight," he said as he took a seat next to Mollie, who straightened her dress and took the opportunity to shift several inches away from him.

Pierce watched her fidget with her dessert, moving the food one way then the other, but not taking a bite. She set the plate down, picked up her cup, and took a sip. That didn't seem to satisfy her either and she set it down next to the plate before standing to walk toward the window.

"Whatever is going on between us isn't going to go away, you know. It's going to hang there until we figure out what to do about it." Pierce walked up beside her and slid both hands in his pockets.

Mollie steeled herself and turned toward him. "I don't know what you're talking about. There's nothing going on between us. The other night was just two people reacting to the situation and the job. We're both stressed from the lack of direction and information. We handled it poorly, that's all." She turned her attention back outside, pretending to enjoy the spectacular garden when her eyes couldn't focus on anything other than the man who stood next to her.

Pierce's emotionless expression didn't change while she spoke, even though inside he was reeling from her words. His reaction to their kiss had been devastating, forcing him to turn away and leave before he did something both would regret.

Mollie was his partner, someone he depended on each day and was tasked to protect if her life was in danger. Neither could afford to tangle their emotions with the need to focus on the assignment.

Even though he accepted that they couldn't get involved, unlike Mollie, he wasn't about to deny how he felt or the strong desire that continued to draw him to her. She obviously didn't feel the same toward him. Pierce stared at her a brief moment before making the decision to leave the discussion where it lay. It wasn't something he wanted to explore further. Letting it drop was the best solution for both of them.

"It's been a long day. I'll see you tomorrow." Pierce closed the door behind him, leaving Mollie and her jumbled thoughts to herself.

******

"Chaz," Lee said as he took a seat across from the other man in the small restaurant not far from their hotel. He looked around. Chaz had selected a table away from most of the others, offering the two men some privacy.

"Good to see you, Lee. How was the trip?"

"Long and uneventful. Tell me how it's going here." Lee signaled a server for coffee.

"We're making progress, but at a pace that's not even measurable," Chaz joked and sipped his coffee, looking over the rim of his cup at Lee. "Does Eva know you'll be her partner?"

A sardonic look passed over Lee's face before he masked it. "No."

"I didn't think so. The four of us met and reviewed what we'd learned. She never mentioned you. I believe she's under the impression Owen will be her partner."

"That would be a wrong assumption." He set down his cup and leaned back in his seat. "Tell me what you know."

Chaz took the next half hour relaying what he'd learned from his source, including the rumors about an American seeking contact with those of questionable character. "The man is like a ghost. No one has seen his face or knows exactly what he wants, except that he is looking for some type of resolution to a problem. Under normal circumstances, I'd ignore it as folklore, people making up a story out of boredom, except the same story has filtered out of several cities within a couple of weeks. That's too much of a coincidence to ignore."

"Plus, it matches similar information we're getting from our East Coast team. No one can identify him, not even a description." Lee's frustration was obvious. "Whatever the man wants, he'll either find someone or do it himself. My guess is he's put too much effort into this to stop now."

Both men were silent as they dug into their breakfasts. Lee finally pushed away his empty plate, crossed his arms, and leaned them on top of the table.

"I'll send Noah a message about the man your source mentioned and get in touch with some people I know. My guess is that it's someone not in the government, but who has access to officials and intelligence, a man beyond reproach and most likely from wealth. He has an unpleasant task to perform and would prefer to find someone else to do it. The question is still why? What is he planning, who are his colleagues, and what resolution is he looking for? You don't reach out to the type of men you've described unless the request is serious and immediate. My gut tells me something big is about to happen. We need to identify what."

"Agreed." Chaz reached into this pocket to extract some bills. "I'll be in touch."

Lee nodded, watched Chaz disappear through the front door, and sat back to finish his coffee. The Mayor's Ball was the following night. He had much to accomplish before facing Eva and the wrath he knew would follow.

Chapter Nine

Pierce and Mollie sat across the breakfast table from each other, he pretending to be absorbed in the paper, and she concentrating on the meal Penelope had prepared. They hadn't spoken since the night before when he'd left her alone in the parlor. He'd gone to his room and let her comments play over and over in his mind. Each time he did, the same answer held firm. She didn't actually believe what she'd said. She'd been as affected by their attraction to each other as Pierce. Mollie had thought they'd come to some resolution, but she was wrong. Her continued silence and obvious discomfort around Pierce told him there was still much to be said.

He studied her for a moment before forging ahead. "It's not like you to lie to me or to yourself, and I believe that's exactly what you did last night." Mollie opened her mouth to protest, but Pierce held up a hand to silence her. "I don't believe either of us knows what's happening, whether it's a passing attraction or something to build on. Whatever it is, we need to either get it out of our systems, so we can concentrate on our jobs, or ignore it. I don't believe it's smart to try the first and I'm not sure we'll succeed at the latter."

Mollie stared at him, her eyes wide, not wanting to accept what he'd said, even though she knew it to be true. She had no intention of letting her feelings for this man go any further. She'd never intended to fall in love with anyone, and certainly not Pierce MacLaren, yet she had.

"What happened the other night was a mistake. At least we had the good sense to stop before we did anything we'd truly regret." She watched his cool eyes assess hers as she spoke. "There will never be anything between us. We're too different and want dissimilar things in life."

Pierce listened, not believing much of what she said. He knew Mollie had developed feelings for him, as he had for her. Their response to each other the other night was all the proof he needed. The difference was that he wanted to erase those feelings with one passionate night in bed, while she wanted to deal with them by pretending they didn't exist.

"What is it you want, Mollie? Surely it isn't a life of being an agent, traveling from one job to another, never having a home or family." Pierce's words were soft, penetrating the emotional armor Mollie had so diligently constructed over many years.

"And why not? It's a good life, lucrative and rarely boring. Don't tell me you want a home, a family? Do you really want to be saddled with children just to pass your name on to?" In contrast to Pierce, Mollie's tone was mocking, almost bitter.

"You have something against families? My four cousins, my brother, and my sister are married and happy. From what I can tell, it can be a good life if you fall in love with the right person."

"I'd expect that sentiment coming from a man who grew up in a large, loving family. The reality is quite different."

Pierce was poised to deny what she'd assumed. The truth of his growing up was so much different from what she'd implied, yet something held him back, prompting another approach.

"How did you grow up? You were born in Boston, right?"

Mollie looked at her plate and the food she'd barely touched, not wanting to get into this discussion. Few people knew of her childhood, and that was fine with her. Except, something about Pierce pulled at her, pushing her to talk about things she knew should be left alone. Then she had a thought. Perhaps sharing something of her past would change his mind, make her less attractive in his eyes.

"Yes, Boston."

"And your family?"

Mollie's gaze focused on his, her eyes never flinching. "My mother abandoned my father and me. Just disappeared one night." To her surprise, Pierce showed no noticeable reaction.

"How old were you?"

"Ten."

"Did your father work?"

"When he could find it. Mainly, he drank, forgetting about me or anything else, including work." She took a deep breath, not realizing her voice had begun to waver with each word. "I got a job in a bakery, delivering bread to restaurants until I was old enough to work inside the kitchen. I must have been about twelve by then. It was enough to put food on the table and sometimes pay our rent, but nothing was left over for much else. There was a family with several children who lived nearby. The husband had something to do with the railroads and they always seemed to do okay. The wife would give me clothes their children had grown out of."

Pierce waited, expecting her to continue. When she didn't, he reached out and placed his hand on hers. "As much as I know you'd like to think we have nothing in common, I believe we have much more than you think."

Mollie looked at him, glanced at their joined hands, and slowly drew hers away. She started to speak when Penelope appeared to take their plates.

When it became apparent their conversation had ended, Pierce stood and pulled Mollie's chair back.

"Don't assume this conversation is over, because it isn't." He strode toward the entrance hall and grabbed his hat. "I'm to meet Carlton Benstead and Gerald Goss for lunch. I'll be back directly afterward."

Mollie watched him leave, perplexed by his lack of reaction to her low upbringing as well as his desire to continue their conversation. Her belief was that their discussion was over. There was no need to bring up the past in any more detail than she'd already shared. Besides, she wasn't some naïve young girl. She understood his interest in her had nothing to do with anything other than alleviating his physical needs. He'd have to find a solution for that from someone other than her.

******

Lee waited for the message from his contact in Washington, a man he'd known since childhood who now worked in the government and contracted with Alex McCann on a regular basis. Clive Hawkins was one of the few good men in Grover Cleveland's government, at least in Lee's opinion. Honest, hardworking, with a sixth sense about anything that could endanger the country. Clive's father had been a general for the Union army during the Civil War. Clive had followed him to West Point, served his time, then decided on a career in government. Lee wished there were more like him.

The clerk handed him the missive and he scanned it quickly, absorbing the information but not quite believing it. Certainly, it was something he couldn't share with most in the present assignment. Clive had provided the name of a man under surveillance for various activities deemed to be not only illegal, but also traitorous. The message warned that the information provided was highly secretive and that only four people knew what he had shared.

Lee folded the paper and slid it into the inside pocket of his coat before penning a message back to Clive. He wanted to share the information with Noah and needed Clive's approval. He knew how he'd like to handle the information if it were up to him, however, he was astute enough to know his reactions might be a little skewed. Noah would provide another perspective, something that might stop Lee from going straight for the man and beating a confession out of him.

He told himself his reaction wasn't out of line, anyone would want to do the same if they'd learned a colleague had committed treason. His gut, however, provided a different answer. He knew his response had more to do with settling an old score and exposing the man for the lowlife Lee knew him to be. If Clive's information was true, revenge would be sweet and come sooner than Lee had anticipated.

******

Mollie had met Henrietta Benstead and Lottie Goss for a tour of what the two women considered the most suitable establishments for ladies of their social standing. As Henrietta had said during their luncheon earlier in the week, one could never be too careful about the businesses they patronized. The caliber of each shop said much about the women who shopped there.

"Here we are." Henrietta stopped in front of a small boutique that specialized in hats and gloves. Before any of them had a chance to grasp the brass handle, the door flew open and a short, slender woman of Asian descent stood smiling at them.

"Enter, my good friends, Mrs. Benstead and Mrs. Goss." She bowed slightly before noticing the third woman. "Ah, you brought a friend today." Her smile grew even wider, sensing another sale.

"Yes, Mei-Li. This is our good friend, Mrs. MacLaren," Henrietta responded and strolled into the store.

"Ah, welcome, welcome," Mei-Li said to Mollie as she pushed the door closed.

Mollie wandered to the back to join the others. They were already pointing out new creations and commenting on each. Lottie liked a particularly bold hat with tall feathers and bright purple ribbon.

"Doesn't she create the most exquisite hats you've ever seen?" Lottie gushed as Mei-Li held out the hat.

Mollie agreed they were amazing hats, and from the prices Mei-Li quoted, quite expensive. The conversation and fittings continued for another ten minutes before the women were interrupted by the sound of a gentleman's voice as the back entrance to the shop was pushed open and a lone man walked through the opening. Thomas Traxton. He glanced behind him quickly, nodded, and shut the door.

Henrietta, Lottie, and Mollie all stood silent, waiting for him to explain why he was coming through the back door of the hat shop.

"Good afternoon, ladies. It's a pleasure to see you all again," Thomas Traxton drawled.

Mollie was the first to respond. "Good afternoon, Thomas. What a surprise to see you here. Is there perhaps another showroom with creations that aren't displayed in front?"

Thomas's smile broadened even more and he walked toward the women, ignoring Mollie's question.

"Virginia is feeling a bit off today. I thought perhaps a new hat would cheer her up. Since I had a business meeting with Mei-Li today, it seemed like the perfect opportunity to find something special." He grabbed a particularly gaudy hat with red and purple feathers. Oddly, it did seem like something Virginia might like.

"Mei-Li, would you mind wrapping this up for my wife? I'll come back tomorrow to settle up what is owed."

Within minutes, Traxton had accepted the boxed hat and left the store for his carriage out front.

Henrietta and Lottie stepped to the front window and watched as he disappeared inside the carriage.

"What in the world?" Lottie asked under her breath. She hadn't spoken a word since Thomas emerged from the back of the millinery.

Mei-Li stood behind a counter at the back of the store, her face red and fear evident by her wide-eyed expression. It took just four strides for Mollie to stand directly across from the shop owner.

"Mei-Li. What is going on?" Mollie indicated with her head to the back door, but all the Chinese woman did was shake her head. "Did you just have a meeting with Mr. Traxton?" she persisted.

Mei-Li put a hand over her mouth and shook her head. Other than that, the shop owner

97

remained silent, refusing to discuss anything about Traxton.

"I believe it's time we left, ladies. Mei-Li, thank you for your courtesy. I'm sure we'll see you again soon."

Mollie herded the other two women outside and signaled for the Benstead carriage. Once inside, each remained silent for several minutes, reflecting on the scene they'd witnessed.

"How incredibly odd," Lottie commented.

"Perhaps he did have business downstairs. It could be nothing." Henrietta huffed. She turned her attention to Mollie, who sat across from her.

"I agree, Henrietta. I believe his appearance just took us by surprise." Mollie's mind raced at the implication that something more was going on with Thomas Traxton than a simple business transaction. "Are the store offices in the back?"

"No. At my insistence, Carlton has done some business with Mei-Li. She normally meets him at the bank, but he mentioned she has an office above the store, in a corner of the apartment where she, her husband, and two children live. Her husband isn't involved in the store and she doesn't have a partner. She uses the back for storage only. I can't imagine why Thomas would be back there."

Henrietta's explanation fueled Mollie's concerns about Traxton and his reason for being at the small hat shop. Something was definitely going on with the man, and she was determined to find out what.

Chapter Ten

Mollie paced her bedroom, waiting for Pierce. She wanted to get his impressions on what she'd seen earlier that day. Something was certainly amiss with Thomas Traxton, and she meant to find out what it was.

She heard a door downstairs close and raced to the entrance. Pierce was just turning toward the parlor when he spotted her dashing down the stairs. For a brief moment, he fantasized she was hurrying to greet him, planning to throw her arms around his neck and place a welcoming kiss on his mouth. He shook that image aside as she stopped a couple of feet in front of him.

"What is it?"

"We need to talk." Mollie turned toward the library, shutting the doors behind them.

"All right, what is so important?" Pierce crossed his arms in front of his broad chest, leaning one shoulder negligently against the door, eyeing Mollie and wondering what had her so agitated.

"Henrietta and Lottie invited me to accompany them to several shops today, one being a fashionable millinery several blocks from your office. We were speaking with the shop owner, looking at hats, when Thomas Traxton appeared through a door in the back of the shop."

"And?"

"There is nothing in the back of the shop except storage," Mollie replied. She walked over to stand in front of him.

Pierce pushed away from the door and dropped his arms. "Why don't you start from the beginning? Traxton being in the back of a hat shop without an office doesn't tell me much."

"You're right." Mollie began to pace, sorting out the details so she could describe her concerns to Pierce. "He walked out of the back room alone, except that there were two distinct male voices coming through the door. American, not Chinese. He quickly shut the door when he saw us and made up some excuse about being in the hat shop to buy a present for Virginia." Mollie snorted at the man's poor attempt to cover up what actually brought him to the shop. She paced back toward Pierce to see his brow lifted in question.

"And?" he prompted again.

"Traxton told us he was in the back to discuss shop business. He said Mei-Li is a customer of his company. The odd thing is, Mei-Li was with us in the front of the shop, not in back with Thomas. Her husband is not involved with the shop and, according to Henrietta, there is no other partner, meaning Traxton had to be lying about his presence. Mei-Li's office is upstairs in her apartment, not on the shop level." Mollie stopped and smiled, a look of triumph filling her face.

"Did Mei-Li provide any explanation for Traxton's presence?"

"She wouldn't say anything, only shook her head when I asked her if she'd met with him. She seemed shaken that we saw Thomas, as if she were afraid of something. I spoke with her for a few minutes, trying to get her to talk to me, without success."

"It doesn't surprise me that Traxton may be involved in something shady after seeing the way he acted toward you at the Benstead's house. He believed you were married and it didn't seem to matter at all to the man. I was close to walking over and punching the sanctimonious smile off his face."

"Really?" Mollie felt her heart pound at the implication of what he'd said, a half-smile on her face as she waited for his explanation.

"Hell, yes. You're my partner. I can't let just anyone make a pass at you, and especially not a married man." He could see Mollie's smile falter and wished he could say what had actually crossed his mind that night.

"Of course." She recovered quickly from the disappointment she felt. "Do you think what I saw has any significance to what we're investigating."

"I'm new at this, but I'd say it's worth bringing up to Eva and Chaz." In truth, Pierce thought Traxton's presence at the small shop may have more significance than either of them realized. He'd never believed in coincidences, and found he was best served by following his gut reactions.

Pierce stood and stretched his arms above his head. "I need to clean up before Penelope calls us to supper. Care to join me in a hot bath?"

His eyes twinkled as a wicked smile replaced his impassive expression. Mollie found herself imagining him running soap over her water-slicked body, her skin heating at the thought. She closed her eyes and shook off the tempting vision.

"No, of course not." Her words were clipped, although Pierce thought her voice sounded thick, husky, as if she was conjuring up the same images as him.

"If you're sure you don't want to give it a try, then I'll excuse myself and see you at supper."

It took several minutes after Pierce left for Mollie's heart rate to slow. He'd surprised her with his comment, which she knew wasn't serious, only meant to shock her, and it had. As ludicrous as it sounded, she'd wanted to say yes, join him in his bath, run her hands down his muscled arms and legs, and kiss away the dampness from his tanned skin. The image made her face burn and body tighten. She knew it would never happen, yet the vision of it made her knees weak.

Perhaps she did need a bath before supper—a cool one.

******

Mollie finished her hair, looked in the mirror, and deciding she looked better than average, made her way downstairs to the parlor. Pierce was already waiting when she walked through the door. He stood by a window, looking out on the darkening night, a glass of whiskey in one hand.

He turned at her entry, and, as was becoming a habit, her breath hitched at the sight of him.

Pierce's eyes followed Mollie as she made her way to the edge of the divan then stopped. He took his time letting his gaze wander from her thin-soled kid slippers, up her dress, over her womanly curves to her slim waist, the creamy skin of her neck, then upward to her face. The heat he saw in her eyes matched his own, and it took all his willpower to stay where he was and not stride forward to pull her into his arms. He'd thought of little else since their conversation that morning. He cleared his throat, walked with slow steps to her side, and offered his arm.

"May I escort you to supper?"

She didn't reply, just slipped her arm through his.

The sight that greeted her in the dining room was a surprise. The room was lit with candles. The large table had been replaced with a smaller, round one, set for two with a stunning arrangement of roses in the center. Her eyes shifted over large vases of roses set on every available table, the candlelight highlighting the petal colors of red, yellow, and peach. The room was magnificent and, in Mollie's mind, meant for seduction.

Her legs seemed anchored in place, incapable of moving the few steps to her chair. She felt Pierce's hand on the small of her back, warm and possessive.

"Do you like it?" he asked as he encouraged her to move toward the table. He leaned down and breathed in her ear, "Happy birthday, Mollie."

Her eyes shot to his then back to the table. She blinked, trying to stem the dampness pooling in her eyes. No one had ever done anything like this for her before. No special suppers, no birthday surprises, no presents, or acknowledgement that today was anything different from all the others. Nobody had ever made this day something to remember—no one except Pierce.

She swallowed, seeking the courage to speak. "This is, well, it's simply..." she stumbled over her own tongue, afraid more than anything that she'd cry and ruin it all. "Thank you," she finally whispered and watched as he pulled out her chair.

Pierce took his seat across from her as Penelope entered the room with an open bottle of champagne and poured some into each of their glasses. He lifted his and tilted it toward Mollie.

"Wishing you many more happy birthdays."

She picked up her glass and touched his before taking a small sip. "How did you know?"

"About it being your birthday?"

She nodded.

"You told me. Back in Fire Mountain. I mentioned that our family was having a birthday party for Niall's daughter, Beth, and you said her birthday and yours fell on the same date." He took a sip of his champagne then set down the glass. "So does this compare with any of your previous birthdays?"

Mollie didn't know how else to respond except with the truth. "I have nothing else to compare it to." She looked up at him. "I can't imagine another birthday ever being as perfect as this one."

Pierce grimaced as her meaning sunk in. It hadn't occurred to him that she'd never celebrated her birthday.

His mother had always made birthdays special for him, Connor, and Meggie. When his parents sent their three children to America for a better life, Connor made sure they kept the tradition, even though there was little money left for special occasions. Connor had told Pierce and Meggie that there would always be money for birthdays.

Their meal was excellent. Mollie ate until she thought she'd burst and laughed at the stories Pierce told about working on the MacLaren ranch.

"What was life like growing up on the ranch?" she asked as Penelope whisked away the empty supper plates.

"Connor, Meggie, and I didn't grow up on the ranch. We landed in New York when we arrived on the ship from Scotland and found a place in Red Hook."

"Is that where your father found work?"

Pierce finished the wine in his glass and set it down, leaned back in his chair, and crossed his arms over his chest. "Our parents didn't come with us to America. We were sent by ourselves in hopes of finding a better life."

"But I thought..." Mollie's voice faded as she absorbed his words.

"I know. Most people not from Fire Mountain assume we grew up there. The truth is we only found our cousins and Aunt Alicia during the last year. We tried to locate them when we first arrived, without success. That's when Connor found work on the docks in Red Hook. I worked for a man who made tools and Meggie cleaned rooms in a boarding house." He fell silent for a moment, remembering the small two-room apartment they'd shared until Meggie had been kidnapped. "One night, Meggie never came home. We looked for her everywhere, for months, before Connor decided it was best to move on—life in Red Hook no longer held any appeal. We did whatever we could to get by, always looking for Meggie. Eventually, we both found work that took us to different locations. He and I always stayed in touch. After years, he located Meggie and brought her to Fire Mountain, where I'd settled with our cousins."

"I'm sorry, Pierce," Mollie murmured.

"For what?"

"Believing that you could never imagine how hard life could be without parents or family. I thought all the MacLarens had grown up with ... well, I guess with..." She looked down at her folded hands, feeling ashamed of the assumptions she'd made.

"With everything handed to us?" he prompted, his voice soft, barely above a whisper.

Mollie raised her head to focus on a man who'd become more important to her than she wanted to admit. "Yes, I suppose so."

Penelope picked that moment to enter the room carrying a cake and place it in the center of the table. She stepped back to watch Mollie's reaction.

"Oh, Penelope, this is beautiful," Mollie exclaimed, staring at the dessert adorned with flowers and bows.

"Thank you, ma'am. May I bring in coffee or tea?"

"Coffee for both of us," Pierce answered. "And thank you. The cake is perfect."

He watched Mollie's eyes as they took in the sweet confection, looking at each decoration as if trying to memorize it.

"You know, it might melt if we don't try some." He grinned at her surprised expression then laughed when she realized he was joking.

"You're right." She reached for a knife, sliced a good-sized piece, and set it on one of the small plates Penelope had provided before handing the serving to Pierce. She cut another slice and set it aside. When Penelope returned with their coffee, Mollie presented her with the portion of cake and asked for a third plate.

Penelope blushed, took the cake, and rushed into the kitchen for another plate.

Pierce and Mollie each had two slices, deciding it would never be as good as it was right now. When they were finished, Pierce pushed up and walked around the table to pull out Mollie's chair.

"Come on. Let's take a walk." He strode to the entrance and came back with her coat before grabbing his own and slipping into it. He escorted her outside into the cool night air and stopped, tilting his head up for a view of the star-filled sky.

He remembered lying on the roof of the boarding house in Red Hook and staring at the same sky, wondering if his life would amount to much. Tonight, he felt it had.

Mollie walked up next to him and looked up. "Beautiful, isn't it?"

Pierce looked down at her glowing face, wisps of golden blonde hair escaping from the loose chignon, her warm brown eyes sparkling in the moonlit night. "Very beautiful," he answered then picked up her hand to wrap it around his arm before starting down the steps to the street.

"Where are we going?" Mollie felt almost giddy with an excitement she hadn't felt in a long time.

"I don't know exactly. Perhaps around the block or further. Does it matter?"

"Not really," she replied, and realized she'd spoken the truth. Being with this man, on her birthday, was more than she'd ever imagined.

******

Pierce opened the oversized entry door an hour later, followed Mollie inside, and escorted her upstairs. He pushed open the door to her room, and then turned her to him.

She looked up into his clear blue eyes, knowing he meant to kiss her, anticipating it as she felt her heart begin to thump in her chest. At least she thought that was his intention until he leaned down to place a soft kiss on her forehead then gave a brief brush of his lips against hers before setting her firmly away.

"I want you, Mollie, more than I've ever wanted a woman, and much more than I should."

He stared into her warm brown eyes and took a deep breath, trying to clear his head and explain himself in a way that would make sense. "We're partners trying to focus on solving the puzzle Noah and Lee have dumped on us. Our job doesn't include the two of us getting involved."

Mollie's face changed from expectant to emotionless as she stepped away from him, her anticipation turning to disappointment in the space of a heartbeat.

"You're right." Her voice was flat, devoid of the light tone that had captivated him most of the night. "It would be a major mistake for us to let anything happen." She took another step backward, resting her hand the door frame, wanting nothing more than to disappear inside. "Thank you for the lovely supper, Pierce. It was the best birthday I've ever had." She offered him a brilliant smile, one, he noticed, that didn't quite reach her eyes. "I'll see you tomorrow." She closed the door, leaving him standing alone with a strange, hollow feeling in his gut.

Chapter Eleven

Lee penned a brief message and handed it to the hotel messenger. "Do not include my name, just the message." He focused on the short, slim man to emphasize his request.

"Of course, sir."

Lee watched the employee take the stairs at a brisk pace. Within minutes, Eva would know the other agent she'd requested had arrived, although later than anticipated. The note recommended that they meet at the Mayor's Ball. Lee had no intention of letting her know who had been sent to act as her partner until it was too late. She was a consummate professional and wouldn't think of making a scene during the highly anticipated social event. No, she'd save her wrath for him, and Noah, until later.

It was mid-afternoon and he had one more errand to run before returning to his room to dress for the ball. Noah had alerted him to a service with an office not far from the San Franciscan hotel that was run by a former government employee. The man and his two partners, who ran the New York and Chicago offices, specialized in providing businessmen and government officials with messenger services, whether over the wires or in person, on an anonymous basis.

The information Lee received from Clive Hawkins had been gnawing at him. He wasn't sure why, no one would be more pleased than him if the person named in the message did turn out to be responsible for the strange activities surfacing on the West Coast. Clive's assumptions about what had been uncovered made sense, yet Lee still felt something was amiss. Perhaps another of his contacts could add some clarity to the mystery.

He stepped through the doorway and strode up to a tall counter. He looked around, and finding no one, rang the bell conveniently placed to the right of the ink pad.

"Be right there," a deep voice answered a few moments before a short, stout gentleman with a long, graying beard slipped sideways through a slim opening between the front and back offices. "What can I do for you?" He leaned forward and placed his arms on the counter.

"I'd like to send a message to a contact on the East Coast. A private message."

"How did you hear about our service?"

"Noah Dodds."

The man nodded. "Silas Springer," he said and offered his hand.

"Lee Hatcher."

"Noah, huh? That's good. Something more interesting than my recent customers. I'm getting mighty tired of sending secret messages between two married lovers—married to others, that is." He reached under the counter to grab a pad and fountain pen. "Write your message and contact here. I expect Noah told you it's cash only?"

Lee nodded as he wrote. When finished, he passed the pad back to Silas and reached into his pocket, pulling out a wad of bills. He looked up in time to see the man's eyes widen when he saw the name of the recipient.

"You know him?" Lee asked.

"Used to." Silas's eyes narrowed on Lee. "Not many know of him outside certain circles. I'd thought he'd retired until someone else sent a message to him a couple of weeks ago."

"From here?" Lee was stunned at the news.

"Yep. Strange message too. No response was received, so it could be that the person sending the message was just fishing. That happens sometimes."

"Can you tell me who sent the message?"

"I'd be glad to, if I knew. Unfortunately, the man didn't leave his name. Told me he'd be back to pick up any reply. I never got a reply and never saw the man again. My guess? He was experimenting to see what would happen." Silas counted the words and named a price for guaranteeing Lee's contact would get the message. "Where do you want me to send a response, if one arrives?"

"I'm at the San Franciscan." Lee closed the door behind him, perplexed and concerned about the identity of the man who'd sent the other message.

Fewer than ten people knew the man had been a government agent for years working for the Treasury and Justice departments. He knew information about people that could get them exiled, imprisoned, or killed. He accepted messages from perhaps five of his old colleagues, Lee being one. Lee knew the identity of the other four and wondered which one of them had been in San Francisco recently, and why.

******

Pierce continued to pace a hole in the library carpet, killing time until he and Mollie would leave for the ball. He'd been in the room for hours, first refining their plan for the evening, then berating himself for the poor way he'd handled the situation with Mollie the night before.

It had turned into the best night he'd had in a long time, and he knew Mollie had felt the same. He'd wanted to kiss her, planned it most of the night, but at the last minute, he couldn't. Not because he didn't want to. Hell, he'd wanted to do a lot more than kiss her—and that was the problem. He knew if they started down that path, it wouldn't take long before they'd be in her room with her laid out on the big canopied bed. The thought of it still sent heat through his body.

Pierce couldn't remember ever craving the touch of woman the way he did hers. For all her stubbornness, Mollie was the most desirable woman he'd ever known. She was bright and fearless, jumping in when others stood aside, seeking answers when everyone else had given up. She excited and perplexed him at the same time.

Last night, he'd lain awake for hours, rethinking the way he'd left her. Or, rather the way she'd closed her bedroom door, leaving him standing in the hall. It had been a remarkable evening, until he'd made his little speech and she'd closed up. Perhaps it would've been best to do what he'd wanted for weeks—kiss her senseless, until they were both on fire, then take her to bed.

He walked to the window, looking out toward a beautiful view, his eyes unable to focus on any of it, and realized the line between right and wrong was fading fast when it came to Mollie. Pierce turned at the sound of three quick raps on the door.

"Mr. MacLaren? Miss Gagnon and Mr. Yarbrough are here to see you and Mrs. MacLaren," Penelope said as she pushed the library door open a few inches.

"Please, show them in and ask Mollie to join us."

He greeted the two, offering them drinks until Mollie arrived. Pierce handed Chaz a whiskey and Eva her sherry, then took a swallow of his drink as the door to the library swung open.

Pierce drew in a sharp breath, almost choking on his whiskey as his gaze locked on Mollie. She stood in the doorway wearing a magnificent, lemon yellow silk gown with small capped sleeves that fell off her shoulders. It dropped low on her chest, exposing just enough creamy skin to immediately heat his blood. The gown fit tight around the waist and down her hips before cascading into soft waves that fell to the floor while tucking into a glorious train in the back. The gown highlighted her golden blonde hair, which she'd pulled up into an intricate chignon, using a pearled clip to secure it in place.

Pierce continued to stare as he attempted to bring both his breathing and pounding heart under control. His hand gripped the whiskey glass so tight it threatened to shatter.

Mollie's gaze landed on Pierce the moment she opened the door. She saw his eyes lock on her, the impact of his stare so great her legs threatened to buckle.

Eva sat back, watching Pierce's reaction to his partner and Mollie's response to his open perusal. She knew in an instant that it was just a matter of time before neither could deny their feelings and one, or both, would act on them.

"Good evening, Mollie. You look absolutely splendid." Chaz walked up, taking Mollie's hand, and gestured toward a chair next to Pierce. "We need to discuss some new developments before we leave for the Mayor's Ball."

"Hello, Mollie. That dress is quite becoming on you. Be prepared, you'll be besieged with suitors before the night is over." Eva smiled at the young woman then turned to Pierce. "Chaz discovered some interesting information through a local contact. Chaz, why don't you fill them in?"

"First, some background. My contact is a gentleman I've known for many years, worked with in Europe briefly, and now makes his home in San Francisco. He was sent here near the end of his career as an agent to help with some difficult foreign relations transactions. Afterward, he retired and stayed. That said, he stays current about what goes on behind the closed circles of the city." Chaz leaned against the large desk and folded

115

his arms over his chest. "There is strong discontent with many of the policies put forward by President Cleveland within the circles my contact frequents—wealthy, well-connected individuals who have the means to make or break a career, and that includes a president. Many of the people he refers to have deep roots in the east and mid-west—New York, Philadelphia, Boston, Chicago, St. Louis, and some ties in the south—and they're organizing their efforts. They've quietly been collecting funds. A war chest, if you will, to accomplish their goal of getting Cleveland out of the White House."

"Do you believe that is what the large withdrawals that Lee and Noah reported are about?" Pierce asked.

"Seems reasonable."

"Did he provide any names or say whether the mayor is part of the movement?" Eva didn't believe for a moment either would be involved in something that would jeopardize the mayor's career, regardless of their feelings toward the president.

"I pushed, but he wouldn't provide names, and said if it got out he'd lose all contact with this group of men. He said it wouldn't be hard to guess at those involved based on wealth and social standing."

Mollie shifted in her chair, glancing around the room at the others. "If that's the case, then there isn't anything illegal happening. Nothing that would necessitate our involvement, correct?"

"Remember, it's input from one contact. We must weigh it against everything we've learned and what Noah and Lee provide to us. It is, however, something we must consider." Chaz dropped his arms to his sides and paced to his chair, standing behind it, resting his hands on the back. "We must continue until we've been told otherwise."

"What do you advise we do tonight? I assume many of the men your contact refers to will be in attendance tonight. Anyone in particular to watch or get close to?" Pierce was impatient to learn whether their involvement was needed nor not.

Eva pulled two pieces of paper out of her reticule and handed one to Mollie, the other to Pierce. "These lists are identical so that you may work together or alone. Mollie will have the chance to get close to some of the men on the list, and Pierce, several of the women on yours will be willing to tell what they know. Keep in mind, many of the women receive little attention from their husbands. A little male flattery can go a long way."

Pierce grinned at what Eva implied, while Mollie's eyes jerked to his. From his reaction, she couldn't help but believe the assignment agreed with him even more than his expression implied. The thought angered and fortified her at the same time.

"Is all of this quite clear?" Eva asked as she stooped to pick up her wrap.

Mollie squared her shoulders and walked toward the door. "Quite clear, Eva." She glanced at the others. "If we're set, I'm more than ready for a change of scenery." She threw a murderous glare at Pierce as she left the room to board their waiting carriage.

******

Pierce sat across from Mollie in their carriage while Eva and Chaz followed behind. Neither said a word as their driver made his way to the ball in San Francisco's downtown district.

Mollie had time to think while riding through the streets, and plan the best way to become acquainted with the men on the list. It wouldn't be difficult—the affair was scheduled to go on well into the early morning, which meant many would be drinking for several hours.

"Are you ready for this?" Pierce asked as the carriage came to stop, surging forward a few more feet before the driver jumped down from his seat and opened their door.

Mollie cocked an eyebrow and offered a brilliant smile as she faced Pierce, who'd stepped down before her. "More than ready. Let's find out what these people know."

The ball was already crowded when they arrived. Mollie watched sophisticated women in stunning gowns and flashing jewels sashay from one group to the next, simultaneously speaking with friends while gauging the others in the room. It was a game to some, business to others, and deadly serious to the four agents who began to circulate through the room.

Eva and Chaz spoke briefly before splitting off, giving each the ability to move freely about the room. She expected to locate Owen Kendall at any time to begin their charade as wealthy lovers. Although she'd never been attracted to the handsome agent, she knew he'd been infatuated with her for years. At least, from his standpoint, it would be an easy performance.

She spotted Pierce and Mollie across the room in deep conversation with two couples she didn't recognize. That's when she noticed the mayor and his wife, standing in a grouping of people, laughing while sipping champagne. She'd met them the year before during a short assignment in the Bay City, and had been to their home a few weeks ago for a private supper party, where she'd met Theodore Crow, who stood in their circle speaking with the mayor's wife, Lydia. They were an amicable couple, political to the core, yet deeply committed to making San Francisco the jewel of the West Coast.

She accepted a glass of champagne from a passing server and turned to maneuver her way across the room to greet the mayor, all the while searching for Owen. The event was intended to accommodate two hundred guests, yet Eva estimated there were closer to three hundred in the crowded space. It took several minutes, pausing to speak with a couple of individuals she'd met over the last few weeks, before she stopped next to the mayor who stood talking with two gentleman Eva had yet to meet.

The mayor glanced at her then turned fully, a smile on his round face. "Miss Gagnon. It is a pleasure to see you again."

"Mayor Pound, I'm so glad to be included." She looked across the mayor to his wife. "Mrs. Pound, good to see you."

"Eva, my dear, where have you been keeping yourself? It seems like ages since we saw you at our home." Like the mayor, his wife was a short woman, rotund, and friendly with a ready smile. No one would suspect the razor sharp mind she hid behind the genial façade.

"You know how it is, Lydia. Most days fill up, keeping me quite busy." She turned to Theodore. "It's nice to see you again, Mr. Crow."

"I'm glad you were able to make the event." Theodore looked to the others in the group. "Miss Gagnon, I'd like to introduce you to our Chief of Police, Robert Curtis, and Mr. Jock Flannigan, captain and owner of one of the most important shipping lines on the West Coast."

"Good evening, Miss Gagnon." Chief Curtis was a tall, lean man with a short gray beard, and eerily translucent pale yellow eyes. His hair was cropped short and the color matched that of his beard.

"Chief Curtis," Eva responded and shifted her eyes to the other man who had made no effort to hide his stare. It was a slow, easy perusal, one meant to show his interest and, perhaps, appreciation.

Flannigan bowed, never taking his eyes from her. "It is a true pleasure, Miss Gagnon."

She opened her mouth to speak, but stopped as several bells sounded, announcing supper. The Mayor, his wife, and the others in the group left to locate their table, leaving Eva and Jock alone.

"May I?" Captain Flannigan inquired and offered his arm to Eva. Even though she was a tall woman, he towered above her. His hair was burnished copper, similar to the colors in the setting sun, and pulled back into a neat queue at the nape of his neck. His deep amber eyes bore into hers, an amused expression flickering across his face.

She had just begun to raise her arm to his when she sensed rather than saw someone come up behind her. Two strong hands rested lightly on her waist as an all too familiar voice wafted over her.

"Eva, my dear, I've been looking everywhere for you." Lee leaned down to place a kiss on her cheek.

The impact of his breath fanning across her neck and the soft feel of his lips against her skin slammed into Eva. She hadn't been this close to him in four years. Four long years, and the way her body responded to him hadn't changed a whit. She closed her eyes to calm the staccato of her heart, but made no move to put distance between them.

Lee stepped back and extended his hand to the tall, ruddy-skinned man who stood next to her.

"Lee Hatcher," he said noting the man's frown and the slight pause before he accepted Lee's hand.

"Captain Jock Flannigan." Flannigan's eyes shifted from Lee to rest on Eva.

"Perhaps you would care to accompany us to the table? We've just recently come to the West Coast and I'm sure Miss Gagnon would enjoy getting to know you better." Lee's suggestion was genuine, although he was particularly interested in learning more about the captain and his shipping business.

"Thank you, Mr. Hatcher. I would also enjoy getting to know Miss Gagnon."

Eva remained silent as the two men conversed, listening as Lee's deep, smooth voice floated over her. Her chest tightened and she worked to control the rapid breathing which had followed him resting his hands on her waist, arousing every part of her body—a touch that was incredibly familiar, painfully so. She swallowed hard, trying to control the grinding ache being this close to him caused.

"Shall we, Eva?" Lee whispered close to her ear, placing her hand through his arm as he started forward.

She had yet to fully look at the one man capable of sending her emotions reeling. She walked beside him, allowing her reaction to move from surprise to anger—fury directed at Lee as well as their boss, Noah Dodd. There was nothing she could do about it tonight, not here at this formal ball with the social elite of San Francisco all around them. No, she would wait, determine the best approach, and make her displeasure known. Her resolve restored, Eva glanced up at the man who would be her partner for this one brief period of time and promised that, no matter what else happened, she'd come out of this with her reputation intact and her heart in one piece.

Chapter Twelve

Pierce watched Mollie's eyes widen as her infectious laughter filled the air at something Gerald Black said. She stood on the other side of Viola Black, creating a distance that allowed her to converse while focusing on the festivities around them. He shifted away from her as his eyes swept the room, identifying people Eva and Chaz had described while listening to personal conversations between the guests in groups close to theirs.

One strikingly beautiful woman behind him introduced herself to another gentleman and Pierce realized he recognized her name from the list. She stood next to Thomas Traxton, her animated conversation catching the man's attention. His wife, Virginia, was nowhere in sight.

"Excuse me a moment. There's someone I'd like to meet. Keep track of my wife, would you, Gerald?"

"Of course, Pierce," Gerald replied and stepped closer to the two women. "He certainly is a restless sort."

"You have no idea," Mollie replied as her eyes followed him. He stopped next to an impeccably dressed gentleman with thinning hair and a full mustache, whom she didn't recognize. She watched as he introduced himself then turned to face a tall, slender woman with whitish-blonde hair.

To say that the woman was lovely would be a gross understatement. Her crimson dress dropped low in the front, to just within propriety. A dazzling combination of rubies and diamonds adorned her neck, ears, and wrists. She appeared to be bored, shifting from one foot to the other and trying to act interested in the story the man next to her was telling.

"Hello, Thomas. I'd hoped to see you here." Pierce moved slightly so that he reached across the woman to shake the man's hand.

"MacLaren." Thomas's greeting was less than enthusiastic.

"Perhaps you'd be kind enough to introduce me to this lovely lady?" Pierce could see the strained look on Traxton's face and enjoyed any discomfort he might be causing the man.

Traxton narrowed his eyes on Pierce before he shook off whatever bothered him and made the introduction.

"Georgiana, I'd like you to meet a friend of mine, Pierce MacLaren. Pierce, this is one of Virginia's dearest friends, Georgiana Grayson."

The woman's eyes swung to Pierce and her expression changed in an instant, giving him her full attention as the other conversation faded into the background. She held up a hand for Pierce to accept and he didn't disappoint. In one fluid movement, he lifted her hand to his lips and lightly touched her skin.

"It's a pleasure to meet you, Miss Grayson."

"Thank you, Mr. MacLaren." She pulled her hand free. "It is Mrs. Grayson, however."

Pierce looked at the others in the group and, judging none suitable as her husband, turned a questioning look at the woman.

"My husband passed away several months ago," she replied to his unspoken question.

"I'm sorry to hear that, Mrs. Grayson." He kept his eyes locked on hers, already certain he'd made a favorable impression.

"I'd be grateful if you would call me Georgiana, or Georgie, it's what my friends call me." Her soft voice and sparkling eyes conveyed more to Pierce than just the offer to be another of her friends.

He marveled at how quickly an innocent introduction could transform into an imminent invitation. Pierce wasn't a conceited man, yet over the years, he'd learned that women found him attractive. It was a benefit and a curse. Tonight, he'd use it to his advantage.

Mollie watched the interaction from several feet away, somewhat jealous that he'd made the first contact and more than ready to do her part, gathering information from the men on her list. She didn't wish to pull out the small piece of paper in front of the others and was relieved when one name popped into her head. "Gerald, would you please point out Lloyd Johnson?"

Gerald cast an odd look her way before letting his eyes gaze around the room. "Ah, yes. There he is in the corner, speaking with an elderly woman, his mother, I believe. Do you see?" He indicated a debonair gentleman about twenty feet away. "Would you like an introduction?"

"That would be marvelous." Mollie gathered her skirts as he took her arm and escorted her across the room.

"Lloyd, how are you this evening?" Gerald asked as he came to a stop.

"Quite well, Gerald. And you?" Johnson replied while his eyes focused on Mollie.

"No complaints. I'd like to introduce you to Viola's good friend, Mrs. Mollie MacLaren."

Johnson made a slight bow. "Mrs. MacLaren, it's a pleasure. I've just offered to get a glass of punch for my mother. May I interest you in something?"

"Punch would be wonderful, Mr. Johnson. Thank you."

Gerald Black said his goodbyes and left to rejoin his wife, still somewhat perplexed at Mollie's request for an introduction.

Johnson returned within minutes, holding two glasses. He handed one to his mother, who looked over her shoulder at Mollie, then turned backed to the other women.

"Excuse me, Mother." He made a slight bow to the women before rejoining Mollie. "Are you here tonight with your husband, Mrs. MacLaren?" Lloyd asked as he handed Mollie her punch.

"Yes. He's right over there talking with the tall woman in the red dress."

"Ah, yes. Georgiana Grayson."

"You know her then?" Mollie asked as she sipped the punch.

"I've known the Graysons for many years. Her husband passed away recently after an accident on one of his ships." He shrugged. "Given her background, I'm sure her current life is quite a change."

"Her background?"

"Excuse me, of course you wouldn't know. Her husband, Walter, was partners with Jock Flannigan, the tall man with reddish hair pulled back in a queue." He motioned across the room and Mollie noted the man who stood next to Eva. "The Graysons used to be quite the social couple. I doubt there was an event the two did not attend. Before his accident, Walter did something quite unusual, which few people know about even though he made no provision that it be kept secret. He drew up legal documents to make her a partner in the company, taking over his half interest. Jock handles the day-to-day operations, but it's my understanding that Georgiana does play some small role."

"That does seem unusual. What business is Georgiana in?"

"The company handles shipping up and down the West Coast. It has been in business for several decades and has quite a colorful past. Grayson and Flannigan bought it from the original owners several years ago and expanded the operation. It's quite profitable from what I understand."

"How fascinating. I wonder what kinds of cargo they carry." Mollie finished her punch and handed the empty glass to a passing server.

"The company started out with government contracts to ship and deliver mail. Very lucrative contracts, I might add. They branched into other types of cargo over the years. One of the lawyers in my firm handles the legal work for the company." He stopped and frowned at Mollie. "All this business talk must be quite boring to you, Mrs. MacLaren."

"Not at all, Mr. Johnson. My husband often talks business at home. I find it quite fascinating, even though I don't understand much of it." She gave Lloyd a modest smile.

Their discussion was interrupted by the sound of bells calling guests to dinner.

"It was very nice speaking with you, Mrs. MacLaren. Perhaps you'll save me a dance later this evening."

"I would be happy to, Mr. Johnson," Mollie answered before turning toward the last place she'd seen Pierce and strolling slowly in that direction.

"Who is that woman, Lloyd?" Mrs. Johnson held her glass tight between two hands, scowling at Mollie's back as she walked away.

"Mrs. MacLaren, Mother. A friend of Gerald and Viola Black."

"What did she want?"

Lloyd took a slow breath, becoming impatient with his mother's constant interrogations. They'd gotten worse since his father died two years before. She questioned almost everything he did, as well as his friendships. Even though he was a good-looking man, a lawyer in his own firm, and quite well off, his mother couldn't seem to understand that he was no longer her responsibility. Indeed, she was his. He supposed the fact that, at thirty-five, he was still single played a role in her continual interference.

Mollie couldn't find Pierce anywhere, or Georgiana Grayson. She wondered if he'd already gone to the dining hall, but discarded the thought quickly. No, he wouldn't leave her alone without an escort to their table. The reception hall was emptying, which made it easier to see those who remained. She took one more turn and then heard laughter from outside.

She walked to the double glass doors, grabbed the handle, and peered out, instantly recognizing the two people standing together—Georgiana smiling while Pierce laughed at something she'd said. The instant clinching of her heart surprised and angered Mollie. She dropped her hand from the knob, deciding it best not to interrupt them, and turned toward the direction of the dining hall.

Mollie told herself Pierce was doing his job, getting close to someone who might have information on the activities being investigated. Her heart had an altogether different reaction. She knew it for what it was—jealousy. She'd heard of it, watched as others had experienced it. The feeling was new to her, and she didn't like it.

She turned at the entrance to the dining hall just in time to see Georgiana place a hand on Pierce's arm as they walked inside. The woman gazed up at him and smiled. Mollie suspected Pierce had made an assignation with Mrs. Grayson and scolded herself for the pain that sliced through her at the thought. She steeled herself as they stopped beside her.

"Mollie, I'd like you meet Mrs. Georgiana Grayson. Georgiana, my wife, Mollie."

Georgiana looked Mollie up and down before an almost feral smile tilted her lips up.

"It's a pleasure, Mrs. Grayson."

"No, dear, the pleasure is all mine," Georgiana responded and tightened her hold on Pierce's arm.

Pierce felt the pressure from Georgiana's hands, watched the scene play out between the two women, and noticed the strained faces even as each tried to hide them. He was doing his job and he believed with every fiber of his being that Mrs. Georgiana Grayson would be able to provide more information about the war chest, as Chaz had termed it.

He'd learned during their brief conversation that the woman adamantly opposed the current president and would welcome his departure from office. If he hadn't misread signs, she seemed to have a profound dislike of the man, almost bordering on hate. Pierce was determined to get close enough to her to learn more about the people behind the money.

"Shall we?" He held out his other arm to Mollie and escorted both women inside.

******

Supper was a magnificent affair with stunning dishes that Mollie couldn't pronounce. She and

Pierce sat at a table with Gerald and Viola Black, Harold and Lottie Goss, a gentleman who worked for Gerald, and Georgiana, who had planted herself on the other side of Pierce.

Mollie tried to act unaffected when, midway through the meal, she saw that Georgiana had rested a hand on Pierce's arm as she spoke. He made no attempt to remove it. She found herself wondering if all women, married and widowed, were as bold when pursuing married men or if Mrs. Grayson and Virginia Traxton were exceptions. The fact that they weren't actually husband and wife helped Mollie deal with the intense dislike she felt for both women, although not by much.

She was thankful when the dessert plates were cleared and the music began. The Mayor and his wife led off the first dance, with other couples joining them. Mollie pretended interest in the couples on the dance floor until she realized Pierce had stood and was offering his hand to Mrs. Grayson, disregarding the custom of the first dance being with your spouse. He didn't even look at her, simply led the beautiful widow onto the floor.

Mollie couldn't define the incredible hurt she felt, even though the rational side of her knew it was ridiculous to feel anything for the man who was her partner, who had a vested interest in solving the case—a man who'd kissed her senseless, leaving her confused and thrilled. He was doing his job, as he should be, and it was time for Mollie to do hers.

"Mrs. MacLaren, would you do me the honor of a dance?" Lloyd Johnson stood next to her, his hand extended, offering a warm, sincere smile.

"I would love to, Mr. Johnson."

The band played a beautiful waltz and Mollie discovered Lloyd was a very good dancer. She also realized he was a very good-looking man. He was older than Pierce, not as tall or as broad across the shoulders as her partner. He had a flat stomach, unlike many of the other men who had allowed their middle to jut out beyond their belts.

"Are you enjoying yourself tonight, Mrs. MacLaren?" Lloyd asked as he kept hold of her when a second song started.

"Immensely, Mr. Johnson. However, I do have one request."

His lips turned up in a slow grin. "And what is that?"

"I'd like you to call me Mollie."

"It would be my pleasure. And you must call me Lloyd."

She nodded up at him as they continued the dance. "Tell me what you do at the law firm, Lloyd."

"That's easy. I am the majority partner, so I work on only the most difficult or highly publicized cases. In addition, I try to bring in new clients and cases." He peered down at her. "I would love to host you for lunch some afternoon. Your husband too, of course."

"That would be lovely. However, I believe my husband may be finding other ways to occupy his free time." She glanced at Pierce who had danced within a few couples of them. If she hadn't mistaken it, Mollie thought she'd seen him glare over Georgiana's shoulder at Lloyd the last time they'd swirled past.

Lloyd followed Mollie's gaze. "I see. Well, I wouldn't worry too much about it. Georgiana's charms wear thin after a while."

"You sound as if you have experience." Mollie's tone was light, non-accusing.

He laughed. "I knew her husband, Walter, for a long time. He was a good friend and confidante. That's the main reason I didn't handle his legal affairs. I'll only say she has a vast appetite and has never made a distinction between single and married men. However, I have no first-hand experience with the woman." He watched Mollie's eyes cloud. "If I were you, I wouldn't worry too much about it. If your husband is a smart man, and I'd wager he is, he'll see through her mischief. Whatever happens between the two won't last long. It's the way of it, Mollie."

She bit her tongue. Mollie had no real experience at this level of society and realized the types of assignations Georgiana sought might be quite common in this world. "Why did Mr. Grayson put up with her, well, activities?"

"The reason most men would, and the reason you might put up with your husband's dalliances, if he has them. Walter was besotted with her."

Mollie fell silent, wondering if it truly was that easy or common for some men and women to ignore their vows and seek pleasure somewhere else. She chose to change the subject.

"What do you think of our president?" Her question took Lloyd by surprise. He chuckled at her seemingly sincere interest in his response.

"You are full of surprises, Mollie. To be honest, I'm not a fan. The man seems pleasant enough and honorable, but I believe a good number of his policies are misguided."

The music stopped and Lloyd escorted Mollie back to her seat.

"If we don't see each other again this evening, please be assured that an invitation will be sent out early next week for our meeting." He kissed her hand before pulling out her chair.

Mollie watched him leave, realizing she was looking forward to seeing him again and discovering what other information he might provide. It was quite obvious he was well connected, moved in the right circles, and most importantly, he wasn't a proponent of the president. Eva and Chaz were right to put the lawyer on the list—there was much she could learn from him.

Pierce had not returned to their table. Mollie looked around the large room, expecting to see him on the dance floor with Georgiana. He emerged a moment later, Mrs. Grayson on his arm, both laughing.

Georgiana dropped her gaze from Pierce long enough to notice Mollie watching them. She pulled Pierce down to place a kiss on his cheek and whisper something in his ear. He stared at her then nodded.

Mollie swallowed the bile forming in her throat as she watched the spectacle they made. *It's just a job to him,* she chanted to herself repeatedly, wishing she could believe it. She didn't understand why she was having such a hard time on this assignment, when this had never been an issue before. Granted, the other case didn't involve beautiful women and Pierce wasn't asked to use his charm and good looks to draw information from the women he targeted. Still, before their current job started, Mollie remembered disliking him to the point of almost walking away. She no longer felt that way and couldn't identify when everything had changed.

"Mollie, would you care to dance?" Pierce asked after he'd seated Georgiana.

"Not now, Pierce. Please feel free to spend your evening with Georgiana as you've done for most of the night." She turned away, pulling out the list from her small purse and looking over the names. Perhaps she had time to meet at least one more gentleman before it was time to leave. She didn't notice that he still stood over her, glaring down and wondering what in the hell was wrong with her.

Pierce did as Mollie suggested and took several more turns on the dance floor with Georgiana. They had made an arrangement to meet later that week for a late breakfast. He believed Georgiana expected they'd move from breakfast to bed, but that wasn't going to happen. He would need to be very careful how he handled this, so it didn't blow up.

He'd never admit it, but a few months ago, he wouldn't have considered refusing an invitation to bed a beautiful, willing woman. It wouldn't have bothered him a whit. Now, he had no desire for the stunningly gorgeous woman he'd held in his arms most of the night. There was just one woman he wanted, and right now, he couldn't have her. When this was over, however, the rules would change and he would go after what he'd desired for months.

Chapter Thirteen

"I was doing my job," Pierce explained for the third time, his frustration evident in the set of his jaw and narrowing of his eyes.

"I know, and you were doing it with obvious pleasure, completely ignoring me. We're still supposed to at least put up a front that we're married." Mollie hissed and tried to slam the door, but his foot stopped it. He pushed the door open, glaring at her and daring her to try to stop him from entering. "Do you know what Lloyd Johnson said?"

"No, but I'm sure you'll tell me." His words were hard, measured, his eyes slits.

She stepped backward, her eyes blazing as Pierce stalked toward her after kicking the door closed. "He told me not to worry. That you'd grow tired of her quickly," she huffed. "That's how obvious it was."

"It wasn't meant to be a secret, Mollie. Georgiana made no attempt to hide her interest in me. I was just returning the attention." He was inches from her now, not backing down at all.

"If that's how this is going to happen, then the same rules apply to me." She matched him stare for stare.

"I believe you've already demonstrated that."

"Demonstrated what?"

"That you are fully capable of playing by the same rules as me." He turned from her, paced a few feet away, squeezing the bridge of his nose between his thumb and forefinger. "You know what?" His voice was low and husky as he walked back toward her with slow deliberation.

"What?" Her sarcastic tone wasn't lost on Pierce.

"I didn't much like the way you threw yourself at Lloyd Johnson, either." His tone was hard, rough.

"I did no such thing," Mollie shot back. "I only did the same as you were doing with Georgiana." She drew the woman's name out in a caustic sneer.

"Is that so?" He was within inches of her, staring down into soft brown eyes that had darkened to a deep chocolate, his lean, tall frame towering over her.

"Yes." Mollie tilted her chin up in defiance. She felt her body warm and tried to back further away from the source of the heat, but he'd have none of it. Her legs hit the edge of her mattress. She felt trapped, glancing around Pierce to locate a means of escape, but saw none.

With dawning amusement, he leaned down. "And what was I doing with Georgiana?" His voice was soft, thick, almost menacing in its intensity. His hands moved to her arms and lightly gripped her shoulders. "Tell me, Mollie. What was I doing?"

She tried to shift her gaze away from the deep blue eyes that mesmerized and scared her all at once. Her heart beat so rapidly she felt like it would explode from her chest. She felt sure Pierce could hear it.

"You were... Well..." Her voice caught.

"What?" Pierce's breath wafted over her, causing heat to pulse through her body.

Mollie lowered her chin before she felt firm, warm fingers grasp it and tilt her face up. She kept her eyes closed, scared of what he'd see in them if they were open.

"Mollie, look at me," Pierce encouraged as his lips brushed softly across hers. Instead, she squeezed them more tightly together. She didn't see the slight smile that crossed his face as he moved his lips over hers a second time without breaking contact, increasing the pressure while his hands rubbed restlessly up and down her arms. He stopped abruptly, pulled back a couple of inches, and waited.

Mollie's eyes drifted open as a slow sigh escaped her lips.

What Pierce saw in them thrilled and terrified him. The look she gave him did nothing to cool his raging desire. If anything, his blood flamed more intensely, and he knew he'd pushed them both further than he'd ever intended.

He lowered his mouth to hers once more. His tongue outlined her lower lip, seeking entrance to the delectable sweetness inside. She opened for him as her hands came up around his neck and pulled his head to her. He plunged inside, tasting a combination of strawberries and sherry, losing himself in the feel of her.

His body was on fire. He couldn't remember ever wanting a woman the way he wanted Mollie. No one had ever caused his blood to boil the way she could.

His hands moved to her shoulders, then her back, to unbutton her gown, pushing the cap sleeves down her arms enough to allow her dress to drift to the floor and pool at her feet. Her trusting gaze never wavered from his as he pulled back to look at her, his eyes darkening to an intense midnight blue. He pulled her to him once more, his mouth reclaiming hers.

Mollie was lost. She couldn't seem to fight the emotions, the heat, the thrumming of her body as his hands and mouth moved over her. She pulled him tighter, feeling his strong, hard body, and wanted to tear the buttons from his shirt and run her hands over his taut chest.

"Mollie." His voice was a mere whisper, ragged and thick. "I want you. Tonight. Now."

"I want you, too." She pulled his mouth back to hers. Their kiss intensified until neither could stop the surging emotions that sparked between them.

Pierce broke contact and took a deep breath. "Are you sure? Tell me you're sure this is what you want. If it's not, I'll leave." His voice was urgent, almost a plea.

She looked into eyes, blazing with passion, and knew this was right. "Yes, I'm sure."

He lifted her into his arms, placed her on the large pillowed bed, and straightened as his gaze wandered over her. She was stunning, more beautiful than any woman he'd ever known, and he'd wanted her since the first day they'd met. He'd take it slow and ensure that neither of them ever forgot this night.

******

"You should have told me." Pierce's steel-edged voice cut through the crisp morning air as he shoved his hands into the arms of his shirt and tucked it into his pants.

Mollie sat stone still in bed after the best night of her life, her hands clasped firmly in her lap, knuckles white, feeling totally miserable. *Yes,* she thought, *I should have told him. Now it was too late.*

He walked to the bed, rested both hands on the mattress, and leaned toward her. "That's not something you keep from a man." He pushed away, grabbed his belt, vest, and jacket, and walked toward the door, hesitating before he turned back to her, his eyes conveying the regret she was certain he felt.

Her heart sank.

"We'll marry." His statement was terse, inviting no argument.

Mollie's jaw dropped, but she quickly regained her wits and jumped from the bed, placing both hands on her hips and glaring at him. "We certainly will not."

She could see his jaw work and his eyes narrow. Pierce took a few determined steps forward, stopping directly in front of her, his eyes sparking.

"We will marry, Mollie, make no mistake about it." Satisfied that he'd made his point, he turned to leave.

"No. I will not marry you and you can't force me to. I'm a grown woman, I have a choice."

"Yes, you are a grown woman, and you made that choice when you accepted me into your bed knowing you were a virgin."

This time, he did open the door and started into the hallway.

"You don't love me."

Pierce turned back to her, the edginess in his voice gone, replaced by acceptance. "It doesn't matter."

He left and stormed to his room, slamming the door behind him. Picking up the nearest object, a glass paper weight, he threw it against the wall, sending pieces of the ornament shooting across the floor.

******

"What do you mean Owen wasn't available? Noah indicated he would be dispatched to help if needed. I'd been led to believe he had no pending assignments." Eva was livid, her eyes dancing with fury and her voice scolding.

"That changed." Lee sat back in their carriage, determined to let Eva vent her hostility to him. She had nowhere to go, no other options. She just hadn't realized it yet.

"Surely there must have been someone else if Owen wasn't available. Doesn't Noah understand that this simply can't work?"

He remained silent.

"Lee?" Eva's voice was firm, disgusted.

"Yes."

"Did you hear what I said? We can't possibly be convincing, not with our past."

Lee stretched his legs out as much as was possible in the moving carriage, crossed his ankles, and settled his hands in his lap. "I would think our past is what would make it that much more believable." His blithe response only served to fuel her outrage.

"I'd expect you to say that." Her bitter sigh was accompanied by a flushed face, an indication of the true deterioration of her patience.

Lee dropped his head back against the seat and closed his eyes. He was tired from the long trip, the work he'd done since his arrival, and most of all, tired of still being in love with his wife—ex-wife now. He'd loved no one before Eva, and didn't believe the deep feelings he had for her could ever be duplicated with another. She was one of a kind, and for a short, exhilarating time, she'd been his.

Lee felt the carriage come to a stop outside the hotel and jumped out, reaching a hand up to Eva. She would have preferred to ignore the gesture, but the long dress and heels prevented her from scorning him completely. She grabbed his hand, navigated the two short steps, then released her grip as soon as both feet were firmly on the ground.

They walked up the stairs together before breaking off to return to their own rooms. She took out her key, and just before inserting it in the lock, glanced down the hall to where Lee was performing the same action, his eyes focused on the key in his hand. He turned his head and caught her watching him. He held her gaze a brief moment, made a mock salute, and entered his room.

Eva continued to stare at the empty spot in the hall where he'd stood then walked into her own room. She tossed her small handbag and wrap on the bed. Instead of removing her dress and meticulously securing it on a hanger, she fell back onto the bed and put an arm over her eyes.

Her heart had raced all night, ever since he'd walked up behind her and turned her world upside down. His deep, rich voice washed over her as it had all those years before, and her traitorous body had responded tonight the same as it had then. She'd often wondered how he was doing, if he'd changed or if he was still the most dangerously handsome man she'd ever met. To her disgust, he'd only improved.

It didn't matter. Tomorrow, she'd send a scathing note to Noah, telling him in no uncertain terms that she'd leave if he didn't find someone else, post haste. She knew there might not be another agent available. It would put her boss in a difficult position, but he'd set it all in motion when he'd approved Lee's participation as her partner. Well, he would just have to find a solution.

******

Mollie sat on the bed, feeling bruised from Pierce's firm admission that he didn't love her. To make things worse, she'd known for a while that her heart belonged to the stubborn, cocky rancher turned federal agent. She'd hoped he might feel the same. Now she knew the truth.

She gripped the edge of the mattress and wondered what else she could have expected after encouraging him without disclosing her total lack of experience. Mollie couldn't even throw the blame on how senseless he'd made her with his kisses, the way his warm, calloused hands worked magic on her body, setting her on fire, and making her feel like she would die from the sensations he provoked.

Even at the point where she thought her body would burst into flames, a warning flashed across her mind, pressing her to confide in Pierce before it was too late. She'd ignored it and was now faced with the outcome of her decision.

Mollie fell back onto the mattress and stared at the ceiling. He'd given her an ultimatum, not a choice. It wasn't the usual demand to do something or else. No, he'd informed her they'd be married and left the room. She'd almost laughed at the thought that Penelope and all of their acquaintances in San Francisco already believed them to be married. How would they explain it? Then she'd sobered, realizing that he was absolutely serious. He demanded they marry and she, just as resolutely, would resist. Even if she wanted to marry her egotistical partner, she'd never agree to it unless he loved her, which he didn't.

Though it had been at least an hour since he'd stormed from her room, Mollie could still hear the slamming of his bedroom door echoing in her mind. She'd abandoned the idea of running after him to explain, knowing he wouldn't hear a word she said in his present mood. No, she'd wait until he calmed down enough to have a rational discussion, and quash his ridiculous idea of marriage in the process.

Chapter Fourteen

Pierce woke with a blinding headache. The sun was high in the sky, indicating it was already midday. He sat up and pushed his palms into his eye sockets, trying to ease the pain while doing his best to remember why he'd drank such a large amount of whiskey. Then reality hit. *Mollie ... marriage.* He fell back on his pillow and groaned.

What had begun as the most incredibly intense sensual experience he'd ever had turned into a painful schooling in trust and honor. He couldn't believe he'd let it happen after telling himself over and over to stay as far away from the alluring woman who commanded his dreams. And why had Mollie stayed silent, not giving a hint that this was her first time?

A part of him felt exhilarated, realizing he'd been her first. Another part felt betrayed. Her silence pushing him into a situation he neither expected, nor wanted. He'd always stayed away from married women and innocents, knowing both would lead to entanglements beyond what his traveling lifestyle could accept. His older brother, Connor, had been firm in his belief to take responsibility for bad decisions, and he'd drilled this same maxim into Pierce. As a young, single man, Pierce had thought it an honorable way to live.

His intentions to take it slow, make it last, were lost as he became consumed in his desire for her. The easy pace he'd envisioned had become frenzied as their need for each other increased. He remembered the sick surprise he'd felt when the truth was revealed—their bodies passionately entwined—already too late to reverse what had occurred.

He sat up, thinking of Mollie, and wondered if she'd accepted that they'd marry or would continue to fight him. It wasn't so much the thought of marriage that bothered Pierce as much as marrying a woman who wasn't in love with him. He knew his response to her about not loving her was a half-truth. He did care about her, most likely loved her, but he wasn't prepared to confess the point. He would do the right thing, though, and marry her.

He dressed then walked the short distance to her bedroom and knocked. No answer. He tried once more. "Mollie, it's Pierce. Are you in there?" There was still no answer.

Pierce descended the stairs and walked through the doors of the conservatory to find Mollie staring at a plate heaped with eggs and bacon. He stopped, watching her, and knew she hadn't heard him enter. She continued to stare at the food, not making any attempt to lift her fork or give any indication she planned to eat.

He took a seat across from her and noticed her eyes lifting to his, haunted, turbulent, and wary.

"Good morning, Mollie." His voice was soft, cautious, as he tried to gauge the best way to approach her.

She didn't immediately respond. Without a word, she pushed from her chair and stood. "I won't marry you," she murmured and turned to leave.

"Sit down, Mollie."

"I don't have anything more to say." She'd planned to discuss his ultimatum in a calm, even tone, explaining her reasons they couldn't marry and letting him know that a future between them was impossible. Instead, all of her good intentions fell away as her eyes took in the incredibly handsome man before her and her traitorous body began to respond as it had last night. She crossed her arms, held them tight to her chest, and willed herself to relax.

"We don't have to discuss what happened last night, not right now. What we do have to talk about is what we learned from the other guests, see if anything we heard is worth pursuing." He kept his voice calm, low, and in what he hoped was a reasonable tone.

It was obvious that she was struggling with what had transpired between them the night before, perhaps regretted it, and even more likely, hated him. No matter. As far as he was concerned, the decision about their future was settled.

Mollie knew Pierce was right. They had a duty to continue their investigation and discover if the activities they uncovered were those of rational men looking for change, or something more

149

sinister. Mollie would finish the assignment then do what she'd planned all along—accept her money and head east, leaving Pierce MacLaren and his demands behind. She sat down just as Penelope entered the room to announce that Miss Gagnon, Mr. Yarbrough, and Mr. Hatcher had arrived.

"Show them in," Pierce instructed and stood. "Your timing is perfect," he said to the other agents as they took seats around their table. He'd spoken with Lee briefly the night before, surprised to see him instead of the other agent Eva had mentioned.

"Lee Hatcher," Lee said to Mollie, not having met her at the ball.

"It's good to have you here, Lee." Mollie smiled at the new addition to the team then glanced at Eva who sat stone-faced, her lips pinched into a thin line. Mollie turned her attention back to Lee. "Eva indicated we should expect a different agent."

"I believe you are referring to Owen Kendall. Unfortunately, he wasn't available. Noah sent me."

"And we're glad to have you, Lee." Chaz had sat in the carriage with Eva and Lee on the way over to see Pierce and Mollie. It was a strained trip and it appeared the atmosphere wasn't going to change anytime soon.

Lee nodded at Chaz then looked around the room.

"It's all right." Pierce answered Lee's unspoken question. "Penelope is the only other person here and she won't bother us."

"There were several people in attendance last night we need to learn more about," Lee began. "Jock Flannigan, Georgiana Grayson, and Lloyd

Johnson are three of them and should be our priority."

"I have an engagement with Mrs. Grayson this week, for breakfast." Pierce felt Mollie's eyes on him, but didn't turn to her, focusing his attention on Lee. "She mentioned her disenchantment with the president's policies and seemed more than eager to see someone else take his place. I'm certain she'll know others who feel the same."

"Good. We also need to learn her true role in the shipping company she owns with Flannigan. For those of you not familiar with Grayson & Flannigan, they are the largest and most profitable shipping company on the West Coast. They specialize in long-haul shipments between Asia and California, as well as shorter trips, many originating in Canada, with deliveries to ports in Washington and California. When Walter Grayson passed away, his percentage of ownership transferred to his widow." Lee stopped and sipped coffee that had turned cold. "According to the chief of police, there are still unresolved questions about Grayson's death, even though it was deemed an accident. Perhaps we can help Chief Curtis close that case along with resolving our own."

"Do you believe Flannigan is one of the men included in the group Chaz's contact mentioned?" Mollie asked.

"He very well could be. His company was hit hard by the ban on Chinese immigration that the government, and the president, continues to support. His business has experienced a significant slowdown of Chinese men traveling to the States to work and a loss of many of his Chinese seamen. The company has always employed a large number of seamen from Asia. He's been able to find good replacements, yet believes that the ban is a poor reaction by the government."

"How do you want to handle Flannigan?" Pierce asked.

"For now, Eva and I will focus on high-profile people such as the mayor and his wife. Learn if they know anything that might warrant more attention." He glanced at Eva, knowing this was new information to her. She showed no reaction. "Chaz will continue to focus on his numerous contacts to learn if there is something more ominous than political disagreements. That leaves you to focus on Mrs. Grayson and Mollie to concentrate on Mr. Flannigan."

Pierce understood his part as he'd already met and made arrangements to see Georgiana again. Mollie was at a disadvantage, as she hadn't met Flannigan.

"Flannigan and I weren't introduced last night. How do you suggest I go about getting close to him?" Mollie asked.

"You didn't meet Flannigan, but you did dance several times with the senior partner of the law firm he uses."

"Lloyd Johnson." Mollie confirmed. "He told me another lawyer in his firm handles the legal work for the shipping business. I didn't get the impression he knew Flannigan well."

"Another lawyer takes care of the day-to-day requirements, however, it was Lloyd who brought

Grayson & Flannigan's business to the firm through his friendship with Walter Grayson. Lloyd Johnson and Jock Flannigan are peers, making Lloyd the perfect person to facilitate your introduction."

Lee reached into a pocket, pulled out a set of folded papers, and handed them to Mollie. "This is what you'll use to make the connection mean something to Flannigan."

Mollie read through them quickly, glancing at Lee a couple of times, but saying nothing.

"Do you have any questions?" Lee asked her.

"No. This is quite thorough and should work well to gain his interest."

Pierce watched the exchange and wondered about the documents Mollie held. He'd ask her about them once everyone had left.

"If there are no further questions, then I suggest we start on our assignments," Lee said. "We'll meet again in a few days."

******

Pierce waited until the others had left then joined Mollie in the conservatory where she sat rereading the information Lee had provided.

"What does he have you doing?"

Mollie looked up at Pierce then back down to the document, ignoring his question and concentrating on the best way to approach Jock Flannigan.

"Mollie?"

She finished then stood to face Pierce. "I'm to make contact with Flannigan as a married woman with considerable assets of my own. I'll pose as a potential customer, ask him about shipments I'd like to make from the east, and see what happens."

Pierce's dubious look triggered her natural defenses, already sensing he'd want to insert himself somehow into this part of the assignment.

"I'm doing this alone, Pierce, at least for now. Lee has it set up that way and that's how I intend to do it." She watched his eyes, hard and assessing, already sensing his disapproval. "I'll let you know if I get the sense Flannigan is involved in something."

"I don't like it." The scenario Lee sketched out meant that Mollie would be going alone to the docks of San Francisco, not a safe place for a woman by herself.

"You don't have to like it."

"In case you've forgotten, we're partners."

"Does that mean you want me to accompany you to see Georgiana?" she shot back, the sarcastic tone stronger than she'd intended.

"You know that isn't going to happen." He shoved both hands in his pockets, protecting himself from reaching for Mollie, then stepped toward her. "Georgiana Grayson is a job, nothing more."

Mollie thought of how he'd left her room, his lack of feelings clear in his parting comment. He may be willing to marry her, out of a sense of duty or honor or whatever it was he felt, but there was no love. She was grateful that he hadn't lied to her.

It would make it easier to walk away when the job was finished.

"I don't care what you feel or don't feel for Mrs. Grayson," she snapped. "You do your job and let me do mine. We'll finish this up and get on with our lives." Mollie turned on her heels, her determined steps underscoring the tension that still lay between them.

"What went on between us last night is significant, something that can't be ignored. I'm willing to take responsibility for my part."

She looked back to him, her face softening. "You'll marry someone you don't love, don't want to live with, to satisfy some sense of male pride? You were right, I should have said something, let you know I'd never been with a man. I'm sorry I didn't, but I'm not willing to throw our lives away over one mistake."

"Is that what you believe, that we'd be throwing our lives away by marrying?"

She clasped her hands in front of her and tried to focus on what she believed was best for both of them. "I won't be a part of a marriage that doesn't include love."

"It doesn't have to be that way, Mollie, the two of us feeling as if we're on different sides." She was his and Pierce was determined it would stay that way.

She turned, her eyes taking on a hard glitter. "It's the only way it can be."

******

"We need to talk about the supper party tonight at Mayor Pound's." Lee spoke in a loud voice as he strode into the sitting area of Eva's hotel suite and took a seat, waiting for her to emerge from the bedroom.

Eva peered through the partially opened door. "How'd you get in here?" she demanded, not pleased with his assumption that he could come and go from her room anytime he chose.

Lee said nothing, just held up a room key and dangled it for Eva to see.

She walked toward him, dressed only in a long silk robe, and tried to grab the key from his hand, but missed when he pulled it out of her reach. "I'll take that," she demanded and held out her hand. "Nothing in this assignment allows you the right to walk into my room any time you please." It wasn't easy to fluster Eva, she was always cool, professional, and in control. It frustrated her that all those traits disappeared whenever Lee was around.

He ignored her, held on to the key, and stretched his long legs out in front of him, making himself comfortable while witnessing her anger escalate.

"Have you heard back from Noah?" Lee's nonchalant tone did nothing to cool her irritation.

She glared at him. "There are no other agents available."

"Guess you're stuck with me."

"Just until this one assignment is over, then never again," she threw back. "Now, tell me why you're here then leave." She sat on the edge of a chair across from him, arms crossed, her eagerness to get rid of him obvious.

"Chief Curtis will be there along with some other guests. As far as I know, Curtis is still unaware of who we are or why we're here. For now, we'll keep it that way." He leaned forward. "We need to keep the mayor and his wife occupied while Pierce checks Pound's office and library. It shouldn't take him long to find anything that might tie the mayor into what we're investigating."

Eva's anger hadn't lessened, but she realized the sooner he told her about tonight, the sooner he'd leave. After he gave her the key.

"What is he looking for, or do you have any idea?" Eva had been able to get through the last few days by telling herself that Lee would be gone once Noah received the message she'd sent. Even though she knew his resources were limited, her boss's response hadn't been what she'd anticipated.

"Anything that would point to the mayor's knowledge of the transfers of large sums of cash being used for actions against the country. There's not much to go on, and frankly, it seems highly unlikely, given what I know of the man. We're mainly trying to rule him out."

Eva stood and walked across the room, sitting down in a window seat and staring at the view below. "We have three things to go on. First, large withdrawals being hoarded for some purpose. The reason could be a legitimate buildup of money to elect someone else, or a cause more sinister. Second, groups of prominent men on the East and

West Coasts meeting to decide the best way to reverse the president's policies and quash his reelection. And third, rumors of a well-connected gentleman traveling from one city to another, trying to gather participation for some action we can't identify. Does that sum it up?" Her gaze shifted from the streets outside to focus on the man across the room.

A frown played across Lee's face as Eva itemized what they knew. "It doesn't sound like much, does it?" he admitted and scrubbed a hand down his face. "I keep wondering if we're on some misguided chase triggered by an over-anxious bureaucrat in the president's administration. I believe we'll find the money is being collected for promoting someone else as a viable alternative to Cleveland in the next election, and nothing more. The meetings are a way to decide who to back and how to get him elected. That takes care of your first two items. The third item is the one that concerns me, and the one I'd like to have as our priority. Unfortunately, we must keep working on all the information to discover if any of it leads to an answer. Follow the funds, watch the people involved, and try to identify the mystery man who keeps surfacing."

"That spreads us very thin."

"I've been having the same doubts as you, Eva. Unfortunately, we're not in a position to simply fold up and leave. We have to wait for Noah to give the order. I have to say, any involvement by the mayor or his wife would surprise me."

Her annoyance at working with her ex-husband dissipated some when she thought of the mayor's wife. She liked the woman. Lydia Pound was the only other person in San Francisco who knew Eva's true line of work. Most believed she was a wealthy widow who spent her time traveling and attending social affairs. Lydia knew different, but only because her brother worked in the Foreign Affairs Office and had somehow let it slip when he'd seen the two woman together during Eva's last assignment in the San Francisco. He'd sworn Lydia to secrecy, not even allowing her to say a word to her husband, Edwin.

"I doubt Pierce will find anything on Edwin. Lydia isn't the type of woman to be saddled with a man who would allow illegal acts to happen, or worse, participate in them. She's not the silent type, and with her family being so prominent in Eastern politics, it would be catastrophic if he were implicated in anything illegal."

"Agreed, but we can't afford not to consider it. Besides, Pierce's background makes him the perfect person to sneak into someone's home or office." Lee shook his head and let out a soft chuckle. "He's actually looking forward to it."

"What of Mollie?"

"She's not involved with this. And I doubt she knows Pierce is."

"Do you think that's wise, leaving her out of it?"

"Pierce and I discussed what was needed. It was my decision for him to work it alone."

"You're in charge." Eva didn't say another word, just shrugged and walked toward a table that held a pitcher of water and glasses. She poured a glass for herself, not offering anything to Lee.

Eva sensed the air around her change a moment before she felt him at her back. Lee's strong, warm hands rested on her shoulders and tried to draw her to him, but she remained rooted in place. It had been four years and she still missed him every single day. He'd been her rock, the one man who could help her sort through difficult memories and past regrets. At least, he had been until she'd learned the truth.

"Are you ever going to let me explain my side of what happened?" Lee's warm breath washed over her through the thin fabric of the silk robe.

She closed her eyes, wishing she'd never listened to Owen's cryptic comments about his friend and partner. "You don't need to explain. I was there, remember?"

"It wasn't what you thought, Eva."

He was gently massaging her shoulders and neck, using his thumbs in circular motions. It was how he'd always relaxed her.

"You were there, she was there." Eva sighed and dropped her head back against his chest. "I understand, truly I do. You were still in love with her when we met, you said as much. I'd thought, hoped, that at some point, the feelings we had for each other would be strong enough to help you forget her. Now, I understand that some losses can never be forgotten." Her heart squeezed as it always did when she remembered that night and

160

the terrible sense of betrayal. She hadn't understood how much she'd loved Lee until it was too late.

"You are so wrong. I loved you, Eva, and still do. Constance was a memory, that's all." He turned Eva to face him. He started to say more when a soft knock on the door stopped him. Lee dropped his hands, but didn't step back. "Promise me you'll let me explain."

Eva didn't answer as she skirted around him, opened the door, and accepted the message from the young man. "Thank you," she said in an absent tone then shut the door.

"The carriage will be outside in two hours. I need to start getting ready." Eva looked to Lee, who hadn't budged. She began to walk past him, but stopped as his hand gently wrapped around her wrist.

"We can work this out if you'll let me explain." His voice was close to a plea. She felt his hand squeeze her wrist lightly before he let it fall back to his side.

Eva studied his rugged face and eyes that had darkened to a deep emerald green, thinking of how many nights she lay in bed dreaming of a chance to be with him again, knowing it would never happen. She shook her head and continued into her bedroom, closing the door softly behind her.

Chapter Fifteen

Pierce finished dressing in his comfortable ranch clothes then hurried down the stairs. The last thing he needed was to run into Mollie on his way to the Pound residence. She wasn't a part of tonight's activities, and he'd been careful to keep his plans from her.

Lee had arranged for a horse to be waiting behind a hotel where his carriage driver dropped him off. Pierce walked through the hotel lobby, out the back door, and around the corner where the horse was saddled and waiting. It would take less time to maneuver the busy streets on horseback than to go by carriage or use one of the horsecars, which most residents rode and were always crowded. His forty-five Peacemaker was hidden in the special holster Noah had sent, and for the first time in weeks, Pierce felt like himself.

It didn't take long to reach his destination. He rode to the back of the property then tied his horse to a post another block away and hidden from the main street. He'd get in and out before anyone discovered his presence. There were to be just a few guests and he'd seen no guards posted, as was the case at the Mayor's Ball. No one was expecting trouble tonight. Truth was, Pierce didn't want any trouble either, just a clean visit without being discovered.

His dark clothes concealed his tall, lean frame as he traversed the short distance through the shrubs and crouched below a well-lit window on one side of the mayor's house. Laughter and conversation flowed from the room, which he guessed was either the dining room or parlor. He looked around and smiled at his luck. There were several large trees within a few feet of the house. The one closest to him had large branches that spread out and touched the upper windows near a second-story balcony. Lee had told him the library, which served as the mayor's office, was downstairs. The mayor also had a small, private study on the second floor. He needed to check both.

Pierce dropped to the ground at the sound of voices near the window.

"How long will you be in the city, Lee?" It was the mayor's voice.

"Weeks or months, neither Eva nor I have decided."

"She's a beautiful woman, a little mysterious for my tastes, but no doubt a most gracious companion. I don't have to tell you how lucky you are."

"No, Mayor, you don't."

"Supper is served," a servant announced.

Pierce could make out the sound of footfalls as everyone moved to the dining room. He stood and peered through the window into the parlor then stooped low to silently traverse the perimeter of the house. He needed to locate the library, then find the upstairs study. The library was on the other side of the kitchen, on the opposite side of the house from where he'd started. Pierce reached up and tried the window, relieved to discover it hadn't been secured. To his relief, it made no noise as he lifted the double-hung window. He pulled himself over the sill and dropped inside.

Pierce moved to the desk, rifling through drawers, and feeling around the bottoms and sides. Finding nothing, he walked the perimeter of the room, locating a small wall safe. He reached into his pocket and pulled out a pouch of tools. Within a minute, the safe was open and he was searching the contents. Again, he found nothing except personal papers and some money. He closed the safe, returned the picture to its place, and took one more careful look around.

A small stand caught his attention. The top shelf was thicker than most, capable of concealing a drawer. He silently approached and noticed what appeared to be a shelf on glides. Pulling it open he found a stack of papers. He searched through them, and again, found nothing except private documents.

It was time to locate the study. He dropped back outside, closed the window, then soundlessly returned to the large tree on the other side of the house. A short time later, he was up the tree and standing on the small balcony. He tried the door. It opened and he slipped into what he guessed was the bedroom used by the mayor and his wife. The inside bedroom door opened to a dimly lit hallway. The third door he tried opened into a surprisingly large study.

Two walls held books, the third was to the outside and had just one window. A desk was pushed up against the fourth wall with tall cabinets on either side—that's where he started.

The third drawer down on the right side of the desk held various files, one labeled 'G and F.' *Grayson & Flannigan?* Pierce wondered as he pulled it out and looked through the contents. His eyes widened as he scanned the documents inside. He read the contents twice, memorizing as much as possible before returning the file to the drawer to search the rest of the room. The file in the desk was the only item of interest. He'd started toward the hallway door when he heard footsteps and voices.

Pierce dashed to the one small window, lifted the bottom half, and peered out. He'd break a leg if he tried to drop from that point. He closed the window and looked around the room, his eyes fixing on the tall cabinets next to the desk. He pulled open the doors at the bottom of one and had just crammed his large frame inside, closing the doors after him, when light appeared from the hallway.

"This is the desk I mentioned. It came over from England. Almost didn't make it when the ship ran into a nasty storm. As you can see, it did survive and required only minor repairs."

"It's magnificent, Mayor, as is the room. This must be where you go to truly get away."

Pierce thought he recognized the somewhat sultry female voice as belonging to Virginia

Traxton and a chill went through him. Something about that woman set him on edge.

"Yes, Virginia, it is. Of course, I receive visitors and do some work in my library, as it is larger and more formal. This room is reserved for my own personal use. Shall we?"

Pierce waited until he heard the door close behind them before pushing open the cabinet doors and extricating himself from the small space. He stretched then pulled open the hallway door and dashed silently to the bedroom where he'd entered. Within minutes, he was outside, moving at a quick pace toward his horse a block away. It wouldn't be long before he'd be back at the house before Mollie could miss him.

This is why he'd been interested in Noah's offer to become an agent. He wasn't any good at biding his time, waiting for actions to unfold. Pierce liked being part of the action, getting in the middle to make events happen. Tonight had gone well. He wasn't sure if the file he read was damaging or an attempt by the mayor to do some investigating on his own, but it was a start. Lee and Eva would know what to do next.

******

Mollie paced the large entry hall, furious that Pierce hadn't told her of his plans. She'd gone looking for him earlier, wanting to clear the air and try to make peace. When she couldn't locate him, she knew his disappearance involved the case and he'd kept her out of it.

Mollie stared at the large entry door when she heard the sound of boots coming up the steps. He'd get everything she had to throw his way this time, she wouldn't hold anything back. The door opened. Mollie was ready, hands on hips, and a don't-mess-with-me aura about her.

Pierce came to a dead stop when he saw her. He pulled his old range hat from his head and tossed it on a nearby chair. "Mollie," he greeted, then made an attempt to walk around her, indicating that he had no time for angry outbursts. She moved into his path, halting his progress.

"Where've you been?" She nearly spit the words at him.

"Working on something for Lee." He tried to move around her again and failed.

"What, exactly?"

He could see she wasn't going to budge. Truth was if it had been her taking off, he'd be mad as hell. "Fine. Let's go into the parlor and I'll explain it all."

Pierce walked straight to the liquor cabinet, poured two shots, and handed one to Mollie. She took it without a word and downed the amber liquid in one gulp. He watched, fighting an urge to smile at how flushed her face got when she was angry. The whiskey would only add to the glow. He hoped it also mellowed her mood. He shot his back and poured one more for each of them.

He sat down in an oversized chair, stretched out his legs, crossed his ankles, and sipped the whisky, hoping she'd calm down.

"Lee asked me to check out Mayor Pound's office. We both knew it was a one-person job. You weren't needed."

Mollie didn't take a seat, choosing to continue to pace while watching her overconfident partner. She stopped to face him. "It doesn't matter if Lee approved one or two, you should have told me, and I should've been there to make sure someone was keeping watch for you. That, Pierce, is what partners are for."

"Lee didn't see it that way. A lookout may have drawn more attention, Mollie. It was a simple supper party, not some major event. Anyway, it worked out fine.'"

"It could've ended up not being fine if you were caught. You'd have gone to jail and it would have taken days for Noah to get you out."

She was right on that count. If any of them were arrested, the procedure was to notify Noah Dodd to handle their release. None of the other agents were to step forward and expose their cover.

"Well, I didn't get caught and I got what Lee wanted."

"Which is?"

"I'll explain when he and Eva arrive, which should be real soon."

They both turned as the door opened. Chaz walked in and glanced around, strode to the cabinet, poured a drink, and swiveled back to Mollie and Pierce. "Not here yet?" he asked, referring to Lee and Eva.

Pierce shook his head.

Chaz downed his drink, looked at the bottle again, decided against pouring another, and set his glass down.

Penelope opened the parlor door to let them know Lee and Eva had arrived and showed them in.

Lee didn't waste time, walking directly to Pierce. "What did you find?"

"Not much, but enough to know that Pound is at least aware of some strange activities at Grayson & Flannigan." Eva took a seat as Pierce continued. "There was a file in Pound's upstairs study. A couple of items were receipts for goods that he and his wife had ordered from the east. One document was three pages long, handwritten, and spoke of his suspicions about Georgiana Grayson. The message was dated before Walter Grayson's death. From the sound of it, the mayor and Walter met for lunch. They apparently were quite good friends. Anyway, Grayson suspected his wife was involved in some activities he knew nothing about, and that Jock Flannigan might be aware of what was going on. Pound mentioned that what Walter told him may have merit—that's where the first part of the document ended. He must have picked up the document again after Grayson's death to add more thoughts. The mayor mentioned that Georgiana and Thomas Traxton were somehow connected. He wrote of his intention to speak with Chief Curtis and have both Traxton and Georgiana watched. That's when the writing stopped."

"Could you tell when the last part was written?"

"It was dated two months ago."

"Interesting. I wonder if he did go ahead with his investigation of the two." Eva stood and walked to the darkened window, aware that the others were continuing their discussion behind her. There was a full moon, with sporadic cloud cover, which cast an eerie glow over the garden area behind the mansion. For an instant, she thought she saw a shadow race through the massive shrubs near the back. She watched another minute, and, when there was no further activity, turned back to the group.

"Eva, it would be best for you to approach the mayor. You've known him and his wife a while. Mention your observations about Traxton and Georgiana and see if he takes the bait."

Lee had taken off his jacket and rested against the edge of the desk, his arms crossed over his solid chest. Eva remembered when she used to hand him a drink when he got home at night. He'd take a sip then set his drink down and rest his hands on the edge of the desk. She'd unbutton his shirt and feel the heat of him while he relaxed. Even now, she could feel her face flush at the thought.

"Eva, did you hear me?" Lee asked, a slight smile curving his lips as if he knew what she was thinking. And he probably did.

"I, uh, yes, certainly. I'd be happy to meet with the Pounds." She'd have to confirm what it was she was supposed to meet with them about at a later time.

"All right. The plan was to have Pierce check the mayor's office downtown. With what he found in the desk, I believe it would be best to have him check out the offices of Grayson & Flannigan instead."

"I'm going this time, Lee. I won't be left out again." Mollie's voice was steel-edged, her face set.

Lee's eyes locked with hers. "You weren't needed tonight, Mollie. I'm sorry if this offended you, but that's the decision I made. Over time, there will be decisions that you may not agree with and will frustrate you. That's part of this type of work and you'll need to learn to handle it." His voice was equally hard. "Do I make myself clear?"

Pierce looked toward Mollie, his face impassive.

"Completely." Mollie hated being called to task in front of others, even though she realized it was her own fault for bringing it up now, with everyone present.

"Good. The search at Grayson & Flannigan is a two-person job. Pierce, you'll take Mollie. We need a layout and the number of men Jock leaves on guard at night. Chaz, you will handle that in the next two days. Pierce will call the shots once you are on the property, no matter who accompanies him. Understood?"

Everyone nodded.

"We'll need at least three days to put everything in place. Plan it for four nights out. Eva and I will do whatever is needed to make sure Jock Flannigan and Georgiana Grayson are out of the office. Any questions?"

When no one responded, Lee continued. "There is something else. President Cleveland is riding the train around the country, building support for his initiatives and meeting with city leaders. San Francisco will be one of his stops. I'd like to have this case closed and all of us out of California by the time he arrives."

Chapter Sixteen

Fire Mountain

"What's the message say, Drew?" Tess stood alongside her husband who'd just picked up a note from his boss, Louis Dunnigan. They'd been in town running errands and were just about to head back to the ranch when he remembered the mail.

Drew pursed his lips as he silently read then looked at his pregnant wife. "He wants me to meet him in San Francisco to review some new business transactions he's considering. Henry Thompson is still back east working on other legal matters and can't get west for several weeks. Dunnigan has already arranged my travel and hotel. I'll need to leave tomorrow."

"Did he say how long you'd be needed?"

"No, but I'd guess a couple of weeks at most. At least it will give me a chance to see Pierce and find out how it's going." He folded the paper before sliding it into his shirt pocket.

Drew hated leaving Tess at this point. She was almost six months along, three months from when the newest MacLaren was expected. At least she would have help from the other women if anything happened while he was gone. Drew had been anticipating a request like this from Louis, knowing how many business deals the man liked to have going at one time. He'd hoped it would wait until after the birth, but that wasn't going to happen.

"Best get back and let everyone know." Drew slipped Tess's arm through his, feeling fortunate in so many ways. The ranch was doing well, their first child was on the way, and, along with the horse breeding operations, his legal work for Dunnigan was lucrative and kept him busy. As Aunt Alicia had commented to everyone the other night, the only thing missing was having the last of the MacLarens back home where he belonged, referring to Pierce.

Drew smiled to himself. This would be a good opportunity to make sure his cousin hadn't gotten himself into too much trouble, and remind him that his family was in Fire Mountain, waiting for his return.

******

San Francisco

Pierce had been restless since the night he'd searched the mayor's study. He hadn't realized how much he missed the excitement of his past life—using his skills to do investigative work that often included backstairs access to people's homes and offices. Sneaking into the mayor's home, going through the library and study, had provided the thrill he'd been missing the last few months. He'd signed on with Noah because his boss had implied the agency needed the types of skills Pierce possessed. Until now, most of the work had been centered on meeting people, attending social events, poring over bits of government-secured information, and trying to make sense of it all. He was looking forward to checking the offices of Grayson & Flannigan—it may prove to be the last adventure he have for a while.

Mollie had made a second appointment to meet with Jock Flannigan that afternoon regarding a contract to bring items to San Francisco from the East Coast. At Lee's request, she'd already met with Jock once—a preliminary meeting to see if his company handled the type of shipping she needed. Flannigan had assured Mollie that her request was quite common and scheduled a second meeting.

This time, Pierce would accompany her. He would get a direct look at the waterfront parcel where Grayson & Flannigan had built their office and warehouses, request a tour, ask seemingly harmless questions, and leave with most of the information needed to access the property a couple nights later. Chaz had already done his part, confirming that Flannigan kept two men on watch each night. They'd have to decide how to distract them while Pierce completed his search.

"Are you ready?" Mollie asked as she walked into the library.

Pierce had been moments away from going to find her. She hadn't invited him to her second meeting with Lloyd Johnson that morning, believing she could get more information out of the man without someone else present.

She'd had her first meeting with the attorney a few days after the Mayor's Ball. As he'd promised, Lloyd had sent her a lunch invitation. That's when she'd asked for the introduction to Flannigan.

Mollie and Johnson had agreed on a second meeting that day. For her, the purpose was to attempt to learn more about Jock before she and Pierce met with the man. Mollie knew Lloyd was attracted to her, yet he'd kept the conversation focused on the potential of securing the MacLaren legal business and providing her with insights on San Francisco society. The information she'd gotten from the attorney had been valuable, indicating that Flannigan was considered to be honorable and an astute businessman. She had left their meeting feeling as if pursuing more information on Jock was a waste of everyone's time.

Pierce pulled out his pocket watch. Somehow, he'd lost an hour in his mental ramblings before Mollie had arrived. "Ready."

Their driver took them down the steep hill to the sprawling dock area on the bay. The Grayson & Flannigan offices were located at the shipping docks of Buena Vista Cove, a rough area that abutted a seedy neighborhood locals referred to as the Barbary Coast. Within its boundaries were concert saloons, dance halls, variety shows, and brothels. Jock had insisted on providing a carriage to and from his office the last time Mollie had met with him, as the area wasn't safe for women traveling alone.

"Mr. and Mrs. MacLaren, it's a pleasure to see you both again." Jock opened the door that lead through a rustic but clean front office large enough for two desks, then through another door to his office which looked out onto the water. It was not built to take advantage of the majestic bay, but to keep watch on the workers as they loaded and unloaded cargo.

"Can I get you anything? Coffee?" He looked at Pierce. "Or perhaps whiskey?"

"Nothing for me, Mr. Flannigan," Mollie replied and set her reticule on her lap.

"Please, call me Jock." He sat behind his desk in an old but sturdy wooden chair and leaned forward, his brawny forearms folded on the desk. "Have you prepared the list of items you need shipped out?"

Jock was a tall man, with broad shoulders and a trim waist. He wore his shirtsleeves rolled up, exposing thick arms dusted with burnished red hair. He wore his hair pulled back in a queue that fell several inches down his back and was the same color as the hair on his arms. Mollie felt now, as she had each time she'd meet him, that his almost translucent amber eyes bore into her, as if attempting to discover long buried secrets. It wasn't a comfortable sensation.

Mollie opened her small purse and handed him the listing of items. "It is several rooms of furniture. I realize this is not your normal load, so there is no hurry for it to arrive in San Francisco."

Pierce listened to the conversation between Mollie and Jock while noting the size of the room, windows, exits, furniture, and where documents such as they sought might be hidden. There were a couple of file cabinets, a wooden cabinet, plus two wooden chests along one wall. The back wall included three windows overlooking the docks and one exit door. The only other door led into the front office. A large bookcase holding various knickknacks, souvenirs, and a variety of books filled the shelves. Pierce guessed they were from the various travels of the two sea captains. He stood and walked over to one group of brass lanterns, compasses, and other small items typically found aboard ships.

"Quite a collection, Jock," he commented and picked up a particularly nice brass compass. "Looks as if you've been collecting for years."

Flannigan watched Pierce scan the room and wondered at his interest in the insignificant items on the shelves. "Yes, Walter and I used to collect many items on our trips. I don't keep much of it now."

Jock picked up the listing Mollie had given him, looked it over, then set the paper down. "Seems very complete. It will need to be packed and at the docks once I have a timeline prepared." He glanced at Pierce once more then his eyes shifted back to Mollie. "You're right that it is not my normal cargo, but I do occasionally handle personal items for friends and business associates. Of course, your other option is to have everything shipped by train. It will most likely cost less and arrive sooner."

"Yes, we've considered it, but I'm not as comfortable with that solution as having someone I've met personally handle my valuables. You understand, of course."

"Certainly. As long as you don't need the items within a couple of months, our services should suit you just fine." He opened a drawer and pulled out a standard contract, handing it to Mollie. "Why don't you and Mr. MacLaren read this over and let me know if you have questions. The items will be added to a separate document and attached once you've agreed to the terms and paid the deposit."

"I'll take care of this over the next few days." Pierce took the document from Mollie, folded it, and placed it in the inside pocket of his vest. "I wonder if you might have time to give us a tour?"

"Be glad to. Just give me a few minutes." Jock pushed from his chair and left the office. They could hear him calling someone's name. A muffled conversation could be heard through the closed office door before he returned.

"If you're ready?" He walked to the back door and motioned them through toward the yard beyond.

It was several acres, with three warehouses and two loading docks. Another building held several horses, tack, feed, and two carriages. They walked inside each of the three large storage buildings, Pierce missing nothing and noting that whatever items they sought would most likely be found in the private office. Jock circled them around until they wound up in the front of the main building.

"Quite an impressive operation. Have you had it a long time?" Pierce asked.

"The company has been in operation for many years, but under a different name. The original owners had government contracts for delivering mail by steamship into San Francisco. They expanded into trans-Pacific shipping between Hong Kong and here, carrying various items of trade. Afterward, they had lucrative contracts for bringing in railroad workers from Asia, mainly Chinese, but some Japanese also. Walter and I bought out the original owners a few years ago, continuing much of the same routes with the addition of more shipments between Canada and the United States."

"Do you use the same ships as the previous owners?"

"Yes, and added others. We had quite an aggressive plan to expand, one that I'm still deciding how to pursue." Jock looked back at the docks as if remembering something then shifted his attention back to Mollie and Pierce. "Let me know when you want to meet again."

He watched as their carriage pulled away and wondered at their real purpose for securing his services. Perhaps he'd just grown suspicious of everyone, an outcome of working with Georgiana after Walter's death. She was bright and greedy. Jock sensed she'd gotten involved in activities that could prove harmful to the business. Her vocal dislike of the president and his policies could do nothing except harm his reputation if taken to an extreme. Right now, he had his hands full running the shipping operation and keeping watch on her. Sorting through his questions about the MacLarens would have to wait.

*****

"There's a message for you, Mr. Hatcher."

Lee was almost to the stairs when he heard the hotel employee call his name. "Thank you." He took the message, noted it was from Silas Springer, tore it open, and read the contents. He'd received a response to the private message he'd sent the week before, and it was good news, at least from his standpoint. Now Lee had two confirmations of who he believed might be the man Chaz had heard about from his contact. Although he'd suspected the man of being involved in some unsavory business for a while, this was the first time Lee had been able to pull enough information together to warrant further investigation. He would have to get a message off to Noah.

Lee started out the door just as Eva walked in, and wondered if he should mention the latest message he'd received. He knew it would be a difficult conversation, that she'd become defensive and refuse to accept the possibility that the person mentioned could be part of what Lee suspected. Eva would think he was trying to settle an old score, get even with someone who'd almost cost him his job as well as his reputation.

He watched her walk up and decided it was best to wait until after he'd contacted Noah to mention his suspicions. "Eva."

181

"Hello, Lee." She gazed up at him and wished she could control her body's response to him each time they were together. For whatever reason, her natural talent for small talk eluded her when he was around. The ease with which she could carry on conversations with perfect strangers vanished when standing alone next to the one person she used to be the most comfortable around. Now, his presence caused her throat to constrict and her senses to go on high alert. "It appears you're leaving for an appointment. I won't keep you." She began to turn away.

Lee reached out and touched her arm. "Walk with me. I need to send a message to Noah and would welcome your company."

It was a bad idea to spend any more time than necessary with her ex-husband. There were too many emotions, memories—good and bad—and regrets that surfaced when they were together. She'd thought about his request to let him explain what had happened that night in New York when she'd found him in his hotel room with another woman.

Eva had recognized the woman instantly. She could still feel her heart clench at Lee's stunned expression when he'd realized she'd had caught him with someone else. It had taken her a few moments to get over the shock, run from the room, and dash down the stairs to find a carriage on a night when the snow was heavy and wet. Her body shook all the way to his large home—from cold, anger, or pain she didn't know. She'd packed and left, leaving the servants to wonder at her rapid exit.

They'd never spoken of it. Eva had refused all of Lee's attempts to contact her. She didn't need Lee to tell her what she'd walked in on. The required documents had been prepared the same week and their divorce was processed without objection on either side. She'd seen him from afar over the years, had contact with him through telegrams and other missives—always work related—but until this assignment, she hadn't been this close in all those years. She found herself wondering at his attempt to explain. Eva didn't see the point, it was over. They'd each built a life without the other. They couldn't go back.

If that was the case, then why did something keep niggling at the back of her mind, encouraging her to let Lee unburden himself? It would be painful to hear, but might bring a finality they both needed.

"All right, a walk might be nice." She slid past him through the hotel entrance. He came up beside her, took her hand, and wrapped it through his arm.

It didn't take long to get to an office where he could send his message. Lee had planned to send it from the hotel before Eva had walked in. This was the only excuse he could think of to get close to her. He penned the note to Noah, paid the cashier, took her hand again, and stepped back into the sunny day. The heat felt good, and for once, the cold San Francisco winds were calm.

He turned away from their hotel and walked toward the water. Neither said a word for a long time before Lee broke the silence.

"I know you don't want to hear this, won't believe it after all this time, but what you think you saw that night was much different from reality." He glanced over at her, waiting for a response that would indicate she might be ready to listen.

Several moments passed before she looked at him. The pain he saw in her eyes was the same as that night four years ago. Her whispered response surprised him. "All right."

He stopped and turned her to him. "I've been waiting a long time for a chance to explain, Eva."

They had come up to the edge of a small park. Lee guided her to a bench a few feet away and stepped back as she sat down. He looked out at the bay, watching a large schooner navigate toward a dock area, before glancing back at Eva and taking a seat next to her. He leaned forward and rested his arms on his knees, clasping his hands together.

"You already know I was finishing an assignment. One or two more days and it would have been over. I was tired, anxious to get home," he looked at her, "to you." His voice was wistful as he broke eye contact and turned back toward the bay. He took a deep breath before continuing.

"It had been a long day. I'd sat in the bar downstairs with Owen for a couple of hours, drinking whiskey and discussing the last things we needed to do. I kept trying to leave. He continued to find one excuse after another to keep me there and drinking. After a while, I'd had enough and left for my room. I had another drink before turning in. I don't know how much time passed before something woke me. There was a light shining in my eyes. I sat up and saw you standing in the doorway, a look I'd never seen on your face. It took a moment before I realized your eyes weren't focused on me, but on something else. I looked to my side. That's when I saw Constance, lying beside me." His gaze focused on Eva. "I swear to you, I did not bring her to my room and she was not there when I fell asleep."

Lee sat up and rested his back against the bench. "By the time I realized what was happening, you were already slamming the door." He stood and turned to face her. "You wouldn't accept my messages to meet. You'd convicted me without ever hearing my side—assumed the worst." He paced a few feet away then walked back. "I know how it looked, but it was not what you thought."

Eva heard every word, trying to reconcile his explanation with what she'd seen. His version and her recollection matched perfectly, except for the reason Constance was in his bed. "You once told me you loved her."

"That was before you, Eva. What I felt for Constance was nothing compared to my feelings for you. I was in love with you."

Eva noted the past tense. She didn't understand why it mattered.

"What was she doing in your room if you didn't invite her?"

"I don't know and I didn't stay to find out. When you left, I told her to get out then went after you. By the time I reached the house, you were already gone. It was days before I learned where you were staying, and by then, you'd submitted the documents for a divorce." He continued to stand, too edgy to relax or sit down.

"You didn't try to stop it. From the scene I'd walked into, I thought you'd be relieved. You were back with Constance. I was certain you wouldn't care."

"Not care?" Lee was incredulous. "I was in love with you, Eva. I didn't want a divorce. You were the one determined to end our marriage, without knowing the truth or giving me a chance to explain."

"It seemed so clear..."

"You never believed I'd be faithful, did you?"

Eva had said as much before Lee asked her to marry him. She'd been joking, saying a man like him could never commit to one woman. He'd read it for what it was, a thin attempt to hide her insecurities regarding marriage, trust, and commitment.

Like Lee, she'd come from wealth and was afforded every opportunity. Unlike him, however, her parents had led separate lives—her father appearing at social events with his current mistress. Her mother was more discreet, keeping her affairs away from public scrutiny.

When Eva was eighteen, she was betrothed to a man her parents considered a perfect match. He was several years older, settled, quite wealthy, and from an acceptable family. He also kept a mistress and had informed Eva that he had no plans to stop seeing the woman after their marriage. They'd discussed it at length, and finally, over protests from him as well as her family, she'd broken the engagement, believing that no man was capable of committing to one woman. She'd carried that belief like a shield until Lee had burst into her life, shattering all her notions of marriage. He'd broken down her defenses, persuading her that he loved her enough to never want another woman.

Over the years, Eva had tried to push the painful memories of that night out of her mind. Now she tried to remember the details.

She'd received a message from Lee telling her the assignment had ended and to join him at the hotel to celebrate. They hadn't seen each other in over two weeks due to the demands of the latest case, an assignment she had no part in. Eva remembered her excitement on the way to the hotel. She'd asked their carriage driver to return the following morning. A key to her husband's room had been set aside for her at the reception desk.

Lee's room was dark. She'd only been able to see the two figures in the bed because of the light from the hallway. Eva focused on that memory. Lee was on his side, facing away from Constance. When the light hit his face, he'd been pulled from a deep sleep, his motions slow, groggy, as if he'd been out for hours. In contrast, she remembered Constance looking wide awake, as if she'd just slipped into bed, wearing a slight smirk on her face.

"Eva?" Lee encouraged. She had yet to answer his question about her lack of faith in him.

She pulled herself from the memories to focus on the man in front of her. "Did you send a message for me to join you that night at the hotel?"

He thought a moment. "No. I still had a few days left on the assignment. Why?"

"That's the reason I went to the hotel. I'd received a message from you saying the assignment had ended and requesting that I join you."

"I never sent a message to you, Eva."

"Then who...?" Her voice trailed off as she tried again to sort through what had happened and make sense of it.

"Are you wondering who sent the note?" Lee asked, believing he knew the answer. "My guess is the same person who persuaded Constance to sneak into my room and climb into my bed. The same person who never wanted us together from the beginning."

She thought a moment. "You can't mean Owen? He was your friend, your partner. Why would he have done something like that?"

Lee walked to within inches of Eva and leaned toward her. "For the same reason he and I are no longer friends, or partners. He wanted my wife," he hissed, the anger he'd kept under control for the last four years pouring out.

Eva gasped at the accusation against Owen. She'd know the man had been attracted to her and would have welcomed her into his life after the divorce. But she hadn't felt the slightest attraction toward him. She'd never thought him capable of the actions that destroyed the life she and Lee had built. "That can't be. You must be wrong." Eva whispered the words even as her mind told her that Lee's accusations had merit.

Lee watched her face as she struggled with what he'd said. It had taken him a long time to realize the extent of Owen's obsession with Eva. What bothered him even more was the fact that Eva had accepted what she'd seen as truth, never questioning it or asking her husband for an explanation. In her mind, all her past fears had been confirmed—Lee had proven to be no more faithful than her father.

"It's time to start back." Lee had accomplished what he'd wanted. Eva knew his side of what happened that night. Now it was up to her to accept his story or not. It mattered little to him. As much as he loved her, would always love her, the fact that she'd judged and abandoned him without allowing him to explain would forever be burned into his heart.

Chapter Seventeen

Pierce needed space, time to clear his head and get away from the job, Mollie, and the social obligations threatening to strangle him. Although he'd lived in New York, Boston, and Baltimore, he was most comfortable away from the cities with their masses of people and lack of concern for those around them. He'd found the home he'd been searching for in Fire Mountain, and longed to return.

After leaving Jock Flannigan, he and Mollie met with Chaz to discuss the best approach to entering the property without being detected. Chaz had made two visits to the docks, noticing that Flannigan kept two men posted at night, and volunteered to do what was needed to keep them occupied while Pierce and Mollie searched the office.

Pierce knew if there was anything at all to find, he and Mollie would locate it and slip out without anyone knowing. He had no idea what they were looking for, much the same as he hadn't at the mayor's house. His gut told him that Flannigan was hiding something. Whether it was related to their current assignment, or even illegal, would be determined once the search was complete.

Now he needed to get out. Pierce dressed in his ranch clothes, grabbed his well-worn hat, strapped his Colt forty-five around his waist, and started downstairs. Mollie had made plans with Henrietta Benstead, so his evening was his own. He was looking forward to it.

He reached for the door handle as a loud knock came from the outside. He pulled the entry door open, stunned to see who stood on the other side.

"Drew! What a surprise." Pierce held out his hand then pulled his cousin into a hug before stepping aside to let him enter. "When did you arrive?"

"Last night. I spent most of today with Louis, reviewing his plans to purchase more property and some other transactions. The man's mind never rests," Drew joked as he looked around the opulent entry and into the parlor. "This really is quite a place."

"Yeah. It is an amazing house. Never thought I'd have the opportunity to stay in a place like this. For all its beauty, I much prefer the ranch. Come on." Pierce led Drew into the library and poured them each a drink.

"You look like you were on your way somewhere." Drew sipped at his drink and leaned against the desk as Pierce lowered himself into a large leather chair.

"No place in particular, just needed to get away. Thought I'd head down to the docks, get lost in one of the saloons, maybe play some cards, and grab some supper." He shrugged.

"Sounds good to me. The last thing I want is to get back to the hotel and find an invitation from

Louis to one of his many business suppers. Your idea sounds much better."

A few hours later the two men sat at a table in one of the many saloons in the Barbary Coast area of San Francisco, watching one of the floor shows after finishing supper. They'd decided to hold off on cards until later.

"How long before you head home?" Pierce asked over the sound of a piano and women's voices coming from the stage.

"Two weeks at the most. I'm certain Tess will be fine, especially surrounded by all the other MacLaren women, but it's our first and I don't plan to be away when the baby comes. Dunnigan agrees. I think that may be why he moved up the timing for his purchases. What about you?"

"I don't know. Could be a few weeks or more." Pierce held up his glass and toasted a pretty brunette who sashayed by their table, then turned his attention back to Drew. "One thing is certain, this will be my last case."

"Not quite what you thought?"

"Guess not." Pierce rolled the shot glass between his fingers, thinking about the last few weeks. "Too much sitting around and waiting."

"And Mollie?"

Pierce's head snapped toward Drew. "What about her?"

Drew chuckled. "The last time we spoke, you couldn't wait to get away from her, didn't want to be partnered with her on this job. Has that changed?"

Pierce thought about it, knowing the answer he'd give today was different from what he'd said a couple of months ago. "It's going all right."

Drew was perceptive. It was one of the traits that made him a good negotiator for both Louis Dunnigan and the ranch. Something had changed between Pierce and Mollie, he just didn't know what.

"You bringing her back to the ranch?"

Pierce glanced at his cousin, the edges of his mouth curving up in a slight smile. "Hope to."

"Good, Pierce." Drew slapped him on the back. "That's real good."

******

An hour later, they stood at the bar of another saloon, talking in low tones and making plans for Drew to come for supper, maybe move out of the hotel and into the mansion while in town.

Although in the same district as the other saloons they'd visited, this one was on the edges of the red-light district, near the more respectable middle-class neighborhoods that surrounded the seedier sections of the docks.

Both turned to look over their shoulders when shouts erupted from one of the tables. Five men played cards, another stood, waving his hands and cursing. From behind him, a tall, dark-haired man walked up and clasped a hand to the man's shoulder.

"Sit down, Jim. Looks to be a friendly game, you're just having a run of bad luck."

193

Jim took in the man who'd spoken, and nodded. "Yeah, Colin, guess I just got a little hotheaded." He took a seat and resumed play.

Drew and Pierce watched as the one called Colin ambled up to the bar along with two others who looked enough like him to be brothers. The three took places next to Pierce.

"Three whiskeys," he ordered before nodding at Pierce and Drew then turning his attention to the two men who'd walked in with him.

"Here you go, Colin," the bartender said as he placed the drinks down. "Quinn, Brodie, good to see you. Didn't expect you'd be back for a while."

"Didn't expect to be back either. Got a few things we need to take care of that can't wait."

The brief conversation ended when Colin picked up his glass and tossed back the tawny liquid, letting it wash down the dust from their ride to the city.

Pierce and Drew went back to their conversation, forgetting the men next to them. The saloon settled into a quite cadence of soft discussions, cards being shuffled and dealt, and drinks being poured. It was late, near midnight, when the door burst open and a rough-looking, burly man, of average height, with a thick, unruly beard pushed his way past several tables and came to a stop.

"MacLaren!" he yelled.

In unison, five heads turned from the bar to look at the man who must have weighed close to three hundred pounds. No one spoke.

"You and me, Quinn. We need to talk."

One of the men pushed away from the bar to face the man. "Not tonight, Edison," Quinn replied, his voice calm, reasonable. "It's late and I aim to get some sleep."

"Now, Quinn. This can't wait."

The other two men on either side of Quinn turned to stand alongside their companion.

"Nothing's going to be finalized tonight, Edison. Get some sleep, we'll talk first thing tomorrow," Colin replied and turned back toward the bar.

"Dammit, MacLaren, this needs to be settled now." Edison wasn't backing down.

Drew and Pierce watched the exchange, stunned to hear the name Edison had thrown out.

"Pierce, you know of any MacLarens up this way?" Drew asked.

"Hell, I'm not aware of any MacLarens, except in Fire Mountain. But damn if the one doesn't look just like my father."

Drew watched as Edison lifted his right hand and settled it on the butt of his gun. "Ah hell," he murmured and stepped forward.

"Look, Edison, I don't know anything about you, but you're beginning to get on my nerves and my cousin's." He nodded toward Pierce. Edison flashed a stunned expression toward Drew, but didn't respond. "These gentlemen have made a good suggestion. Why don't you take them up on it?"

Edison's jaw worked a few times before he spoke. "This conversation's got nothing to do with you, mister. It's between me and the MacLarens. I suggest you stay out of it."

Drew sighed. "You may be right. But know if you push this any further, you'll be up against five MacLarens, not three."

The three men at the bar—Colin, Quinn, and Brodie—turned their full attention on Drew, their eyes narrowing as they absorbed his words.

Pierce faced the man, his face as firm as Drew's. "Believe me, those are odds I wouldn't want to face."

Edison let his right hand drop to his side and backed up a step. "Who the hell are you?" He aimed his question to Drew.

"Drew MacLaren. This is my cousin, Pierce. Now, I don't rightly know these three gentlemen," he nodded toward Colin, Quinn, and Brodie, "but if they're anything like the rest of the MacLarens, you'll be in a world of hurt if you keep pushing this issue. Go home, Edison. Save it for tomorrow."

Everyone watched as Edison let Drew's words sink in then backed up. "Tomorrow, this gets settled," he yelled as he stomped out the door.

No one in the saloon moved, including the five MacLarens.

A tense moment passed before Colin walked up to stand in front of Drew and Pierce. "This wasn't your business, mister," he directed at Drew.

"Probably not." Drew reached toward the bar and picked up his whiskey.

"Could've gotten yourself killed," Colin tried again.

"Doubtful," Drew drawled. "Anyway, the man's gone. Now, Pierce and I can get back to our conversation." He didn't take his eyes off the tall, broad-shouldered man who stood before him. The dark, wavy auburn hair and moss green eyes were eerily familiar.

Pierce noticed the other two MacLarens move in front of him and stop.

"Where you boys from?" the one called Quinn asked.

"Fire Mountain, Arizona," Pierce responded. "You?"

"About twenty miles east of here in Settlers Valley."

Pierce stuck out his hand. "Pierce MacLaren. This is my cousin, Drew."

"What do you say we get a table and talk?" Brodie suggested and led the way.

******

Three hours later, the five men had sorted through the family history to learn they were closely related and had come to America within a short time of each other.

Although each of their paths had been unique, the MacLarens in California held ranchlands to rival those in Fire Mountain.

"When do you head back to Settlers Valley?" Pierce asked as they stood to leave.

"Not sure. A week, two at the most," Colin responded. "We're staying at The Palace Hotel. We expect to see you before we leave." He smiled for the first time that night.

Drew and Pierce watched the three cousins mount their horses for the ride to The Palace, looking forward to seeing them again.

******

Two nights later, Pierce, Mollie, and Chaz quietly approached the dockside location of Grayson & Flannigan. Chaz split off to locate the guards while Pierce and Mollie watched from a distance, confirming they had a clear path to the office.

They stayed low, moving from one building to the next, avoiding one guard before reaching the front entrance to the office. There were no lights, only those visible from the nearby ships that were docked and waiting to load or unload. Pierce reached up and turned the knob. Locked. He pulled out his tool pouch, opening the door within seconds and slipping in, Mollie close behind.

They checked the front desks, and finding nothing of interest, moved to the back office. Pierce started with the unlocked desk while Mollie searched the file cabinet. Although the desk held numerous files, it failed to provide anything that would point to Captain Flannigan being involved in anything of interest to their investigation.

Mollie rifled through one file cabinet then moved to the second, finding nothing in either one. Her eyes lit on the two chests next to her. She tried to open one, then the other, and found both locked.

"Pierce, I need you to open these." She nodded to the two chests.

He used his tools to open one and nodded for Mollie to start with it. Pierce took the second chest. His was full of clothing, a couple of old blankets, and some rolled up maps. He'd just closed the lid when he heard Mollie gasp. She'd moved from the chest, which held little, to the bookshelf.

"I may have found something." She held up a large bound book. As she thumbed through the pages, a stack of papers fell to the ground.

Pierce snatched them up and began to read.

"What is it?" Mollie stood at his side, looking over Pierce's shoulder.

"It's not what we expected to find." He continued to read then looked at Mollie. "Seems Jock suspects Georgiana of being involved with some others in illegal activities that could impact Grayson & Flannigan. He mentions Thomas and Virginia Traxton as possible partners with Georgiana. There are some other names I don't recognize. Jock believes there is someone else involved, a man from the East Coast. He doesn't list a name." He glanced up at Mollie. "I wonder if this ties in at all with the person Chaz mentioned."

"Does he say what it is he suspects?"

"No. Only that he is trying to find out what she's doing and protect himself and the company."

"Anything about the mayor or his wife?"

"Nothing." Pierce grabbed a piece of paper and pencil from the desk, jotting down names and dates.

"It appears we may need to focus on your lady friend, Georgiana Grayson." Mollie smirked as she walked to the window and peered out. "We'd better leave."

Pierce ignored her comment and slid the book back onto the shelf just as gunshots sounded outside. "Get down," he hissed and pulled his forty-five from its holster before moving to the back door.

Another gunshot rang out. He looked behind him to see Mollie holding her gun while trying to look through the dirty glass to the outside.

"I can see a large man with a rifle crouching near one of the warehouses. He's sighting on something, but I can't see what."

"Any sign of Chaz?"

"No." She continued to watch while Pierce pushed the back door open and peered out.

"I need to find him—" Pierce began before a noise from the front office stopped him. They turned and aimed their guns in that direction.

Chaz pushed open the door then stopped and held up his hands. "Don't shoot."

Pierce and Mollie lowered their guns as Chaz shut the door and crouched beside the desk. "I only saw two guards. Both are tied up under the docks behind the main warehouse. The third must have shown up after you two got inside. We need to leave, now." He dashed toward the office door. "Out the front is best."

Mollie and Pierce followed, staying low, guns drawn. They slipped through the front door and plastered their bodies to the side of the building. Chaz looked around a corner, and seeing no one, broke for the unlocked gate and the street beyond. Pierce and Mollie were close when shouting came from the office.

"Stop!" A bullet ripped into the wooden fence next to Pierce, sending splinters flying in all directions, followed by a second that sliced through his upper arm. He cursed as blood seeped through his shirtsleeve, then crouched and took aim.

"Go!" he spat at Mollie before pulling the trigger three times in succession. He looked around to see her follow Chaz into a darkened alley. Pierce waited another moment, fired two more shots then ran after them.

They didn't stop for several blocks, running through damp backstreets, past open doorways where loud music and raucous laughter filtered to the outside. They stopped behind a small boarding house where Chaz had hidden a carriage. Chaz jumped onto the small bench and took the reins while Pierce and Mollie piled into the seat behind, Pierce still holding his gun and looking around to be certain no one followed.

Chaz slapped the reins with a light touch. Within moments, they had escaped and were on their way back to the relative safety of Torie's mansion in Nob Hill.

Chapter Eighteen

Lee and Eva were waiting when Pierce, Mollie, and Chaz entered the house. Penelope stood nearby, clearly confused at the odd activity so late at night and the blood she saw on Pierce's sleeve. She didn't say a word, just dashed to the kitchen for what was needed to treat the wound as the others moved past her into the parlor.

Lee and Eva stood at opposite sides of the room, clearly concerned at the appearance of their three team members.

"What happened?" Eva asked and dashed over to Pierce's side. Penelope appeared a moment later, handing her a bowl of water, towels, bandages, and a small brown bottle of antiseptic. Lee handed Pierce a shot of whiskey as Eva got to work cleaning the wound.

"There was a third guard who arrived after Mollie and Pierce were in the office. We were almost away when a bullet hit Pierce." Chaz stood next to Eva and looked down at the bleeding arm. "A flesh wound. It could've been worse."

Pierce stared up at him and tossed back the second whiskey. "The guy's shot was lucky." He grimaced and let his head fall back against the chair as Eva finished bandaging his arm.

"Find anything?" Lee asked. They'd kept Jock and Georgiana at supper as long as possible before returning to wait for the others.

Mollie explained what they'd found.

"Mollie, grab the list of names from my pocket," Pierce said.

She handed the list of names and dates to Lee, who took it and reviewed it quickly. "Georgiana Grayson, Thomas Traxton, and Virginia are the only names I recognize." He gave the paper to Eva to look over.

"Same here. I don't recognize any of the others."

"Let me take a look." Chaz glanced over the names. "Besides the Traxtons and Georgiana, I do recognize William Hardy. He's active in state politics, a friend of Mayor Pound's, and from what I've heard, quite vocal in his opposition to current policies. I don't recognize the others." He handed the list back to Lee.

Lee paced behind the desk, taking a seat in the high-backed chair. "We need to find out more about the people listed and identify the man Jock mentions." He looked at the others. "It may be coincidence that the mention of a wealthy, well-connected man keeps coming to our attention, however, I doubt it. Someone must know who he is and what he plans."

"Do we bring Jock in?" Mollie asked.

"No. We can't afford to bring in anybody not working through Noah." Lee's eyes narrowed. "That doesn't stop us from using him as a source."

"And the mayor?" Pierce asked.

"There's no need to bring him in either, and there's no reason to suspect he's involved in anything illegal. He has the same suspicions as Jock. There is something happening, we just need to figure out what it is and determine if it poses a threat." Lee looked at Pierce. "I want you to pay a visit to Georgiana. Say whatever is needed to make her nervous. Push her enough to lead us to the others. I'll be prepared to follow her after you've left her home."

Pierce nodded, his gaze focusing on Mollie, and wondering what she was thinking. The original invitation to visit the widow had been postponed at her request. Georgiana had sent a second invitation, which still awaited his response. He'd send her a message the next morning.

"Chaz, you focus on William Hardy. Learn what you can about him and keep watch on the man. Perhaps he'll lead you to something that may be relevant."

Chaz nodded.

"And the Traxtons?" Eva asked.

"You and Mollie follow the Traxtons." Lee didn't want Eva or Mollie anywhere near Thomas Traxton or his wife. Unfortunately, there was no one else and time was short. He knew the women would do whatever was needed to get some answers.

"Of course."

Lee nodded at her and started toward the door to the entrance hall, indicating it was time he and Eva left. "We'll be in touch."

"I'll go with you," Chaz said and followed them out, leaving Mollie and Pierce alone.

Mollie watched Pierce stand. The bleeding from his arm had stopped, even though his face still held a greenish tint.

"Are you all right?"

"Yeah. Just need to get upstairs to bed." Pierce's eyes focused on hers. "Care to join me?" His voice was steady and serious.

Mollie should have been surprised by the comment—she wasn't. She wanted to accept, share another magical night with him before the assignment ended and she left for good.

"You're hurt. It wouldn't be a good idea."

He walked up to her and extended a hand. "Sleep with me tonight, Mollie. We won't do anything you don't want to."

She glanced at his hand, hesitating for an instant before threading her fingers through his.

******

Pierce watched her walk past him toward the large bed. He thought she'd hesitate, change her mind when they passed the door to her room. Instead, she gripped his hand tighter and smiled up at him. His heart clinched in response and Pierce realized he had to find some way of convincing her to accept his proposal. He also realized he felt no pressure to marry her. No, he wanted to make her his wife and build a life with her. The thought pleased and terrified him.

Mollie sat on the edge of the bed, surprised at how much she wanted to be here, with Pierce, in his room. He was all she'd thought of since the morning he'd made the ultimatum that they marry. It would be so easy to say yes, become his wife, and build a life in Fire Mountain. She loved him, there wasn't any doubt in her mind. The problem was he didn't love her.

Pierce paced to the other side of the bed, not letting his wound hinder him at all as he removed his boots, then his belt, pants, and shirt. He turned to see Mollie's intense gaze wash over his body and could feel himself tighten at her open perusal. He pulled back the covers and climbed underneath before patting the mattress next to him.

"You don't have to stay if you're uncomfortable." Pierce wanted to give her a way out. He didn't want to pressure Mollie. At the same time, he desperately wanted to be with her.

"I'm not uncomfortable," she whispered, and began to undo the buttons on her dress. She slid it off her shoulders, letting it pool at her feet, then climbed under the blankets to join Pierce. She stayed on her side of the mattress, suddenly unsure of what to do.

"Come here," he murmured and reach his uninjured arm out to her.

Mollie slid into his embrace, settled her head on his shoulder, and rested a hand on his broad, solid chest. The sense of how right this felt overwhelmed her and she began to doubt her previous decision.

Pierce lowered his head to breathe in the sweet smell of her hair, then rested his chin on her head and pulled her more tightly to him. He'd never been like his brother Connor, believing he wouldn't settle down or have a family. Pierce had always felt there was someone out there for him, a woman he wouldn't be able to leave behind, someone to spend his life with. He just hadn't expected it to be this woman.

Pierce closed his eyes then opened them, trying to stem the wave of exhaustion that flowed through his body. He could feel Mollie's warm hand as it lay across his chest, her soft breath drifting over him, and the rapid beat of her heart. If she wanted something more, it was up to her to let him know. He wasn't going to push, no matter how much he ached to have her.

He heard her breathing slow and her body relax into his as he drifted off.

******

Mollie awakened to the sound of measured breathing. Her eyes opened and a smile played at the edges of her mouth when she remembered where she was and with whom. Her body felt warm and she nestled closer to the source of the heat.

She looked up to see Pierce's eyes closed, his face peaceful in sleep. Her eyes moved back down to his chest, feeling the coarse hairs under her hand and marveling at the solid bands of muscle. She let her hand travel down to his hard stomach, then lower.

Pierce's eyes shot open at the same time his hand moved quickly to grasp her wrist.

"Be sure of what you want, Mollie. I don't have much willpower when it comes to you," he breathed in her ear, then placed a kiss on her forehead.

She lifted her eyes to meet his. "I know what I want, Pierce. You."

******

Chaz sat alone, sipping coffee from a small china cup and waiting for his prey, William Hardy, to complete his breakfast meeting with a client. It had been two hours of sitting and waiting—a man could only handle so many cups of watered-down coffee. He watched as Hardy paid for the meal, shook his client's hand, and walked outside.

The agent had been following him since first light. Hardy kept a busy schedule even though it was apparent he had no real job. His wealth came from his family, money accumulated from the time the first Hardy set foot in the Americas in the early seventeen hundreds. So far, he had yet to do anything that caught Chaz's interest.

He stayed behind Hardy, far enough back not to be noticed, even though the man had an annoying habit of looking behind him every few minutes, as if he expected to be followed. Three blocks from the restaurant, Hardy jumped onto one of the many horsecars and Chaz had to run to catch up, barely making it aboard before the crowded horse-drawn car started up one of the steep streets.

Hardy stood near the outside as if ready to jump off at any moment. Several blocks later, he did just that and took off at a brisk pace into what had become known as Chinatown. Chaz kept watch on the man as he too jumped from the horsecar and disappeared into the densely populated section of the city.

It was late morning by the time Hardy stopped in front of a small store, situated on a busy corner. He looked into the decorated window, turning his head one way then the other before stepping into the store and closing the door.

Chaz took his time walking up to the shop. He glanced inside through the large glass window and watched as Hardy spoke to a stooped, elderly Chinese gentleman. A moment later, a younger Chinese man joined them from a back room and nodded for Hardy to follow him.

When Hardy didn't return, Chaz dashed around the corner and into an alley half a block away. He found a back entrance, tried the knob, and finding it locked, checked one of the two windows that faced the alley. Neither budged.

He had no choice. Chaz hurried back around to the front, intending to enter the shop, when he spotted Georgiana Grayson walking toward him. He stopped and moved back around the corner out of sight.

******

Pierce woke early, feeling better than he had in weeks, other than the pain from the wound to his left arm. Mollie was curled around him, his good arm holding her close. He watched her sleep, mesmerized by her soft breaths which fanned his chest. If it were up to him, he'd stay like this all day and into the night with her lying next to him.

He slid his arm from under her and maneuvered himself off the bed. His breakfast appointment with Georgiana Grayson was still three hours away, plenty of time to take care of his other business.

An hour later, Mollie woke to find herself alone in Pierce's bed. She sat up, rubbing her eyes, and looked around. No sign of him. Then she remembered his breakfast engagement with Georgiana. Her stomach clenched briefly before she gained control of her wayward emotions and slipped from the bed.

She and Eva were to meet in an hour to confirm their plan for following the Traxtons. It was a job Mollie was anxious to take on, especially while working with Eva. She admired the experienced agent, the way she handled herself, and the respect given to her by other agents. The men saw her as important to the team and sought her input. Mollie knew it could take years to gain that kind of reputation. As Noah said, there were just three women in the agency, and Eva was the best.

She dressed and walked downstairs as Penelope opened the door to admit Eva.

"Good morning, Eva. Have you had breakfast?"

"No, and I'm famished."

"Penelope, we'll take our meal in the conservatory."

Once served, the two women went right to work. Eva had already learned that Thomas would be at his office until late morning. She had no idea of Virginia Traxton's plans. It was decided that they would both follow Thomas, believing it would be easier to explain themselves if they were seen together rather than one woman alone.

An hour later, they sat in a small restaurant across from Traxton's office. The location afforded them a good view of both the front and side entrances to the building, which housed offices for various businesses.

They were on their second cup of tea when Eva touched Mollie's arm and nodded toward Thomas's office. He was just leaving, walking away from the downtown area at a brisk pace. The two women hurried to catch up, pausing once or twice to look into a nearby shop when he would stop to speak with someone. It didn't take long for them to realize he was headed into the heart of Chinatown.

******

Pierce arrived at Georgiana's beautiful home overlooking the harbor, stepped from the carriage, and stopped to take in the magnificent view. It was a clear, sunny day, and he could see what appeared to be hundreds of ships in the bay. He glanced down the drive to the street in time to see another carriage pull to a stop. Lee Hatcher.

He turned when the front door opened. A tall, slender gentlemen greeted him, took his hat, and asked that Pierce follow him into the dining room where Georgiana waited.

"Pierce, it's good to see you. Apologies for canceling our last appointment, but it couldn't be helped." She stayed seated, lifting her hand so he could take it and brush a kiss across the back.

Pierce pivoted at the sound of the door closing then turned back to his hostess.

"Not an issue, Georgiana. I know you keep a busy schedule. I'm thankful you had time this morning." He took a seat next to her, noticing that she wore a lightweight dressing gown, which covered a sheer chemise underneath. It was something a woman would wear for breakfast with her husband, not for a married man who'd come at her invitation.

"Please, have some breakfast. I know this is a later hour than you're used to, so you must be famished." She sipped tea while picking at the eggs on her plate and watching her guest take a couple of bites then set his fork down. "It doesn't suit you?" she asked.

"The breakfast is fine, but the reason I came has nothing to do with food." He relaxed in his chair, ready for his work to begin.

Georgiana shifted in her chair, allowing her dressing gown to part a few inches, exposing her creamy skin. "And what would you like, Pierce, if not food?" Her voice had turned low and sultry as she reached out a hand to stroke the top of his.

"Perhaps friendship." He leaned forward and wrapped his free hand around hers.

"I think we can work something out." Her voice was husky, anticipation clear on her face.

"And information," Pierce continued, never taking his eyes off hers.

"Information?"

"Yes, such as your association with Thomas Traxton and William Hardy."

The expression on Georgiana's face turned from desire to stunned surprise as she snatched her hand from his and sat back in her chair.

"I have no idea what you're talking about. Thomas and William are friends, that's all."

"Oh, come now, Georgiana. Although you and I have just met, it's no secret that the three of you share a strong dislike for the policies of the current president."

"As do many people."

"Does their dislike extend to secret meetings the way yours does?"

Georgiana stood and walked toward the door. "I don't know what you've heard or what you're accusing me of, but I think it's time you leave, Mr. MacLaren."

"Of course." Pierce stood and bowed slightly. "Let me know if you change your mind."

Georgiana stared at the closed door. No one knew of the twice a week meetings in Chinatown she attended with a group of people dedicated to changing the current policies. They were small in number, and perhaps a little more vocal and active than others who were unhappy with the president and more organized in their efforts to make change occur. However, they did have one advantage that other groups of dissenters might not—a man on the inside.

Georgiana dashed to her room, changed, and called for her carriage. She needed to let the others know of her strange meeting with Pierce MacLaren.

Chapter Nineteen

Lee watched as Pierce's carriage left the Grayson property. He hadn't been in the house long, indicating to Lee that the meeting to fluster Georgiana and push her to action may not have gone as well as he'd hoped. He continued to watch, hoping the woman would make a move. He didn't have to wait long.

Georgiana came sweeping out the front door and stepped into her waiting carriage. Lee followed as her driver turned toward the downtown district, making good time on the uncrowded residential roads. Travel became slower as they approached Chinatown and the dense late morning traffic. Her carriage stopped. She stepped down, looked around, and then began walking down a narrow, crowded street.

Lee followed at a discreet distance, assuming Pierce had done his job, flustering the woman enough to lead him to the answers they sought.

******

Chaz checked once more around the corner of the alley where he hid to see if Georgiana Grayson was still in sight. She had stopped at the front of the same shop William Hardy had entered. She looked around. Satisfied she hadn't been followed, Georgiana walked into the shop.

Within moments, Lee followed, and seeing Chaz, joined him around the corner.

"Is Hardy already inside?"

"He is," Chaz replied and scanned the front of the street once more. That's when he spotted Thomas Traxton a block away. "Stay back." He moved an arm across Lee's chest, emphasizing his words. "Traxton is walking toward us."

They waited until the man had entered the same shop as Georgiana and Hardy then searched the street for Eva and Mollie. The women joined Lee and Chaz moments later.

Mollie looked around. "Where's Pierce?"

"Right here," an out of breath Pierce said as he came to a stop next to them. "I had my driver follow Lee's carriage. Thought I'd lost him a few blocks back, then I spotted the ladies." He nodded at Eva and Mollie.

Noticing that their group of five was beginning to garner attention, Lee pointed to an area of the alley further from the street where they'd draw less notice. "Grayson, Hardy, and Traxton are inside. Someone needs to find out what they're doing."

"I'm the most logical," Chaz offered. "Pierce can't, as Georgiana would recognize him, and the ladies appearing would seem more out of place than a lone man. Besides, none of those inside know anything about me and it's doubtful I'd be recognized. If needed, I'll make it appear that I stumbled onto their gathering and see what happens."

Lee agreed and watched as Chaz walked toward the front of the shop.

"What now?" Mollie asked. She wasn't comfortable with Chaz going in alone, even though there was no indication that the meeting could turn violent. She still doubted that all of their work would uncover anything besides a group of intense, vocal citizens planning how best to move someone else into the White House after the next election.

"I'm staying here," Lee said. "I'd like the three of you to go back to the house and wait. We're already drawing more attention than I'd like. Besides, it's unlikely more than two people will be needed to handle anything Chaz learns."

All three hesitated before doing as Lee instructed.

******

Chaz entered the store and began to look around, picking up one item then another, in an attempt to appear as any other customer. A man, who Chaz assumed to the owner, scurried up, asking if he could help.

"I'm to meet a friend here. William Hardy, do you know him?"

"Yes, yes. Mr. Hardy. He is with the others." The owner began to escort Chaz to the back when another customer walked in and the man excused himself to walk up front.

Chaz took the opportunity to disappear into the back, closing the door behind him. He saw no one in the small room although whispered voices filtered through a curtain several feet away. As he got closer he could make out one female voice, who he assumed to be Georgiana, and three or four male voices. Chaz tried to pull the curtain aside enough to see who was in the room then stopped when he saw the closest person was a mere two feet away.

"He'll be here in a couple of days. That's when we'll learn what's being planned." The voice was deep, raspy. Chaz didn't believe he'd heard it before.

"That doesn't give us, or Wang Tao, much time," Georgiana said.

"Wang Tao will need little time to organize his group. A day, maybe two."

"And if our source doesn't show up?"

"He will. His message indicated this was the best opportunity to achieve our goal."

"And we're certain the others won't join us?"

"They've made it clear that, although their beliefs are the same as ours, they can't risk publicly demonstrating their discontent. They've provided money, now it's up to us to get our message out."

Georgiana and Thomas glanced at each other, aware that only three in the room were aware of what would happen once their source gave the signal. They were more than a vocal group of malcontents, so much more.

"There's something else," Georgiana said. "Pierce MacLaren visited me and mentioned my meetings with William and Thomas. I have no idea how he found out about us or if he means to cause us trouble."

"Really, Georgiana. What can one man do against a group of committed citizens?"

"I don't know that he plans anything, Thomas. However, I thought it best that you all know he is aware of our meetings. It seems odd, given that he is new to the city."

"I will do what I can to check further into his background, however, our time is short. There may be little we can discover before our plans go into effect." Thomas rubbed his jaw between his thumb and forefinger, wondering if MacLaren was more than he seemed.

The group stayed silent, leading Chaz to believe they were ready to adjourn.

"My recommendation is that we all keep watch for him. If you find him following you, let me know." It was the owner of the deep, raspy voice. "If there's nothing else, I suggest we leave and wait for further word from our contact."

Chaz wasted no time exiting the back room, nodding to the shop owner, and slipping out the front door to find Lee.

"Let's go." Chaz started walking at a brisk pace up the alley and away from Chinatown.

******

"I don't know, Lee. From what Chaz is telling us, it appears to be a group of unhappy citizens, nothing that would warrant our involvement. Perhaps this has been a waste from the beginning." Pierce sat with his arms on his knees, hands clasped.

"Except for the mention of the man who appears to be their leader," Lee responded.

"I have two concerns." Eva stood behind a chair, her hands grasping the back. "First, the comment about this being the best chance to achieve their goal. What goal is that? Second, Wang Tao's group."

"Who is Wang Tao?" Mollie sat near Pierce, absorbed in the details Chaz had provided.

"He's a well-known Chinese organizer. Highly vocal in his opposition to the law against Chinese immigration. He and his son came to America several years ago. Now, he is unable to bring his wife and daughters to the States. If he leaves, odds are he won't be allowed back in." Lee had met Wang once, understood his frustrations and his desire to see the law overturned.

"Is his group capable of violence?" Pierce had little knowledge of the regulation or its impact on the Chinese community.

"Any group can turn violent, given the right motivation," Lee answered. He lowered himself into the chair behind the desk and leaned back. "The large sum of money collected would seem to be targeted toward the candidate the contributors support in the next election. We've uncovered no information to believe otherwise." He thought for a moment. "The president will be in San Francisco soon. It now appears that the activities of Hardy's and Wang's groups are to take place during that visit."

"And the man leading their efforts is to arrive shortly beforehand." Chaz pulled out a cheroot and rolled it between his fingers. "I don't know. It seems as if we are simply chasing our tails."

"Perhaps, but we're here and there's no reason not to carry this through until the end of the president's visit. I'll get a message to Noah. Until then, we wait." Lee stood to leave. "Chaz, I do believe it would be wise to continue to watch Thomas Traxton. Something about him doesn't seem right. I wish I could identify what."

"I agree. I'll stay on the man and let you know what I find."

******

Pierce walked into the offices of Taylor-Dunnigan then continued down the hall to find Drew working on final purchase agreements with Miss O'Connell for the property Louis planned to buy. He took a seat and waited for his cousin to finish, nodding to his assistant when she looked over at him.

"That's it, Miss O'Connell. I'd appreciate it if you'd make these changes and send everything to Mr. Dunnigan."

"Of course, Mr. MacLaren." She looked at Pierce. "Is there anything you need from me, Mr. MacLaren?"

"Not right now, thank you." Pierce watched her leave the office, remembering the first time he'd met her, when he'd wondered if she were single. It no longer mattered. He'd accepted his feelings for Mollie, now all he had to do was convince her to share a life with him in Fire Mountain.

"Look at you," Drew drawled, his eyes taking in the suit and tie Pierce wore. "Didn't know you owned anything so fancy." He chuckled even though he wore essentially the same outfit when working for Dunnigan.

"Don't get used to it. As soon as this job is over, the suit will be packed away, only to be brought out for special occasions."

"Like a wedding?'"

"Perhaps." Pierce picked up a picture on Drew's desk. It was taken a few months ago, at Connor's wedding.

Drew watched his cousin look at the picture that included all the MacLarens. He was struggling with something. He waited, knowing Pierce would say something when he was ready.

"How did you know Tess was the right one?" Pierce didn't take his eyes off the photograph.

Drew relaxed into his chair and thought for a few moments. "It felt right. Whenever I was around her, I felt good, as if there wasn't anything else I needed to be happy. When she was gone, there'd be a void I couldn't explain. It took a while to come to terms with how I felt. There were other things weighing on me at the time."

Pierce nodded, remembering the struggles his cousin had faced. "Was it the same for the others?"

"Not quite. Jamie took one look at Torie when they were teenagers and that was it. He carried a torch for that woman for years, wouldn't even consider anyone else. And Will, he pretty much felt the same about Amanda, although he had his own demons to fight at the time. Niall took a little longer with Katie. He almost lost her because of his stubborn streak and sense of duty to the family. And you know Connor and Grace's history. I guess everyone's experience is different."

Pierce stayed quiet, taking in Drew's words and not responding. He took a deep breath and pushed up from his seat.

"I told Mollie I want to marry her."

"That's great."

"She wants no part of it." Pierce sighed, feeling an ache in his chest that was becoming more familiar than he'd like.

"I see. She give a reason?"

"She wants a marriage based on love."

"That sounds reasonable. You don't love her?"

"I don't know. Hell, how do you know if you're in love with someone or not? The kind of love like our parents had, where they stuck by each other no matter what."

Drew thought a moment. "Guess you never know for sure until there's some kind of tragedy or crisis. What will you do?"

"I'm not sure. Looks like our assignment will end soon. She plans to leave for Boston afterward and I'll go back to Fire Mountain."

"You don't have much time."

"No, I don't." Pierce walked toward the door. "I sent a message to Colin, Quinn, and Brodie. They'll be at the house for supper tonight. You too." He didn't wait for an answer before closing the door behind him.

******

Eva opened the message from Lee. He wanted to take her to supper, someplace quiet, away from the hotel. She folded the note and placed it on her vanity.

Their time was short. All of them believed their job would be finished within a week, and then they'd leave for their next assignments. The odds that she'd work with Lee again were slim. Most jobs were meant for one agent, and rarely for a man and woman. She might see him on an occasional trip to New York. Beyond that, it could be years. Her heart constricted at the thought.

His room was just down the hall. She penned a quick response, walked to his door, and slipped it underneath before returning to her room.

She'd thought almost non-stop about what he'd said on their walk, his suspicions about Owen and that he knew nothing of a note inviting her to his room at the hotel. Eva wondered if she'd been wrong all these years, condemning him as guilty and not allowing him even five minutes to explain.

She sat on the edge of her bed, wondering if what Lee suspected was true. If the actions that destroyed their marriage were set in motion by Owen, would he allow her to apologize, perhaps consider trying again? It was doubtful. He possessed a great deal of pride and had no need for the permanent ties of a wife and family.

Although he'd been eager to have children when they were married, it hadn't happened. Now, well, she didn't know how he'd feel about any of it. She might never learn the truth about that night, if Owen had been the one to send the message and persuade Constance to go to Lee's room or if Lee had been the one to invite her. It was up to Eva to make a decision. Either she believed his story or she didn't.

Eva checked the small brooch which held her watch and made a quick decision. Grabbing her reticule, she dashed out of her room, down the hotel stairs and ordered a carriage. Whether life worked out for them or not, she would look her best tonight and see what happened.

Chapter Twenty

Pierce waved Penelope away to answer the loud knocking himself. He pulled the door open to find his three MacLaren cousins—Colin, Quinn, and Brodie—staring at the ornate front portico before walking into the equally elaborate entrance hall.

"Who did you say owns this?" Brodie asked as he hung his hat on the hallstand and shook Pierce's hand.

"Victoria MacLaren, Jamie MacLaren's wife. He's our Uncle Duncan's second oldest." Pierce greeted the others and showed them into the parlor where Mollie and Drew already waited.

Pierce made the introductions, poured everyone a drink, and took a seat next to Mollie.

"It's such a coincidence that you all met in San Francisco. And none of you knew the others had made it safely to America?" Mollie was surprised at the story Pierce had told her about his cousins. There was much he didn't know about them except that they had come to America close to the time he, Connor, and Meggie had made the trip, and that most of them lived in an area known as Settlers Valley.

"No, ma'am. We'd all met when we were small, but our lands in Scotland weren't close. My father came from a large family with four brothers," Colin explained. "Quinn and Brodie are my cousins, as is

Pierce. Pierce's father, Hugh, was one of the brothers, as was each of our fathers. As we understand it, Drew's father, Duncan, was a cousin to our fathers. It's a might confusing, I'm afraid."

"Nonetheless, it's good we met up." Quinn shot back his whiskey.

"Are there more of you?" Mollie asked.

"Quite a few more, I'm afraid. It would take a piece of paper to draw it all out for you." Colin still carried a slight brogue which Mollie found quite engaging.

They all turned as Penelope entered the room and announced supper was ready.

Mollie watched the men's faces change as they spoke—sometimes in low, almost conspiratorial tones, then broke out into animated discussions about their families, land, and journeys to America. She found herself fascinated by it all, how quickly strangers could become connected by a common last name and family ties. Mollie hadn't had any brothers or sisters, or even cousins that she knew of, and she'd never felt the loss either. Her life had been consumed with working, putting food on the table, and making it from day to day. She'd never thought how life would've been if she'd had siblings.

"Now, tell us again why you're in town, Drew." Quinn sat back, enjoying the wine and company.

"I work for Louis Dunnigan, a businessman with holdings in San Francisco."

"I've heard of him," Colin said. "I thought he was out of Denver."

"His home and main operations are in Denver. He has businesses in various states and he's always looking to expand."

"And you also ranch?" Brodie asked.

"My twin brother, Will, and I run the horse breeding part of the ranch, while the others, Niall, Jamie, and Connor, concentrate on the cattle business. I'm hopeful when Pierce returns that he'll join Will and me. Don't want it to get too lopsided." Drew smiled as he saluted Pierce with his glass of wine.

"How long have you and Mollie been married, Pierce?" Colin asked and glanced at his cousin.

Pierce's eyes shot to Mollie then back to Colin. "Not too long."

"Months, then? Newlyweds," Brodie added.

"Maybe a month, or two," Pierce murmured.

Colin's eyes narrowed on Pierce. "Is that a fact?"

Mollie cast a look at Drew then Pierce, realizing the other MacLarens knew nothing of the true reason for their time in San Francisco.

"We're not truly married." Mollie saw the surprised expressions and wished she could pull her words back.

Pierce closed his eyes and a grim expression crossed his face.

"Not truly married, is it? You'll have to explain this to us." Colin crossed his arms and leaned back in the tall upholstered chair, waiting for their answer.

Drew's face was impassive, wondering how Pierce and Mollie would respond. Their assignment wasn't public knowledge, but their marriage was, at least to those who didn't know the truth.

"Why don't we all go into the library and let Pierce explain exactly what's going on." Drew stood and left the room, leaving the others to follow.

It didn't take long for Mollie and Pierce to clarify their true reason for being in San Francisco and the cover they'd been given. Colin, Quinn, and Brodie didn't say much during the explanation, asking an occasional question, nodding as the tale unfolded.

"Do you think the significance of all you've learned may point to an assassination attempt on the president?" Colin asked, his voice level.

"Why would you ask that?" Pierce stared at his cousin. The thought of an assassination had never crossed his mind.

"No reason, except there have been two assassinations since we've been in America. The president is expected in San Francisco at any time. You have prominent citizens speaking out against him and his policies, and a Chinese group ready to engage in a demonstration. There's also a man no one can identify who's leading it all. It may all be coincidence." Colin shrugged and downed the last of his wine.

Pierce thought about what Colin said, amazed that his cousin had been able to summarize a possible scenario in a few minutes that five agents hadn't been able to tie together. Granted, it was a theory pulled together with the slimmest bits of information, yet there was a ring of truth to it that caused chills to course through his body. He looked to Mollie.

"We need to find Lee."

******

"I was surprised you accepted my invitation to supper." Lee sat across the small table from Eva in an intimate restaurant minutes from their hotel. His eyes met hers for a moment and held. "I'm glad you did."

He'd gotten her message after returning from sending messages to Noah, Clive Hawkins, and the other contact who'd mentioned the man Lee suspected of being the one leading the group in San Francisco, and perhaps elsewhere. He'd waited. Clive, his childhood friend and government contact, was the first to respond. The man his agency was investigating had indeed been spotted on the West Coast. Clive had dispatched men from his department to detain him, but they weren't expected to arrive for two or three more days.

Lee hadn't received a response from the other two and had decided to return to his room. He'd seen the note under the door and braced for a rejection. There was no reason for her to see him outside of the job.

Their walk had allowed him a chance to tell his side and explain. Lee hadn't expected anything more from her. His invitation to supper had been an impulsive and brash request which he expected to be declined.

Lee knocked on Eva's door a couple of hours later and came to a halt at the sight before him. He'd always thought her to be the most beautiful woman he'd ever seen. Tonight, she'd dressed in a beautiful gown that accentuated her exotic features—she was the most stunning vision he'd ever seen. His appreciative gaze moved over her gown, up the slim column of her neck, to her face. Her smile caused his stomach to tighten and he wished he could hold this picture in his mind forever.

Eva felt her face redden at his obvious appraisal. "I wasn't sure at first if it was a good idea for us to be together like this." She gestured toward the surrounding room with her hand. She lowered her thick, black lashes before opening them to let her eyes lock on his. "The truth is, I've missed what we had, missed being with you for too long. I don't know if we'll ever see each other again after our job is over, and I didn't want to throw away this opportunity."

Lee stared across the table at Eva, the candlelight enhancing her eyes and skin. He noted the slight moisture in her eyes and reminded himself this was just for tonight, not anything they would continue after leaving San Francisco. Their life together was in the past. He told himself she would always look at him with suspicion, never be able to trust him the way he needed her to.

The hopeful look on her face told him that none of that mattered, at least for tonight.

They talked of their jobs, their impressions of Pierce and Mollie, and the way Chaz always fit, no matter what the assignment. Eva was surprised to learn that Lee expected Pierce and Mollie to somehow stay together. She wasn't aware he'd even noticed their attraction.

Time ticked by while they enjoyed the food and being together, even if there was no future left for them. They'd finished dessert and coffee, there wasn't anything keeping them at the restaurant any longer.

"Are you ready to start back?" Lee asked and set down his empty cup.

"Yes, I'm ready. Thank you for a lovely night. It was all perfect." Eva waited while Lee walked around her chair to pull it out then extended his hand. She looked at it briefly before resting her hand in his. He didn't let go as they walked outside. It was a warmer than usual night, lacking the normal chill expected from the brisk breeze off the San Francisco bay.

They walked toward the hotel, their joined hands clutching tighter with each step.

"Eva..." Lee began as he pulled her around to stand in front of him.

"Yes?"

His breath hitched. Everything he wanted stood before him, gazing up into his eyes, waiting. He couldn't speak. All he seemed capable of doing was lowering his mouth to hers.

Eva responded eagerly, wrapping her arms around his neck, and pulling him down. The feel of his lips, warm and firm, sent a tremor through her. His arms tightened, drawing her against him until their bodies were perfectly aligned, the heat emanating from his warming every part of hers. His mouth devoured hers, as if he could never get enough and would never let her go.

He edged away on a ragged breath, his breathing fast and uneven, then rested his forehead against hers, not loosening his hold. He started to lower his mouth again when a procession of carriages moved past, coming to a halt in front of their hotel.

"What's going on?" Eva asked as she pulled her arms from around his neck and let them drop to her side.

"I'm not certain, but it appears the president may be staying at our hotel." Lee grabbed her hand in his and started to walk the additional block to the hotel entrance. He spotted Mayor Pound and his wife climbing from their carriage and walking toward the front of the procession as the police spread out to keep away curious onlookers.

Moments later, a medium height, bull-like man with a thick neck and large stomach stepped from the lead carriage. Lee had seen him several times. The man's unique characteristics made the president recognizable to anyone who'd met him in the past.

"We'll wait until everything calms down," Lee suggested.

"Lee!"

They turned to see Chaz move up to them at a rapid pace. "We have another visitor." He gasped, trying to catch his breath.

"Besides the president?" Eva asked.

"Yes. We need to deal with this before morning. Before Cleveland makes any speeches."

"What is it?" Lee pressed.

"The man Traxton and Hardy have been waiting for arrived in the city. They met with him briefly."

"Did you get a good look at him, learn his name?"

"No, but I have enough to start the search."

Lee flagged a carriage. "We'll need to bring Pierce and Mollie into this." He wrapped his arm around Eva and helped her into the carriage. The ride to Nob Hill wouldn't take long.

******

Conversation stopped as everyone turned in the direction of pounding on the front door. Pierce waved Penelope aside and opened the door to let Lee, Eva, and Chaz enter. He directed them to the library. The three stopped when they saw four unfamiliar men.

Pierce quickly introduced Drew, Colin, Quinn, and Brodie. "It's all right to speak in front of them. They're aware of what's happening."

"Not the latest," Chaz added before taking a seat and glancing at Lee.

"Chaz has been following Thomas Traxton, believing he may be the main contact to the man we've been unable to identify. Chaz's work may prove important, especially given that the president arrived this evening. Chaz?"

"I followed Traxton to a home on the other side of the city. William Hardy was already inside. About an hour later, another gentleman arrived. I wasn't in a position to get a good look at his face and they never used his name. I can, however, provide a description. We'll need it for what they plan."

"Which is?" Pierce asked.

"Assassinate the president."

Pierce glanced at Drew, and they both turned their gaze to Colin, who sat stone-faced between Quinn and Brodie. A chill passed through the room.

"When and how?" Lee paced the floor.

"I don't know how, but they did say it would be tomorrow during his speech."

"Where will the speech take place?" Eva moved next to Lee and placed her hand on his arm.

"The police station, at noon," Lee responded and wrapped his hand around hers. No one seemed to notice except Chaz.

Mollie walked to the desk to pick up a piece of paper and pen. "You said you can describe the man?"

"I'd estimate a little over six feet tall. His shoulders sloped a little. Blonde, wavy hair, long— to his collar. No beard. I couldn't tell if he had a mustache. His accent is what you hear in the upper class of New York or Boston. I believe it was closer to a Boston accent. And expensive clothes, like Lee wears." He looked at Lee, but there was no amusement in his expression. "He had a large ring on his right hand, huge ruby in the middle. One last thing. I did see a thin white scar that ran from the edge of his ear to his chin on the right side, then cut into his mouth. That's the most I saw of his face."

"It can't be?" Eva murmured and searched Lee's eyes seeking confirmation or denial. What she saw turned her stomach. "Why? The man has everything."

"Not everything, Eva," Lee whispered.

"Do you know the man, Lee?" Pierce asked.

"Eva and I believe it is Owen Kendall."

"But, isn't that the agent Eva mentioned to us? The one she believed Noah would send instead of you?" Mollie put down the paper and sat on the edge of the desk. What they'd thought of as a futile assignment had turned into a critical, life-or-death situation.

"The same. What I can add to Chaz's description is that he has a thin mustache, close-cut, that matches his hair. He is an expert shot with a handgun and can hold his own in a fist fight."

"And you're sure he's the man?" Quinn MacLaren had stayed silent, not wanting to interrupt those who'd been involved for weeks on this case.

"The description, the ring, and the scar all point to him. Plus the fact that our man has connections in the government and can move around at will," Lee replied.

Eva was still reeling from the realization that Owen was behind everything, still not comprehending why he would jeopardize everything or be involved in murder.

"Why would a man like Kendall risk it all on a plot to kill the president?" Pierce couldn't understand why anyone with so much would throw it all away.

"He was never satisfied with his life, always craving what he couldn't have and believing he was entitled to whatever he wanted. Everything came too easy to Owen." Lee mourned his old friend, but not the man he'd turned into. "Now, we must determine what to do about him and his partners. Before tomorrow."

Chapter Twenty-One

It was almost six in the morning. No one had slept and the rest of the MacLarens never left. Lee had sent a driver to the police station to pick up Chief Curtis, along with several others, and bring them to the house. Meeting at the police station wasn't an option—Owen could have eyes everywhere.

Lee introduced Curtis to everyone. He'd met some of them before at the Mayor's Ball, and was familiar with the MacLarens in Settlers Valley even though he'd never met them.

At first, the police chief was reluctant to believe what he considered an ill-conceived theory. It took quite an effort to bring him around. The urgency, and the fact that he knew Traxton and Hardy, guaranteed he couldn't turn his back on their idea. Curtis decided he must put his full energies into locating and arresting those involved before the deadline.

A message was sent to the president suggesting that he postpone or cancel his speech because of the threat. He'd sent back a note firmly declining the proposal and stating that he'd go forward with his speech. The only concession the president made was to change the location from the police station to the front of the hotel, eliminating the need for him to travel across the city.

Police officers were dispatched to pick up Thomas Traxton and William Hardy. Neither man was found at his home or office. Virginia Traxton hadn't been seen in several days. The servants had mentioned it several times to her husband, yet no police report had been filed. Police were posted to keep watch for both men as well as Mrs. Traxton.

According to her butler, Georgiana Grayson had left the city earlier that day. None of her servants had any idea of her destination. Wang Tao had also disappeared. His son hadn't seen him since the day before. Police were posted at both the Grayson and Tao residences.

The group turned their attention to finding Owen Kendall. Unless his disguise was extraordinary, his personal features were distinct enough to help identify him, especially the scar that ran from his right ear to his mouth. It was assumed he'd remove the ruby ring, cover his head, and wear clothing dissimilar from his normal attire.

Curtis noted that everyone had useful skills. Though some of those present—Drew, Colin, Quinn, and Brodie—were volunteers, their help was welcomed. Curtis ordered several sketches with a description of Owen Kendall be prepared and passed around.

"I'd suggest that the MacLarens, except for Pierce, be located here, here, and here." Lee stood at the desk, pointing to specific locations on a rough drawing of the area where the president would be speaking. "Pierce, Mollie, Chaz, Eva, and

I should circulate through the crowd along with some of your officers."

Curtis glanced around the room. "Sergeant Flynn," he called to an officer across the room who'd been speaking with Brodie MacLaren.

Flynn broke off and walked over to Curtis. "Yes, sir."

Curtis outlined Lee's proposal for locating the MacLarens and his group. "I need you to identify the best officers to be part of the president's detail and let them know what we expect."

"Yes, sir."

Curtis leveled his eyes on his sergeant. "The best and most trustworthy, Flynn. I know many of the current officers were assigned in an honorary capacity. We now require men who are crack shots and prepared to protect the president with their lives."

"Understood, sir." Flynn nodded at his boss and Lee before turning to leave.

"Flynn. One more item. Take the MacLarens with you. I want our men to recognize them and know they are part of our group and not random spectators, or worse, part of the conspiracy."

Pierce watched as Flynn spoke with Drew, Colin, Quinn, and Brodie, and saw them nod in agreement before they followed the sergeant to a waiting police wagon.

"Drew, what's going on?"

"Chief Curtis has asked us to join his men near the front, where the president will be standing. We're leaving to meet the other officers, make sure they recognize us and don't shoot us by mistake,"

Drew explained, aware of the danger he and his cousins were walking into.

"You don't have to do this." It was clear to Pierce that everyone involved would be putting themselves at risk. He wasn't prepared to lose a family member to some maniac bent on murder.

Drew turned to Pierce. "We wouldn't be doing this if we didn't believe it was right." He clasped his cousin on the shoulder. "You do what is needed and so will we. I'll see you afterward." He squeezed Pierce's shoulder once, dropped his hand, and followed the others outside.

Pierce let the reality of the peril he'd put his family in take root and hoped he hadn't made a mistake by bringing them into it.

******

"Is everything clear?" Lee asked the others as they stood a block away from the hotel, finalizing their roles and locations. The president was due to speak in one hour, and already the area was flooded with people.

"Clear." Chaz answered for everyone.

"All right. Let's go." The others dispersed to their assigned locations as Lee took Eva's arm to guide her through an open doorway and into a secluded corner. He turned her to him, searching her eyes for something—he wasn't sure what—and suddenly, he was at a loss for words.

Eva saw the turmoil in Lee's face—concern, fear, and, what four years ago, she would have thought was love—and placed her hand on his arm.

"It's going to be all right." The confidence in her voice was what he needed to hear. "We'll get through this. Afterward, if you still want to..." Her voice trailed off.

Lee offered a half-smile. "I'll see you in your room at the hotel after this is over." He kissed her once then grabbed Eva's hand to lead her outside toward the job they had to finish.

******

Pierce followed Mollie across the crowded street in front of the police station and stopped beside her as each took a slow turn around, looking for anything that might be considered a threat. Seeing nothing except curious onlookers, he took her elbow and guided her to a spot sixty feet away from the podium at the top of the steps.

"Lee and Eva believe Owen will use a handgun, which means, in a crowd this big, he'll need to get close. Watch for men tall men with wavy blond hair. Don't rely on clothing. I'll be on the other side of the podium," Pierce finished, realizing Mollie was already aware of everything he'd said but unable to control his need to confirm it once more.

He tried to swallow the growing lump in his throat. His concern for Mollie and her safety grew with each passing minute, encouraging him to ask her to step aside and let the others handle it. Pierce remained silent.

Mollie could see the growing agitation on Pierce's face—the way his jaw worked, the narrowed eyes that refused to stay still, and

242

breathing that had become uneven. She acknowledged her fear that one of them might not make it through this assignment and reached out to touch his arm.

"You'll be careful?"

Pierce stopped scanning the crowd and looked into eyes that expressed the concern each felt. He gripped Mollie's arms and pulled her to him, his mouth coming down on hers, letting it move against her lips, almost desperately, before he set her away.

"We'll both be careful," he replied and kissed her once more before leaving to find his position on the far side of the hotel.

******

Lee searched the crowd once again. He knew Owen better than anyone and wanted to be the one to find and arrest him.

A commotion from the crowd pulled his attention back to where the president was to appear. The plan was for him to walk from the hotel, take a seat while the mayor provided an introduction, then stand and take his place behind the podium.

Lee watched as Mayor Pound, accompanied by his wife Lydia, walked outside followed by Chief of Police Curtis, a few other dignitaries, and finally, the president. Loud applause erupted as the crowd recognized the squat, rotund figure of the man elected to lead the country, followed by cheers and a few jeers as he waved and took his seat.

The agents continued to scan the crowd, watching for anything suspicious or out of place. Lee located Eva about forty yards to his right, standing alone with a parasol to ward off the midday sun, and knew she held a pistol in her other hand. Mollie held her position straight across the square from Eva, to one side of the police station, her eyes searching the crowd, which now stood elbow to elbow. Pierce was on the opposite side of the station, to Eva's right, his height giving him an advantage. Lee noted his eyes shift for a moment to his four cousins who were spread out directly in front of the podium, their watchful eyes focused outward toward the throng of people who were attempting to move forward, wanting to get closer to the president. Pierce nodded to one of them before turning his eyes back to the crowd.

To his left stood Chaz, his face set as he made a complete turn, checking behind him then facing forward. Lee knew he would be carrying at least two handguns and a knife. It was his preferred weapon when there was a need for a fast, quiet solution.

The crowd roared once more, indicating the mayor had completed his introduction.

******

Pierce felt his heart pound as the president stood, shook hands with the men on either side of him, then turned toward the crowd. Movement drew Pierce's attention first to Eva then Lee who had left his position and was steadily moving forward. His eyes followed Lee's path. He was heading straight toward Colin and Quinn who were centered in front of the podium. Pierce's gaze retraced the path toward Lee, who'd stopped, watching someone several feet ahead.

That's when Pierce spotted Owen. He was dressed in clothing typical of the dock workers, white shirt tucked into dark pants, suspenders, no jacket, and a small brimmed dark hat. His thick blonde hair was clearly visible under the hat, and even from this distance, Pierce could see the thin scar running from his right ear to the edge of his mouth. He wasted no more time.

Chaz held his ground as Lee and Pierce cut into the crowd, drawing little attention as they focused on Owen Kendall. From experience, he knew that if his colleagues missed their target, Owen would run, most likely toward him or Eva. He caught her attention, signaling for her to stay where she was until Lee and Pierce had a chance to apprehend their target.

Mollie focused on a small group of men several yards behind Chaz. She was certain one was Thomas Traxton and another, William Hardy. Without hesitating, she left her position, skirting the crowd while keeping the men in sight. Mollie was almost halfway there when she glanced toward Pierce's location and realized he was gone and so was Lee. She came to an abrupt halt and scanned the area. From her current spot, Mollie couldn't find either and felt her heart rate quicken as her concern for Pierce increased.

She swung her attention back to where Traxton and Hardy were standing a moment before. Both had disappeared.

Mollie took off at a run toward the last spot she'd seen them, rounding a corner in time to see Traxton disappear down an alley. She dropped her parasol, gripped her gun in one hand and her skirt in the other as she tore down the backstreet after him. Mollie stopped when the alley turned, peering around the corner as Traxton stepped through a doorway and out of sight.

******

The four MacLarens stood in a line in front of the podium, each with a hand on the butt of their weapon as Lee and Pierce converged on the man they'd identified as Owen Kendall. They knew if the assassin pulled a weapon, he'd be dead where he stood. It was now a question of who would take him down first.

"Stop, Owen!" Lee's voice rang out, drawing the crowd's attention away from the president and toward the tall, dark-haired man near the center. Lee pulled out his badge, waving it in front of him as he kept walking. Owen didn't stop. "Owen Kendall, stop where you are!" Lee shouted once more. The crowd began to part as Lee continued to display his badge while lifting his other hand, the revolver aimed toward his ex-partner.

Pierce saw the crowd move and heard the screams of onlookers as Lee positioned his gun. He swung his eyes to Owen in time to see a pistol clearly visible in his right hand.

"You don't have a chance, Owen. Stop now and drop your gun," Pierce said as he continued his path toward the man, pushing his jacket aside to display the badge secured to his belt.

Owen focused on the man at the podium, the object of everything he'd worked toward the last year. He'd seen his ex-partner standing near the back of the crowd, aware that Lee was searching for him. He'd heard Lee's shouts and those of another man, ignoring both in his quest to rid the world of a man he believed had no place as his country's leader. Owen no longer cared about his own life. He'd convinced himself that his actions were right, knowing he'd go down in history as a hero. Owen ignored the screams around him as he stopped, began to lift his gun, and aimed at the man on the stage.

"For God's sake, Owen, put the gun down," Lee yelled once more and held his ground not twenty feet away.

Pierce was to Owen's right, his gun leveled and ready.

Drew, Colin, Quinn, and Brodie started forward, moving in slow deliberation toward their target.

Chief Curtis ordered his men to surround the president and move him into the safety of the hotel. The president resisted at first, wanting to face the man who'd threatened him. Curtis grabbed hold of the president's arms as first one, then another shot rang out, chipping the columns around them, missing the president and his protectors by inches.

Lee turned in the direction of the shots, both coming from behind and above him. He spun back around toward Owen as a shot ripped through his shoulder. He faltered, his eyes blurring as he stared at Owen Kendall, the man's gun still pointing at Lee. His second shot never left the barrel.

A split second later, Owen spun one direction then another as bullets tore into him. His body crumbled to the ground.

Drew, Colin, Quinn, and Brodie continued forward, their guns still smoking.

Pierce ran to Lee, kneeling to check his wound.

"You need to find the other shooters," Lee ground out as he began to lose consciousness. "I'll be fine. Go, now."

Eva appeared next to Pierce, lifted Lee's head, and cradled him in her lap while pressing a hand over his wound to help stop the bleeding. "Go. I've got him," she said focusing her attention on Lee.

Pierce focused his attention on the buildings across from the hotel as his cousins formed a perimeter around Lee. "We have to find who fired those other shots."

He pointed to a building on the left. "Colin and Quinn, check in there. Drew and Brodie come with me."

Chapter Twenty-Two

Chaz turned and crouched at the sound of shots from overhead. He looked up to see a man, gun in hand, standing at a window three floors up. Chaz raised his gun and fired twice before running into the building, taking the steps two at a time to reach the gunman before he escaped.

A block away, Mollie moved into position behind the man she'd been following.

"Drop the gun, Traxton." Her voice was hard, uncompromising.

Thomas Traxton turned toward her, gun in hand, an almost maniacal look in his eyes.

"There are police everywhere and they're looking for you. You'll never get away."

"Oh, he just might."

The familiar female voice came from behind Mollie as hard metal pressed into her back.

"I'd suggest you set down your weapon, Mrs. MacLaren. Or is it Agent Jamison?"

Mollie stared at Traxton in front of her, his gun pointed at her chest. Behind her stood Georgiana Grayson, her gun at Mollie's back. The situation was bleak, yet Mollie didn't feel the fear she expected. They stood in the middle of a three block area thick with police and federal agents, and her guess was that most of them would be looking for those who'd shot at the president.

She bent down, laid her gun on the ground, and turned slowly toward the woman behind her.

"Where's Virginia?" Mollie asked, wondering how Thomas's wife fit into the conspiracy.

Traxton kept his gun trained on Mollie, picked up her weapon, placed an arm around Georgiana, and pulled her tight to his side. "Virginia made a choice to pursue her own interests, elsewhere. I'm sorry to say it's doubtful anyone will ever see my wife again." His smile was evil, making Mollie's skin crawl.

"We need to leave, Thomas. The police are everywhere." Georgiana flinched at the sound of shouting from the street.

"You're right, of course." He waved his gun toward the stairs. "Agent Jamison, please follow me. I hope I don't have to tell you to stay quiet. At this point, we have little to lose by killing you."

******

Chaz stopped on the top floor, listening to what sounded like furniture being dragged across the floor in a room down the hall. He started forward then turned at the sound of footsteps coming up the stairs. He plastered himself against the wall and aimed his pistol.

Moments later he lifted his gun as Colin and Quinn MacLaren joined him in the hall.

"Down the hall, the last room," Chaz whispered. "I think he may have barricaded himself inside."

"Who?" Quinn asked.

"My guess is either Traxton or Hardy."

They moved to just outside the door and listened. Nothing. Chaz tried the knob. Locked.

"Police. Open up." Chaz pounded on the door, and waited.

When there was no response, the three kicked in the door then ducked back into the hall as the air exploded. Colin and Quinn turned as one and aimed their guns into the room, waited, then moved inside. William Hardy's body lay sprawled on the floor.

******

Pierce, Drew, and Brodie entered the building from the back street, located the stairs, then stopped when voices sounded from above. They stepped back into the alley, hiding in two small alcoves several feet away, and waited.

The door from the building to the alley creaked open as Traxton took a glance around and then looked over his shoulder at Mollie.

"Do not say a word," he warned before stepping outside while Georgiana nudged Mollie in the back to keep her moving as they exited the building.

"Stop where you are Traxton," Pierce hissed as the three MacLarens trained their guns on Thomas and Georgiana.

Traxton swung toward Pierce and fired, nicking the wall beside him. Pierce and Drew fired as one. The impact knocked Traxton backward and onto the ground. Brodie continued to aim his gun at Georgiana.

Georgiana held her gun with both hands, pointing it at Mollie's back, her body shaking violently as she tried to focus on the men in front of her.

"Don't do it, Georgiana. You can still get out of here alive." Pierce's voice was low, calm. Drew and Brodie's weapons were aimed at the woman. They didn't want to kill her, but would if it meant saving Mollie.

Pierce held up his hand to ward off a group of police who came to a stop when they saw the scene in front of them.

Georgiana's eyes shifted up and down the alley, looking for any means of escape. There wasn't one. For a moment, Pierce thought she would fire. Instead, she backed away from Mollie and dropped the gun, then slumped to the ground.

He dashed to Mollie, turning her around and looking for injuries. Finding none, he pulled her into his arms.

Drew kicked Georgiana's gun away while Brodie hauled the woman up and pushed her against a wall.

"Do not move," he advised, his voice hard.

"You're all right?" Pierce asked Mollie.

She didn't answer. Instead, her head swiveled toward the woman Brodie guarded. Her eyes blazed with the fury radiating through her body. She took three quick steps forward and landed a punch so hard on Georgiana's jaw that the woman's eyes rolled back in her head and she fell to the ground unconscious.

"I'm all right, now." Mollie grimaced while rubbing her sore knuckles, then lifted her face to the others and smiled.

******

The president wasted no time boarding an afternoon train, never having finished his speech or taking the tour planned in his honor. He headed east, his next destination unannounced.

Georgiana Grayson was the lone participant in the assassination attempt in custody. She resisted interrogation attempts at first. It took a long while to obtain details of the murder plan to a point where Chief Curtis felt comfortable that she had told them all she knew.

According to Mrs. Grayson, many prominent citizens across the country disliked the president's policies and were building a large fund to remove him from office at the next election. These individuals were content gathering money and waiting, not seeing the imminent threat to the nation Cleveland's agenda posed.

Owen's group believed the man was a supreme menace to the country and that change was required sooner than the next election. It was a small group who decided to take the matter of eliminating the president into their own hands.

Owen Kendall had known of the president's plans to ride the rail across country to gain support for his policies. The trip was to culminate in San Francisco.

He pulled those he identified as the most radical into a circle of seven—Thomas and Virginia Traxton, Georgiana Grayson, William Hardy, Wang Tao, Owen, and Hardy's brother, Harrison, who was the man Chaz heard with a deep, raspy voice at the small store in Chinatown.

Over months of preparation, working together to sort through each detail, Owen felt comfortable moving forward. He'd tried to locate others to handle the actual assassination, traveling from one city to the next, speaking with those he knew had no qualms about carrying out plans such as his. Unfortunately, no one was willing to kill such a high-profile client as Owen described without three times the money the group had available. Most believed he was targeting a senator or member of the president's staff. No one, except those in his circle, knew the objective was the president himself.

Something Owen had not foreseen was the involvement of the Treasury Department's Secret Service group. He believed he'd been too careful in the planning to alert those in the very department where he worked. Owen had been wrong. He got to work covering his tracks as much as possible, taking care of those he believed knew too much or were a threat to his plans. This included a banker in New York who'd overheard a damaging conversation. Georgiana believed the man's name was Edward Franks.

She confessed that she and Thomas Traxton had begun an affair within months of the Traxtons arrival in San Francisco. Her husband, Walter Grayson, had learned of the affair weeks before he died. Georgiana professed she was innocent in setting up the shipboard accident that killed her husband. It had all been Thomas's doing.

A week before the president's visit, Virginia Traxton discovered Thomas and Georgiana's involvement and threatened to expose the entire group as well as their plans. She'd disappeared the following day. Thomas told Georgiana he'd taken his wife's threats seriously, hiring men he knew to be trustworthy, and the problem had been handled. She knew no other details.

Wang Tao backed out the day before the president's arrival, saying he hadn't fully understood the plan involved murder. Although Tao was adamantly opposed to the law against Chinese immigration, he had no desire to jeopardize his family by an attempt to eliminate Cleveland.

Harrison Hardy had been present at their last gathering the morning of Cleveland's speech. He was to go into the building across the street with his brother, William, and provide backup to Owen, the same as she and Thomas. Georgiana was surprised to learn he wasn't present with William when Chaz, Colin, and Quinn broke down the door.

Georgiana had no idea what had happened to either Wang Tao or Harrison Hardy, guessing each was in hiding.

She was surprised when Curtis asked if Jock Flannigan had any involvement in the murder attempt. Georgiana scoffed at the notion, saying the man was too honorable for his own good. She had gripped Curtis's arm, however, imploring him not to tell Jock of what had transpired, saying she'd lose her ownership rights in the company if it were found she'd participated in anything illegal.

Curtis laughed, telling her it was doubtful Flannigan would hear the news from the police. The Chronicle, San Francisco's main newspaper, would be more than happy to provide him with details.

******

It was late by the time all the formalities were behind them and the agents and MacLaren cousins were free to leave the police station.

Lee's wound wasn't serious, although it hurt like hell. He ordered carriages to take everyone to the hotel for a meal and liquid sustenance, as Chaz termed it.

A message from Noah awaited them at the front desk, congratulating the team on their success, and letting them know he'd expect a full report from each within the week. The agreed upon funds for the assignment would be in their accounts by the end of the month. New assignments would be made once he'd had a chance to review the current requests from Treasury, as well as some of the other departments who now seemed to count on his agents for most of their investigative work.

It was a quiet meal. Everyone was exhausted, glad it had ended well. All were looking forward to moving on to new assignments, or in the case of Colin, Quinn, and Brodie, getting back home. Drew had a few more days remaining to complete his work for Louis Dunnigan before his trip home to Fire Mountain and Tess.

Pierce had been unusually silent, not voicing any opinion about obtaining another case or his desire to continue as an agent. His mind was consumed with thoughts of Mollie. She hadn't spoken much since they'd finished their meetings at the police station and had barely touched her meal. He had no idea if she still planned to return east to Boston or stay with Noah as an agent.

Colin stood, followed by Quinn and Brodie, and addressed the others.

"Thank you all for a very memorable trip to San Francisco. I can't remember when we've been able to return home with such great stories."

"Let us know if any of you ever get tired of ranching. I'm sure we can find something for you to keep the stories flowing," Lee quipped before shaking their hands and watching them walk outside.

Drew and Pierce followed their cousins to a waiting carriage.

"Plan a trip to Fire Mountain as soon as you can. I know the family will want to meet everyone and learn of your experiences since arriving from

Scotland." Drew held out a hand, hoping they'd take him up on the offer to travel south.

Pierce said his goodbyes, telling them to expect him in Settlers Valley at some point. He had an urge to see more of California and what his cousins had built over the years.

Colin, Quinn, and Brodie boarded the carriage and nodded to Drew and Pierce. They'd be leaving for Settlers Valley in the morning.

Pierce turned at the sound of voices behind him. Mollie emerged from the hotel followed by Lee, Eva, and Chaz. He waved for another carriage, waited until Mollie had boarded, then said his goodbyes to the other agents, not sure when, or if, he'd ever see them again.

Their ride was short, perhaps fifteen minutes. Pierce escorted Mollie inside and up the stairs to her room before turning her to face him. He rested his hands on her shoulders, making no move to draw her closer. Pierce noted the sadness in her eyes. The sparkle he'd grown to count on, whether from anger or something else, had disappeared.

His jaw shifted as he struggled with all the things he wanted to say.

"Will you go back to Boston?"

"I'm not certain." Her quiet response gave him hope. "You?"

"I'm going back to Fire Mountain. It's home now. That's where I want to build my life."

She nodded before letting her head fall forward to rest on his broad chest.

"Come with me, Mollie," he breathed in her ear. "I'll make a good life for us."

He could feel her chest expand and contract on a ragged breath. She lifted her head, eyes locking with his, and took a step back.

"Without love?"

"Do you love me, Mollie?" Pierce asked. He needed to hear her say it even though he wasn't certain of his own emotions.

"I have feelings for you, Pierce," she lied. Mollie knew she had more than mere feelings for him, she was in love with him. She needed Pierce to love her in return.

"Just feelings? Nothing more?" His eyes flickered, waiting for her response.

Mollie looked away, no longer able to lie, yet unable to voice what she felt. She couldn't bear to love a man who didn't feel the same for her. It wouldn't be fair to either of them.

He grasped her chin between his thumb and forefinger, drawing her gaze back to him. The desolation he saw tore at his heart. She didn't love him. The realization triggered an intense pain that squeezed his chest, causing his breath to hitch. He swallowed the lump in his throat as a finger traced a tentative, soft line down her cheek to her jaw.

Her eyes searched his. Mollie wanted with all her heart to say what she felt, but her stubborn pride held her back. She would not make her heart vulnerable, not to a man who had the power to crush it if he were never able to return her love. She reached up and let her warm, soft lips brush across his. Mollie couldn't give him a lifetime, but she could give him one last night.

Pierce felt the flutter of her lips against his, creating a heat that flowed through him. His response was quick. His arms tightened around her, drawing her softness up against his hard chest. The blood in his veins turned to molten fire, pounding through his temples. He bent, lifted her into his arms, and walked with slow determined steps to his room, kicking the door closed behind them.

Chapter Twenty-Three

Pierce woke to the bright, warm rays of the sun beating onto his face. He pulled the covers up, trying to put off the morning, and then remembered the night before. Mollie. He reached over to find the bed empty and the sheets cold.

"What the hell?" he mumbled and rolled from the bed. He jammed his legs into his pants, stabbed his arms through the sleeves of a shirt, and stormed to her room.

Pierce grabbed the knob and threw the door open, knowing instantly that she was gone. The room was as clean as the first day they'd arrived, as if she'd never been there at all. He slammed the door and dashed down the stairs.

"Penelope!"

She came running from the kitchen, a towel gripped in her hand.

"Where is she?" he demanded, his voice fierce, his disposition worse.

"You mean, Mrs. MacLaren, sir?"

"Yes, who else?"

"She left, sir. About two hours ago. Took her bags and ordered the driver to take her to the train station."

Two hours. How had he slept through it?

Pierce opened the entry door and looked out, hoping to find.... Well, he wasn't certain what he thought he'd see. Mollie had made her choice. She was gone and out of his life.

"Shall I get you some breakfast, sir, or coffee?"

He looked at Penelope, reclaiming his calm and letting his eyes sweep the parlor, knowing he'd find it empty. "Coffee is all. Please bring it to my room. I'll be leaving within the hour."

His steps felt heavy on the stairs, but not as heavy as the dreadful thumping in his chest. He pushed open his bedroom door, grabbed his satchel, and began to cram clothes inside without thought to anything except the dull ache in his heart.

An hour later, he entered the San Franciscan Hotel and asked for Chaz, Lee, or Eva. Any one of them would do. He waited in the restaurant, the coffee in his cup getting cold from lack of attention. The sound of a cough brought his head up.

All three stood beside his table.

"She's gone."

Lee, Eva, and Chaz looked at each other then took their seats, waving for a server to bring coffee.

"Did she say where?" Eva asked as she laid a comforting hand on his. It had been obvious to all of them how much Pierce and Mollie cared about each other, even as they fought their feelings.

"No. She left before I got up. I suspect Boston, that's where she's from."

"You could go after her," Chaz put in as he waited for his coffee to cool.

"It's a big city. I'd have no idea where to start." Pierce shook his head then let it fall back against his chair.

"That's a joke, right?" Lee asked, his eyes crinkling at the corners.

Pierce stared at him.

"We have access to some of the most incredible resources for finding people and you say you have no idea where to start? Not including the fact she still works for the Treasury Department," Lee reminded him.

Pierce ran a hand through his dark brown hair. "Guess I'm not thinking too clearly." His half-smile was the first sign of the Pierce each of them had worked with for the past couple of months.

"You want a suggestion?" Eva asked.

"Anything..." His voice trailed off.

"Give her some time. Go home to Arizona. Decide what you want, where your life stands, and if she is truly the woman who will make you happy. If she is, we'll be available to find her. There's no possibility she'd be able to hide from all of us." Eva smiled at him while her heart ached for the young couple who was so obviously in love and unable to admit it.

She reached for Lee's hand under the table and squeezed it lightly. After everyone had left the night before, he'd escorted her upstairs, to his room, and hadn't left until they'd gotten the message from Pierce. They'd leave for New York in a few hours, together. Neither had made any promises, knowing they had a long journey ahead of them to reestablish the trust they'd lost years

263

ago. Both were hopeful they'd be able to put the past behind them and build a future.

Lee reached into his pocket and pulled out an envelope. "Noah sent this a few weeks ago, in case you and Mollie needed it. Not important now, but you may want to save it for later." He handed it to Pierce then stood. "Eva and I have plans to spend a couple of quiet hours in San Francisco before boarding the train for New York. Let us know if you need any help at all." He reached out a hand to Pierce, then Chaz. Each man stood. "You two have a safe journey."

"It was as pleasure, Lee," Pierce said, glad he'd had the chance to work with such a remarkable man.

"We're going to try to work things out." Eva sent a meaningful look at Chaz before kissing the cheek of each man then slipping her arm through Lee's and following him outside.

Chaz and Pierce stood at the table, their eyes following the couple to the street.

"What did Eva mean when she said they were going to try to work things out?" Pierce asked.

"You don't know?"

"Know what?"

"They were married once, very much in love. Owen Kendall was the cause of the breakup." Chaz watched as Lee assisted Eva into the carriage, sat next to her, then took her hand in his before pulling the door closed. "This assignment has given them a second chance. Maybe it will work out for them this time."

"I'll be damned," Pierce muttered as he watched the carriage pull away. "You going back to Fire Mountain?"

"Not yet. I think I'll stay in San Francisco a while. See what mischief I can get into before returning to help Dodge and Meggie at the hotel. I'll see you soon."

Pierce sat back down, finished his cold coffee, and made a decision to do as Eva suggested. He'd give it some time. If he still felt the same in a few weeks, a couple of months, well, he'd figure out what to do then. Pierce glanced at the envelope Lee had left for him, picked it up, and shoved it in the pocket of his jacket. No hurry, Lee had said. He decided to read it another time.

******

One month later, Fire Mountain

Pierce never knew his muscles could ache so much. He, Drew, and Will had been working non-stop on a new horse breeding area ever since Drew had returned to the ranch. It was Tess's idea, something she'd been reading about and wanted to try. So far, all of her ideas had proven successful. There was little doubt this one would work out well also.

"What do you say?" Will drawled. "Time to call it a day?"

"Fine by me," Drew replied and poured some water over the hot, tired muscles in his back.

"Three more days of this and we should be done." He chuckled, hearing the other two groan.

It was Saturday and they'd all been invited to Dodge and Meggie's hotel for supper. Aunt Alicia said they had some news to announce and everyone was pretty sure what that meant.

"So is this a fancy shindig or are ranch clothes okay?" Pierce asked.

"Hell, she's your sister. You tell us," Will replied and slipped on his shirt before climbing atop his horse, Justice, for the ride home.

******

Pierce's older brother, Connor, had completed a home on a beautiful piece of land within the MacLaren Ranch while Pierce was in San Francisco. He and his wife, Grace, lived there, and now, so did Pierce. Both Drew and Will had offered him rooms. For now, he'd chosen to be near his brother, who spent much of his time in Fire Mountain managing the three saloons his oldest cousin Niall owned.

Tonight, Pierce would tie his horse, Bandit, to the back of a wagon and drive Grace to the hotel where Connor would be waiting. Getting the MacLarens together was no small task. He figured they were close to needing their own private dining room.

The news of the MacLaren cousins in Settlers Valley was unexpected to everyone. Aunt Alicia was already making plans to visit. Mr. Jericho had said he'd be honored to accompany her. Niall and

Kate, and possibly Jamie and Torie, thought they might go along also. It was an odd feeling to know that more MacLarens had made the arduous journey across the Atlantic to start a new life about the same time as Connor, Pierce, and Meggie. Everyone was anxious to learn their full story.

Pierce's life had settled into a routine that now seemed to fit him. As much as he enjoyed the adventure that sometimes accompanied the life of an agent, he felt at home in Fire Mountain, on the ranch with his family. One day, he hoped to have what each of them had found—a good person to love, marry, and the expectation of children.

His mind had rarely left Mollie. He wondered how she was, where she'd settled, and if she ever thought of him.

A message from Noah, asking him to continue with the agency, had revealed that Mollie had decided to take some time off, needing a break to decide if she wanted to continue as an agent. Pierce understood her feelings.

He found the work exhilarating and challenging. The agents he'd met were dedicated, willing to put their lives at risk for their beliefs, and committed to each other. The camaraderie had its appeal and he'd learned much from the more experienced agents.

Pierce worked from dawn until supper each day. It exhausted his body and kept his mind off the woman he'd come to realize he loved. He hadn't been prepared to confess his feelings earlier, needing to know how Mollie felt before risking his heart to a woman who might not feel the same. She'd told him she cared for him, and at the time, he'd taken that as proof she didn't love him. Now, he wasn't certain.

The way her gaze followed him, the smile she flashed when he'd enter a room then conceal in hopes he hadn't noticed, the way her eyes sparkled, and most of all, her uninhibited response to his touch when they made love, all told Pierce more about her true feelings than she'd been able to put into words. He believed she had the same fears as him when it came to putting her heart at risk.

Pierce finished cleaning up and was slipping into his best clothes when he spotted the envelope Lee had handed him from Noah. He'd forgotten all about the note, which had gotten buried in a drawer after his return. He picked it up, started to open it, then set it back down, believing it to be an offer for continued work at the agency.

"Pierce, you ready?" Grace called from downstairs.

"On my way." He grabbed his coat and left for the ride to Fire Mountain.

******

"I don't think I can wait much longer to hear your news," Aunt Alicia warned as they finished a delicious meal Dodge Delaney's chef had prepared for the MacLarens.

The comment brought everyone's attention to Dodge and his wife, Meggie, who sat together on one side of the long, rectangular table, between their cousins.

268

"Then we won't make you wait any longer," Dodge replied and stood, holding a wine glass in one hand as he pulled out Meggie's chair with the other and helped her stand. He wrapped an arm around her waist and pulled her close. "As you may have already guessed, Meggie and I are pleased to announce she's pregnant." His smile was broad as he raised his glass into the air.

The room erupted in cheers, toasts, congratulations, and hugs.

Grace walked to Meggie, her best friend since their time together in Utah. She was thrilled for her and Dodge, and gave Meggie a warm hug before whispering something in her ear. Meggie leaned back, a gasp springing from her mouth, before she grabbed Grace and pulled her into another quick hug. She turned to Dodge, pulled his head down, and whispered in his ear.

Dodge walked over to Connor and slapped him on the back before addressing the family again.

"It seems there's another announcement." He nodded at his brother-in-law.

Connor motioned for Grace to join him then turned to the others. "We didn't want to infringe on Meggie and Dodge's announcement, but I've just been given the approval to make our own announcement." He smiled at his wife. "Grace is pregnant, too."

Again, the family responded as they had with Dodge and Meggie's news.

Mr. Jericho slapped Connor on the back and hugged Grace. He couldn't remember a night like this in his life. It had taken a long time, and now it was all coming together for Connor and Meggie. Now, it was just Pierce he had to concern himself about. His gaze drifted down the table to the young man, wondering what he was thinking.

Pierce was thrilled for his sister and his brother. Both would be adding more MacLarens to the growing brood. Tess MacLaren was due within a few weeks.

It had been a wonderful evening. The celebratory mood continued through dessert until it grew late.

Connor watched as Pierce sat alone at one end of the table, nursing a whiskey. He'd been concerned about his younger brother ever since he'd returned from San Francisco. He hadn't asked, but suspected Pierce's long hours on the ranch, quiet, introspective mood, and long walks after supper had something to do with Mollie Jamison and not his decision to leave the agency.

He pushed from his chair and walked toward Pierce. "Mind if I sit?"

"Up to you, Papa." Pierce's grin didn't quite reach his eyes.

Connor nodded and sat down.

"You hoping for a boy or girl?" Pierce asked as he finished off his drink.

"Hell, I don't care. Either works for me." Connor looked down the table at Grace laughing at something Will had said, then back to his brother.

"You haven't mentioned Mollie since you got back. She handle herself okay up there?"

"Yeah, she did real good. Mollie's a professional."

"Seems like a different story than what you told us before you left."

"Well, I was wrong about her." His jaw tightened and Connor watched as Pierce's grip on the edge of his seat tightened.

"That's all there is to it?" Connor asked, pushing for his brother to get out whatever he'd bottled up inside.

Pierce's head turned toward Connor and he saw the concern in his brother's eyes. "No, there was more. It's over now and she's moved back to Boston." He looked down into his lap and the whiskey glass he rolled between his palms.

"Boston. You lived there for a while. How long has it been?"

"How long?"

"Since you were back there? I guess maybe five, six years."

Pierce thought a moment. "Maybe. I don't know exactly."

"Seems like it might be a good time to find a reason to return. Take a break and return to the east for a bit. 'Course, I'm not suggesting you stay, just go for a visit."

Pierce's eyes narrowed on his brother. "You looking to get rid of me?"

"Nope. Just looking to see you back the way you were before heading to San Francisco. Appears you and Mollie may have some unsettled business. Might be best to find an excuse to visit. You could probably think up something if you tried hard enough."

271

"This coming from the man who almost lost Grace due to pride and misunderstandings?"

"Yep, and that's exactly why I'm telling you this. You once told me that the right woman would come along, and when she did, I'd better reach out and grab her. I almost missed my chance. I don't want to see you miss yours." Connor stood and clasped Pierce on the shoulder. "Doesn't have to be tomorrow or next week. Just think about it."

Chapter Twenty-Four

Pierce spent Sunday riding Bandit through the heart of the ranch, thinking about what Connor had said and wishing he did have a good excuse to head east to Boston. Maybe his brother was right about Mollie being the one for him. He'd been thinking the same. The problem was he had no reason to go back—except Mollie. He no longer had friends in the city, and it wasn't a place people went to visit. The bustling city teamed with action at all hours, much like San Francisco, which he'd been anxious to leave.

It was getting dark. He turned Bandit toward home, or rather, Connor's home. Pierce groomed his horse before heading up the back steps and into the kitchen. They'd built it large, hoping for a passel of kids, and it appeared they were on their way toward that goal.

"Supper will be ready in a bit, Pierce. Let Connor know. He's in the study." Grace stood at the stove, stirring a pot and checking the skillet biscuits. The fried chicken waited in the warming oven of the cook stove Connor had ordered from back east.

"Just let me wash up and I'll be down to help." Pierce dashed up the stairs, stopping briefly to let Connor know about supper. He was ready to head down within ten minutes. He checked the small mirror above the dresser, ran a hand through his damp hair, and noticed the envelope he'd ignored for over a month.

"Hell," he muttered and picked it up, deciding he might as well take a look and get back to Noah on whatever he wanted Pierce to consider.

He tore it open and pulled out the paper. Only it wasn't just any piece of paper. It was a marriage certificate, and from the looks of it, either a perfect forgery or the genuine article. It was between Pierce and Mollie, signed and dated by both of them. Noah had decided to make sure it was real in case there was any reason someone would doubt their marriage. He'd said he probably wouldn't file it—he had. Noah had included a short note saying he'd decided to file the document as he preferred to err on the side of caution.

Pierce stared at the certificate. It had been filed, stamped, and as far as he could tell, was a legal statement of his marriage to Mollie. What he held in his hand was the reason he needed to head east to Boston—to bring his wife home.

******

Pierce stepped off the train at the Boston station, feeling better than he expected after his cross country trip.

He'd been fortunate. Drew contacted Louis Dunnigan and learned his boss was leaving Denver for New York in three days. If Pierce could get to Denver in time, he was welcome to share

Dunnigan's private car. He'd packed and been on his way to Colorado within hours.

He picked up his satchel and walked to the street, flagging a carriage, and providing an address to the driver for a hotel Dunnigan had recommended. Before leaving Fire Mountain, Pierce had sent a message to Lee and Eva, requesting whatever assistance they could provide in locating Mollie. From New York, he'd sent them the name of the hotel in Boston where he'd be staying.

He was surprised to find a reply waiting for him at the front desk. Pierce ripped open the envelope to find they'd located an address. He remembered little about Boston neighborhoods from his brief stay several years before.

"Excuse me? Can you tell me how to find this location?" he asked the clerk.

"Let's see. Oh, it isn't too far, a few miles to the northeast, I believe. Shall I order a carriage for you?"

"Yes. Thank you." Pierce looked at the inside pocket of his jacket, reassuring himself the marriage certificate was still in place.

******

The carriage bumped along the wide, busy streets before the road narrowed into a middle-class neighborhood consisting of well-kept brownstones. It was early evening. The carriage stopped several times as children followed errant balls into the street, riders exited overflowing horsecars, and merchants made last minute deliveries.

"Won't be long now, sir," the driver threw over his shoulder as the brownstones gave way to one-story shanties in an area where gas lights were few. The sun was beginning to descend and he noticed more than one home missing an address. He hoped the looming darkness wouldn't impede his search.

Pierce knew there'd be hell to pay once Mollie saw the document. He'd wrestled with what to say throughout his entire trip and still wasn't certain how to approach her. It still irritated him that she'd left their bed without a word, skulked out as if what they'd had meant so little. Hell, he'd offered marriage and she'd flatly refused.

Perhaps he'd take one look at her and not feel any of the stirrings of desire that had plagued him for months. Maybe her appeal would have diminished to the point he'd find himself wondering why he'd made the long trip east.

"Here it is, sir." The driver halted the carriage in front of small, rundown home.

Pierce's eyes roamed over the structure. He had a hard time imagining Mollie living in a place such as this when the money she'd earned on their last assignment would allow her so much more.

"Wait for me," he instructed the driver then walked the few steps to the front door. The first knock brought no results, so he pounded more forcefully and waited.

Pierce heard the gruff voice as the door cracked opened a mere inch.

A stooped, thin-haired man peered out. "What you want?" he growled, his puffy, yellow-edged eyes looking out from under bushy eyebrows that matched his graying hair.

"I've come to see Mollie Jamison. Is she here?" Pierce tried to look around the man and into the house.

"She ain't here." He started to close the door, but Pierce stopped it with his hand.

"Wait, please. It's important that I find her."

The man opened the door a fraction more. "How important?"

Pierce understood and reached into his pocket, pulling out a roll of bills and peeling off a one hundred dollar bill. The man snatched it from his hand and stuffed it into his pants.

"She's been here twice to leave money then left. Told me where she was staying." He rubbed his stubbled chin between his thumb and fingers. "Wait a minute. She wrote it down." He shut the door, leaving Pierce to wonder if he'd return. He could hear the sounds of papers shuffling before the door was pulled open and a scrap of paper shoved outside.

"Take it. I don't need it," he said before shutting the door in Pierce's face.

He read the paper—the Tudor Hotel, Beacon Street. Pierce uttered a muffled curse then handed the address to the driver. The driver read the address and cast a questioning eye at his rider.

"Just take me there."

"Yes, sir." He snapped the reins, turned the carriage around, and started back in the direction of Pierce's hotel.

******

The night had turned cold and damp. Pierce stepped out of the carriage, settled with the driver, walked into the Tudor and up to the reception desk.

"Good evening, Mr. MacLaren. Did you find the address?"

"Yes, I did." Pierce cleared his throat. "Do you have a Miss Mollie Jamison registered?"

"Ah, let me see." He grabbed the book and ran a finger down the page. "Yes, and her room connects to yours."

"Is that so?" Pierce thought a moment, then pulled out the marriage certificate and set it on the desk. "She's my wife. I'd like a key to the connecting door, please."

The man took a cursory look at the document, handed it to Pierce then reached into a drawer for the key. "Here you are, sir. Best of luck to you." The man's amused smile was lost on Pierce as he took the steps two at a time and disappeared into his own room.

He tossed his hat on the bed, rolled up his sleeves, poured water into a basin, and scrubbed his face, trying to think. She was in the room next to him and he had the key to the connecting door. It was late, after ten, and he could hear nothing through their common wall.

Pierce paced to the door and put his ear to it, listening. The room was quiet. Perhaps she was out for the evening, or asleep. He wondered if he should wait until morning, as his head instructed, or charge ahead tonight, as his heart demanded.

He slid the key into the lock and opened the door. The room was dark, with only the light of the moon filtering in through the half-drawn curtains. His eyes adjusted enough to make out a form under the covers of the bed. He took one, then two cautious steps forward. The form shifted slightly and he could see Mollie's golden blonde hair peek from under the covers. He walked to the edge of the bed and stared down.

Pierce watched her for several minutes, debating before taking a seat next to her. She stirred and turned her head toward him, a soft sigh escaping her lips. His breath hitched as he took in the sight of her after almost two months. His musings about whether she still affected him were answered in a half-second, his heart thundered and his body hardened.

He reached down to brush errant strands of hair off her face and stroked a finger down her cheek. She stirred again, her eyes fluttering at the contact. He did it once more. This time Mollie's eyes flew open fully and stared in shock at the figure on her bed. She rolled to the other side, grabbed her gun from the nearby table, and aimed it at the intruder.

"What the hell do you want?" she demanded as her eyes tried to adjust and focus on the man before her.

Pierce stood, his hands up, palms out, at chest level.

"Hello, Mollie." The words were smooth, not affected by the pounding he could hear coming from his chest.

"Pierce?" She held the gun steady while swiping at the hair hanging over her face. She took one cautious step closer.

"Yes." He kept his hands up and his face set.

"What are you doing here? How did you find me?" Her voice calmed as she lowered the weapon and placed it back on the table.

He dropped his hands to his sides, making no move to get closer.

"I needed to find you and bring you back to Fire Mountain." His voice was nonchalant, almost bored in its tone.

"Are you crazy? I'm not going back to Fire Mountain with you."

"I'm afraid you have no choice. You're my wife, and as any judge will tell you, your place is with me."

She stared at him. "That's ridiculous. Our marriage was a cover, part of our assignment. I'm not your wife and I'm not going back to Arizona." The pitch of her voice rose which each sentence.

"Do you recall the document Noah had us sign before leaving for San Francisco? The one he said we might need if anyone questioned our marriage?" He arched his brows in question.

"Yes, of course. He kept it with him and said he'd send it to us if needed. Why?"

He reached into his pocket to extract the certificate and held it up to her. "He filed it. It's a legal document. We are man and wife." One corner of his mouth crooked upward as he watched her expression turn to disbelief.

"No. He wouldn't, couldn't, do that to us." She snatched the document from his hand and read it. She glanced up once at him before returning her gaze to the certificate and tossing it on the bed. "How could he do this to us?" She moaned and dropped her face into her hands, coming to terms with the fact that she was legally tied to this man. Mollie looked up at him. "You did this! You persuaded Noah to file the form, make it legal." She stood up and pushed Pierce backward with both hands, causing him to fall, landing in the chair behind him.

Mollie watched in stunned disbelief as he started to laugh. "What is so funny?" Her temper hadn't eased a bit.

Pierce couldn't control himself. He watched Mollie's face scrunch in dismay, then turn to anger, then confusion, and all he could do was laugh harder. "You. Us. The mess we're in."

"It's your fault, Pierce MacLaren, and you're going to be the one to fix it." She plopped back down on the bed in disgust.

"Sorry, sweetheart, but this is our mess, and you're going to have to travel back to Fire Mountain with me to fix it." He pushed himself up from the chair and looked down at her. "I did not put Noah up to this. It was his own doing."

"Then he can fix it."

"Won't work. You and I have to do this together. Assuming, of course, that you truly do want the marriage to end." His expression had turned somber.

Mollie looked up at him, the serious expression, the intense look in his eyes, and wondered—for only a brief moment—if staying married to him would be so bad. It was clear Pierce cared for her. The looks that passed between them, the way he touched her and made love to her, as well as the concern that was always present in his eyes. But would he ever love her?

Her initial outrage at the reason for his presence turned to hope.

She was in love with him. The last two months had been miserable. It had taken all her willpower not to purchase a ticket and board the train for Fire Mountain. Now, Pierce was in Boston, in her room, and encouraging her to go back with him.

"Is that what you want, Pierce, the marriage to end?"

"No, I don't want to end it."

"But you don't love me," she whispered.

He knelt beside her, took her hands in his, and pressed them to his lips. "Come back with me. We'll see what happens. If in time you want out, I won't stop you."

Chapter Twenty-Five

Mollie had seen the reality of their situation within moments of Pierce asking her to return. Regardless of whether she decided to give their marriage a chance as he wanted, or end it, as she thought was best, Mollie had no other choice. She had to travel across country to Fire Mountain. Her presence was required no matter which decision she made.

They stepped off the train to find Aunt Alicia, Meggie, and Connor waiting. Pierce had sent a message to Connor before leaving Boston, telling his brother Mollie was returning with him, as his wife. Connor had wasted no time passing the message around to the other MacLarens.

Aunt Alicia gave Pierce a hug then held out her arms to Mollie. "Welcome home. We're so glad you're now a part of our family."

Mollie glanced at Pierce as she returned the hug, wondering what he had told his family. She hadn't yet committed to staying, however, she'd learned something from Eva during their assignment, and that was to try to hold off saying anything until the time was right. Mollie hoped she could do it.

Meggie stepped forward to hug her new sister-in-law. Connor held back to the end.

Mollie had seen him on a couple of occasions, as both Pierce's brother and the manager of the Desert Dove saloon, owned by Niall. He'd always been pleasant, but she'd noticed an edge, a hardness not typical of Pierce or Meggie.

"Hello, Mollie. Welcome home." He stepped up and gave her a brief hug. "You'll be staying with Grace and me until we're able to get Pierce's house finished." He turned to his brother. "You're going to like the spot Aunt Alicia picked out."

Alicia had already planned a lavish supper that evening and everyone was present. Chaz had returned from San Francisco during Pierce's absence and rode out to the ranch with Dodge and Meggie. Neither Chaz nor Drew seemed surprised at the news of Pierce and Mollie's marriage, sparking the curiosity of the rest of the family.

"When did you get married, Pierce?" Kate, Niall's wife, asked.

"About five months ago."

"But, that would have been before you left for San Francisco," Aunt Alicia commented.

"That's right." Pierce kept eating his dessert, resisting the temptation to look at the faces he knew would show surprise.

"Why didn't you say anything back then, and why didn't Mollie come back with you from San Francisco?" Will's wife, Amanda, asked.

"It's complicated," he answered and glanced over at Mollie who sat stone still, her hands in her lap, and looking like she wanted to disappear under the table.

Connor leaned back in his chair and studied the two. Pierce hadn't confided in him why'd he'd suddenly decided to leave for Boston. He had thought his brother had finally figured out he loved Mollie and had gone to tell her. That didn't fit with what he saw tonight. Connor knew something had been amiss, now he thought he understood what it was.

Connor let the front legs of his chair hit the ground as he leaned forward and crossed his arms on the table. "Why don't you share with us exactly what's going on, Pierce."

Pierce set down his fork and looked around at the family who'd gathered to celebrate his marriage to Mollie. He wondered if it was wrong to continue acting as if nothing was different from any of their marriages or if he should tell them the truth, that this was just a trial run. He decided they needed to learn the truth.

"Mollie and I signed a marriage certificate before leaving for our assignment. Our cover was to make people believe we were a married couple." His narrowed eyes locked on his brother. "After a while, we acted on our feelings, becoming a true married couple."

"Oh, God," Mollie whispered and started to stand. Amanda placed a hand on her arm, encouraging her to stay.

The room fell silent as each person absorbed what Pierce had said. Jamie sipped at his coffee, Will and Dodge picked at their dessert, Niall and Drew waited, figuring there was more to come.

Connor let a half-smile cross his face and shook his head.

The women watched Mollie, knowing how hard it was to come into the MacLaren family under the best circumstances and empathizing with the young woman. Each of them had crossed through their own personal fire with the MacLarens they'd married. No one at the table could to point fingers at anyone else. They were, after all, only human.

"You're confident the license you have is legal?" Drew asked, the attorney in him taking over.

"According to Noah, yes, it is. He filed it with the court in Fire Mountain."

"And you've both decided you want to continue with it?" Jamie asked.

Pierce swung his gaze to Mollie. "Yes, that's what we've decided."

"Well, it seems all worked out fine. The only thing missing is a true wedding, which the girls and I can arrange. We've certainly done it enough times," Alicia quipped and pushed from the table.

"Um, Aunt Alicia, maybe it would be best to—" Pierce began before a hard look from his aunt stopped him.

"You will have a wedding, with a preacher, Pierce MacLaren. And it will be soon. I suggest you prepare yourself for it."

******

286

Pierce and Mollie sat on their bed, conflicted as to the turn of events at supper. Mollie understood why Pierce felt the need to share the truth with his family, he wasn't the type to keep secrets. Now that everyone knew how the marriage had come about, and Alicia had made no apologies for insisting on a wedding, they had to make a decision. Somehow, walking out on a marriage based on a piece of paper seemed easier than walking out on one performed by a preacher, in front of God, and, well, everyone.

"What are we going to do?" Mollie asked and fell back onto the mattress, crossing an arm over her eyes.

"Don't see that we have much choice." Pierce fell back to join her.

"Marriage in front of a preacher is a little more permanent than the paper we signed for Noah, don't you think?" She lifted her arm off her eyes and turned her gaze to Pierce.

"Oh yeah, big difference."

Each lay there a while longer before she sprang from the bed and walked to the wardrobe where she'd stowed her luggage. Mollie pulled out one of her satchels and threw it on a chair, then opened the dresser and started to gather her clothes.

"What the hell are you doing?" Pierce sat up, watching her cram her things into the bag.

"Packing."

"I see that. Why?"

"I'm leaving."

He walked up beside her, grabbed an arm, and turned her to him.

"You're leaving. Just like that? Because the family wants a wedding?" He shot her a killing glare and started to pull her clothes out of the bag and return them to the wardrobe.

"No, not just like that. I shouldn't have come in the first place. It was wrong." Mollie grabbed the clothing from his hands and threw it back in the satchel.

"Wrong, how?" He dropped his hands to his sides, palms facing out.

"Because you don't love me!" she fumed, her voice rising as the tension in her peaked.

"The hell I don't!" he shot back.

Time seemed to stop.

Her jaw dropped and Pierce took a slight step backward.

He squeezed the bridge of his nose between his thumb and forefinger, accepting what he'd said as true.

"I love you, Mollie, and that's God's truth."

"You love me?" she whispered.

"Yes, I do." He took a deep breath, "Look, I know you don't love me, but in time, maybe..." Pierce's voice trailed off.

Mollie launched herself at him, wrapping her arms around his neck, brushing brief kisses across his cheeks, chin, eyes, and nose. She pulled back and looked into his beautiful blue eyes.

"I love you, too, Pierce MacLaren, and that's God's truth."

Epilogue

One last wedding, Alicia thought as she pulled the last pie out of the oven. Everyone is married, finally. She sat down and picked up the lemonade she'd made that morning.

They expected quite a number of people at the ranch today, neighbors they'd known most of their lives, and newcomers who'd somehow discovered Fire Mountain and made it their home. She figured the next big shindig wouldn't be until Beth, Niall and Kate's oldest, got married. She hoped that was years away.

"Aunt Alicia, where do you want the rest of these flowers?" Torie walked up with her arms full. "Chaz sent them."

Alicia shook her head. Now that was one man who needed to meet the right lady and settle down. He was just too darn good looking and smart to stay single. "Please put them on the table next to the hallstand in the entry."

Torie turned to leave as Jericho strolled into view.

"Good, you're resting, Alicia," Mr. Jericho stood in the door of the kitchen. "You've been working much too hard on this wedding. Let the others do more." He continued to stand.

"Sit down, Lawrence, you've been doing more than your share, too." Alicia smiled up at the large man who'd become such a good friend since they'd first met. He'd helped Drew to overcome the paralysis he'd suffered when a bullet ripped through his body and he'd been a fixture in Connor and Pierce's lives since their days in Red Hook. Everyone called him Mr. Jericho, but when they were alone, he preferred she call him by his first name, Lawrence.

"Won't be long and everyone will be here. Didn't think I'd see the day when Connor, Pierce, and Meggie would all be married." He poured himself some lemonade and sat back. "Guess my job here is done."

Alicia's eyes flew to his. "What do you mean, your job's done? From what I can tell, it's just getting started. There's still plenty of young ones to help with and more on the way. If you think you're cutting out and leaving me to do all the work, well, you had just better think again." She set down her glass with a thud. "Now, I'm going to get dressed for the wedding. I suggest you do the same."

Alicia placed a hand on his shoulder as she walked past him to the stairs.

He watched her, glad in more than ways than he could count, that he was a part of what he considered an extraordinary family.

******

Everyone was in place, the music started, and all eyes turned to where Mollie stood. She was a vision in her stunning gown, golden hair pulled up in a soft chignon, wearing the pearls Pierce had presented her with the night before. He'd purchased them in San Francisco, hoping she would one day consent to be his bride.

Connor escorted her between the rows of guests, then stepped aside as they came to a stop in front of Pierce.

Everyone listened as the preacher spoke the same words they'd heard many times over the last several years as each of the MacLarens had married.

"Repeat after me. I, Pierce Mungo MacLaren, take this woman..."

Mollie's eyes shot to Pierce's. "Mungo?" she mouthed as the sounds of muffled laughter could be heard behind them.

Pierce's face turned red. "Later," he mouthed back and shrugged.

Several minutes later, they'd completed their vows, and he slipped a simple gold band onto her finger.

"You may now kiss your bride," the preacher finished, motioning for them to turn toward their guests. "Ladies and gentlemen, I now present to you Mr. and Mrs. Pierce MacLaren."

Pierce let out a loud whoop before grabbing Mollie in a tight hug and swinging her around.

******

Pierce sipped a whiskey and looked on as Mollie sat with the women and looked over the gifts that had been left for them. He'd been stunned at the generosity of the townsfolk and neighbors he barely knew.

Connor came up beside him and clasped a hand to his shoulder. "You did good, real good." He smiled and lifted his glass in salute to his brother. "She's a wonderful woman, which makes her an excellent match for you."

Pierce accepted the veiled complement as he saluted Connor in return.

"Pierce, there's a card here from Settlers Valley, California," Mollie called and held up an envelope.

He walked forward, opened the envelope, and read the brief message.

"What's it say, Pierce?" Alicia asked from her seat next to Mr. Jericho.

He looked up, a smile spreading slowly across his face. "Says congratulations and that they can't wait to get all the MacLarens together to share our stories of coming to America and settling in the west."

That will be quite a reunion, Alicia thought. *Yes, quite a reunion indeed.*

The End

Watch for Shirleen's continuation of the MacLaren clan
in her new series,

The MacLarens of Boundary Mountain
Book one, Colin's Quest

Scheduled for release in early 2015

About the Author

Shirleen Davies writes romance—historical, contemporary, and romantic suspense. She grew up in Southern California, attended Oregon State University, and has degrees from San Diego State University and the University of Maryland. During the day she provides consulting services to small and mid-sized businesses. But her real passion is writing emotionally charged stories of flawed people who find redemption through love and acceptance. She now lives with her husband in a beautiful town in northern Arizona.

Shirleen began her series, MacLarens of Fire Mountain, with Tougher than the Rest, the story of the oldest brother, Niall MacLaren. Other books in the series include, Faster than the Rest, Harder than the Rest, Stronger than the Rest, and Deadlier than the Rest. Book six, Wilder than the Rest, is due for release in early summer, 2014. Her contemporary romance series, MacLarens of Fire Mountain Contemporary, opened with book one, Second Summer. Book two, Hard Landing, released in April 2014, and Book three, One More day, is scheduled to release in midsummer, 2014. Book one of her newest historical western series, Redemption Mountain, will release in the fall of 2014.

Shirleen loves to hear from her readers.

Write to her at: shirleen@shirleendavies.com
Visit her website: http://www.shirleendavies.com
Comment on her blog:
http://www.shirleendavies.com/blog.html
Facebook Fan Page:
https://www.facebook.com/ShirleenDaviesAuthor
Twitter: http://twitter.com/shirleendavies
Google+: http://www.gplusid.com/shirleendavies
LinkedIn:
   http://www.linkedin.com/in/shirleendaviesaut
   hor

Other Books by Shirleen Davies

Tougher than the Rest – Book One
MacLarens of Fire Mountain Historical Western Romance Series

"A passionate, fast-paced story set in the untamed western frontier by an exciting new voice in historical romance."

Niall MacLaren is the oldest of four brothers, and the undisputed leader of the family. A widower, and single father, his focus is on building the MacLaren ranch into the largest and most successful in northern Arizona. He is serious about two things—his responsibility to the family and his future marriage to the wealthy, well-connected widow who will secure his place in the territory's destiny.

Katherine is determined to live the life she's dreamed about. With a job waiting for her in the growing town of Los Angeles, California, the young teacher from Philadelphia begins a journey across the United States with only a couple of trunks and her spinster companion. Life is perfect for this adventurous, beautiful young woman, until an accident throws her into the arms of the one man who can destroy it all.

Fighting his growing attraction and strong desire for the beautiful stranger, Niall is more determined than ever to push emotions aside to focus on his goals of wealth and political gain. But looking into the clear, blue eyes of the woman who could ruin everything, Niall discovers he will have to harden his heart and be tougher than he's ever been in his life...Tougher than the Rest.

Faster than the Rest – Book Two
MacLarens of Fire Mountain Historical Western Romance Series

"Headstrong, brash, confident, and complex, the MacLarens of Fire Mountain will captivate you with strong characters set in the wild and rugged western frontier."

Handsome, ruthless, young U.S. Marshal Jamie MacLaren had lost everything—his parents, his family connections, and his childhood sweetheart—but now he's back in Fire Mountain and ready for another chance. Just as he successfully reconnects with his family and starts to rebuild his life, he gets the unexpected and unwanted assignment of rescuing the woman who broke his heart.

Beautiful, wealthy Victoria Wicklin chose money and power over love, but is now fighting for her life—or is she? Who has she become in the seven years since she left Fire Mountain to take up her life in San Francisco? Is she really as innocent as she says?

Marshal MacLaren struggles to learn the truth and do his job, but the past and present lead him in different directions as his heart and brain wage battle. Is Victoria a victim or a villain? Is life offering him another chance, or just another heartbreak?

As Jamie and Victoria struggle to uncover past secrets and come to grips with their shared passion, another danger arises. A life-altering danger that is out of their control and threatens to destroy any chance for a shared future.

Harder than the Rest – Book Three
MacLarens of Fire Mountain Historical Western Romance Series

"They are men you want on your side. Hard, confident, and loyal, the MacLarens of Fire Mountain will seize your attention from the first page."

Will MacLaren is a hardened, plain-speaking bounty hunter. His life centers on finding men guilty of horrendous crimes and making sure justice is done. There is no place in his world for the carefree attitude he carried years before when a tragic event destroyed his dreams.

Amanda is the daughter of a successful Colorado rancher. Determined and proud, she works hard to prove she is as capable as any man and worthy to be her father's heir. When a stranger arrives, her independent nature collides with the strong pull toward the handsome ranch hand. But is he what he seems and could his secrets endanger her as well as her family?

The last thing Will needs is to feel passion for another woman. But Amanda elicits feelings he thought were long buried. Can Will's desire for her change him? Or will the vengeance he seeks against the one man he wants to destroy—a dangerous opponent without a conscious—continue to control his life?

Stronger than the Rest – Book Four
MacLarens of Fire Mountain Historical Western Romance Series

"Smart, tough, and capable, the MacLarens protect their own no matter the odds. Set against America's rugged frontier, the stories of the men from Fire Mountain are complex, fast-paced, and a must read for anyone who enjoys non-stop action and romance."

Drew MacLaren is focused and strong. He has achieved all of his goals except one—to return to the MacLaren ranch and build the best horse breeding program in the west. His successful career as an attorney is about to give way to his ranching roots when a bullet changes everything.

Tess Taylor is the quiet, serious daughter of a Colorado ranch family with dreams of her own. Her shy nature keeps her from developing friendships outside of her close-knit family until Drew enters her life. Their relationship grows. Then a bullet, meant for another, leaves him paralyzed and determined to distance himself from the one woman he's come to love.

Convinced he is no longer the man Tess needs, Drew focuses on regaining the use of his legs and recapturing a life he thought lost. But danger of another kind threatens those he cares about— including Tess—forcing him to rethink his future.

Can Drew overcome the barriers that stand between him, the safety of his friends and family, and a life with the woman he loves? To do it all, he has to be strong. Stronger than the Rest.

Deadlier than the Rest – Book Five
MacLarens of Fire Mountain Historical Western Romance Series

"A passionate, heartwarming story of the iconic MacLarens of Fire Mountain. This captivating historical western romance grabs your attention from the start with an engrossing story encompassing two romances set against the rugged backdrop of the burgeoning western frontier."

Connor MacLaren's search has already stolen eight years of his life. Now he is close to finding what he seeks—Meggie, his missing sister. His quest leads him to the growing city of Salt Lake and an encounter with the most captivating woman he has ever met.

Grace is the third wife of a Mormon farmer, forced into a life far different from what she'd have chosen. Her independent spirit longs for choices governed only by her own heart and mind. To achieve her dreams, she must hide behind secrets and half-truths, even as her heart pulls her towards the ruggedly handsome Connor.

Known as cool and uncompromising, Connor MacLaren lives by a few, firm rules that have served him well and kept him alive. However, danger stalks Connor, even to the front range of the beautiful Wasatch Mountains, threatening those he cares about and impacting his ability to find his sister.

Can Connor protect himself from those who seek his death? Will his eight-year search lead him to his sister while unlocking the secrets he knows are held tight within Grace, the woman who has captured his heart?

Read this heartening story of duty, honor, passion, and love in book five of the MacLarens of Fire Mountain series.

Wilder than the Rest – Book Six
MacLarens of Fire Mountain Historical Western Romance Series

"A captivating historical western romance set in the burgeoning and treacherous city of San Francisco. Go along for the ride in this gripping story that seizes your attention from the very first page."

"If you're a reader who wants to discover an entire family of characters you can fall in love with, this is the series for you." – Authors to Watch

Pierce is a rough man, but happy in his new life as a Special Agent. Tasked with defending the rights of the federal government, Pierce is a cunning gunslinger always ready to tackle the next job. That is, until he finds out that his new job involves Mollie Jamison.

Mollie can be a lot to handle. Headstrong and independent, Mollie has chosen a life of danger and intrigue guaranteed to prove her liquor-loving father wrong. She will make something of herself, and no one, not even arrogant Pierce MacLaren, will stand in her way.

A secret mission brings them together, but will their attraction to each other prove deadly in their hunt for justice? The payoff for success is high, much higher than any assignment either has taken before. But will the damage to their hearts and souls be too much to bear? Can Pierce and Mollie find a way to overcome their misgivings and work together as one?

Read Wilder than the Rest, another heartening story of duty, honor, passion, and love in book six of the MacLarens of Fire Mountain.

Second Summer – Book One
MacLarens of Fire Mountain Contemporary Romance Series

"In this passionate Contemporary Romance, author Shirleen Davies introduces her readers to the modern day MacLarens starting with Heath MacLaren, the head of the family."

The Chairman of both the MacLaren Cattle Co. and MacLaren Land Development, Heath MacLaren is a success professionally—his personal life is another matter.

Following a divorce after a long, loveless marriage, Heath spends his time with women who are beautiful and passionate, yet unable to provide what he longs for . . .

Heath has never experienced love even though he witnesses it every day between his younger brother, Jace, and wife, Caroline. He wants what they have, yet spends his time with women too young to understand what drives him and too focused on themselves to be true companions.

It's been two years since Annie's husband died, leaving her to build a new life. He was her soul mate and confidante. She has no desire to find a replacement, yet longs for male friendship.

Annie's closest friend in Fire Mountain, Caroline MacLaren, is determined to see Annie come out of her shell after almost two years of mourning. A chance meeting with Heath turns into an offer to be a part of the MacLaren Foundation Board and an opportunity for a life outside her home sanctuary which has also become her prison. The platonic friendship that builds between Annie and Heath points to a future where each may rely on the other without the bonds a romance would entail.

However, without consciously seeking it, each yearns for more . . .

The MacLaren Development Company is booming with Heath at the helm. His meetings at a partner company with the young, beautiful marketing director, who makes no secret of her desire for him, are a temptation. But is she the type of woman he truly wants?

Annie's acceptance of the deep, yet passionless, friendship with Heath sustains her, lulling her to believe it is all she needs. At least until Heath drops a bombshell, forcing Annie to realize that